SILENT COUNT

WALKER UNIVERSITY STALLIONS
BOOK 4

AVA SUTTON

COMPASS PRESS

Visit my website at avasuttonbooks.com
Cover Designer: Enchanting Romance Designs
Developmental Editor: Jeannine Colette, www.jeanninecolette.com
Editor: Jovana Shirley, Unforeseen Editing, www.unforeseenediting.com

ISBN-13: 979-8-9999643-1-1

Dear reader,

While **Silent Count** is full of flirty fun and heart, the story does touch on some deeper, real-life issues. These include themes like the loss of a parent, family incarceration, addiction, abuse (mentioned, not graphic), adoption, and childhood trauma. There's also some explicit sexual content. If any of these are sensitive topics for you, just know they're handled with care, and you're always welcome to skip ahead.

I want to thank my friends and colleagues for consulting with me regarding the legal and psychological aspects of the storyline. Some liberties have been taken for the sake of privacy.

*For those who learned silence as a means of survival,
who hid their bruises behind smiles,
and still somehow grew hearts big enough to love.*

And for DK. You know why.

PROLOGUE
TWELVE YEARS OLD

CHELSEA

THE EARLIEST MEMORY I have is of my parents fighting. I remember it because that was the first time I saw my daddy hit my mama. I don't know why he did it. I just remember him hitting her, and then ... she hit him back. This pattern became normal in my life, so I learned to stay quiet and get out of the way. I kind of liked feeling invisible, so that's what I became during the times they fought. I'd hide in my room under the bed or in the closet.

Then my little sister, Torie, came along when I was six years old. When she was really little, my parents got along well—or at least as well as they could get along. But as Torie got older, Mama began drinking again, and the fighting resumed, so I sort of took over the role as my sister's protector and caregiver. I made sure she was safe when our parents fought, that she was fed and bathed, and I also put her to bed at night because our parents were usually too busy getting drunk, fighting, or passed out.

Both of my parents drink a lot, and I think my daddy does

drugs sometimes, but I'm not sure what. I've just heard them talking about it. Like tonight. After we ate supper, Mama and Daddy argued about money, and she asked him where the rent money had gone and something about cocaine.

I'm old enough now to understand that not having rent money means we might not have a place to live. I really don't want to switch schools, and my sister doesn't adjust as well as I do, so I don't want her to have to start a new school either if we have to move.

As soon as they hit each other, I grabbed my sister by the hand, and we went into our room. I locked the door, like I always do, and tried to get my sister to calm down. She'd held her tears in until we got inside, which I was grateful for.

After a while, we heard the door slam, some glass shatter, but then it was quiet, other than the loud sound of the TV. So, we tiptoed to the bathroom, took care of business, and then hurried back into our room. I put my pajama shorts and T-shirt on, then helped Torie get her Elsa nightgown on.

I finally got Torie to fall asleep after reading to her for what seemed like hours, but she's still holding tightly to my hand across the space between us. Then just as I begin drifting off, I hear the door slam and my daddy's voice.

My parents are fighting again, and this time, it sounds pretty bad. I can make out some of what they're saying, but not all of it. They're screaming so loud that I'll be surprised if no one calls the police. That's happened more than a few times, but the police never do anything because when they get here, my parents act like nothing happened.

"You fucking bitch, you won't tell me how to spend my money! You sit on your ass all day, drinking, and expect me to go out there and work every day!" Daddy's voice sounds like it does when he's really drunk.

"I hate you! I hate you so much! You're a useless piece of shit! Just go. We don't want you here! Don't come back! You ruined my life!" Mama yells back at him.

When I hear crashing sounds like glass and furniture being thrown, I recognize that it's getting physical, and my hands start to shake. Then I hear hitting and more yelling. I squeeze my sister's hand gently to try to wake her, surprised she hasn't woken up yet.

"Torie, wake up," I whisper.

I know we can't walk out of the room, and I need to keep my sister safe because something about their fight tonight feels different. She stirs quickly once she hears her name because when you live in a home like this, you learn how to move fast when you need to. I help her off the bed and lead her into our small closet.

I pull back the clothes hanging off the rod and push her in gently. "Get in and be as quiet as you can be," I say as softly as I can so she can hear me, but we aren't making too much noise. I double-check that the bedroom door is locked and then follow her inside, closing the folding door behind me.

Other than the light coming through the small window in our room and through the slats of the door, it's completely dark, so hopefully, he won't remember we're here.

My sister is leaning against the wall that is shared with the hallway, so I move her to the other side, just in case someone or something comes through the wall, and position myself in front of her. She's being quiet, but tears are running down her face, and her hands are shaking, just like mine.

"It's okay, Torie. We'll be okay. Just sit still and don't move until it's quiet. Plug your ears." I'm practically mouthing the words to her, but she does as I say. I'm trying not to cry for her, but my stomach feels tight, and I'm starting to sweat.

Trying to calm myself down, I begin to count in my head. *One. Two. Three. Four. Five. Six. Seven …*

Before I can get to eight, I hear a loud bang. Torie gasps, so I slap my hand over her mouth to stop her from screaming. I'm biting my bottom lip so hard to prevent myself from making noise that I taste blood in my mouth. Then another shot goes off, and another, then another. I pull Torie into my arms and onto my lap and cover her head as much as I can. We're both shaking, and I feel warm liquid running down my legs. Still, I don't move or say a word.

"FUCK! Motherfucker! Goddammit, why did you make me do that, huh? You couldn't keep your fucking mouth shut!" Daddy yells.

Then, a few minutes later, silence.

I'm not sure how much time passes, but I hear knocking on the door to the apartment. I'm frozen, and I'm afraid to move Torie anyway, so we just stay where we are.

The knocking comes again, and we hear, "This is the police. We received a call about a disturbance. Can you come to the door, please?"

I want to go to the door and let them in. I want them to save my sister and me from seeing whatever is on the other side of our bedroom door. But I can't move.

When we hear the door getting kicked open, we both jump.

"Chels," Torie whispers.

"It's okay. Just stay with me." I squeeze her tighter and kiss the top of her head.

We hear a man and a woman talking outside our bedroom door, but I don't really understand what they're saying, and their voices are muffled.

"We have a potential homicide. Gunshot wounds to the head and chest. No pulse," the man says.

"I'm going to search the premises," the female says.

Torie looks up at me, eyes wide, lips trembling. I just nod and squeeze her to me tighter.

We hear our bedroom door open and footsteps outside the closet. When the door is pulled open, the female police officer is standing there with a gun in her hand, but she quickly lowers it.

"Jones, we have two females, minors," she calls out.

Torie and I are shaking. Torie lets out a sob, and this time, I don't try to stop it.

The officer holsters her gun, then squats down to look at us. "You're okay, girls. We got you."

CHAPTER
ONE
NOW

CHELSEA

FOUR YEARS AGO, when I came to Walker University, I finally felt like I was free. Free to live my life as I wanted and free from my past. I could start over. Make friends like a normal person. And I have. I love the little bubble I've created for myself —away from the news reports, the whispers, the stares. Away from the reminders of all that happened.

Oklahoma is far from home, and I like it that way.

I was a little awkward when I first stepped on campus, still shaking off the rebellious streak of high school—hair pink, a tattoo, the usual angsty choices from a kid with my kind of childhood. But deep down, I knew it was time for a fresh start.

Now, thirteen hundred miles away, I'm four years into my new life. My roommate, Noelle James, is amazing. When we moved in together last year, she was fresh off a breakup, and I was itching to escape the dorms. We'd been friends since freshman year, but I never clicked with her old crowd—loud oversharers who lived for gossip and Instagram likes. Noelle was the one person I stayed close to—and thank God for that. Moving in together was the best decision.

Now we're in our last year of undergrad, still sharing the same apartment as last year, and I have a whole new group of friends because of her, including half of the Walker football team. They're all kind, generous, and a lot of fun to hang out with when I'm feeling social.

My major is prelaw, although it's not really called that. I want to become a lawyer and advocate for children coming from circumstances similar to the one I grew up in. And I want to help be the voice for children who aren't as fortunate as Torie and I were.

My sister and I got lucky with an estranged relative, but that isn't the norm. My dad had a younger sister, Laura, who we didn't know about. When the authorities contacted her when they were searching for our father, she was notified that Torie and I were on the premises during the crime. She'd had no idea about us either, but she quickly became our hero and rescued us from a life in the system. She gave us the love, stability, and structure we craved … which is probably why my rebellion never went much further than pink hair and a little ink.

Still, I don't regret leaving to come to Walker. Between school, applying to law schools, and finding time to chill with friends, I tutor other students struggling with courses in language arts and psychology. It's a decent job, considering I'm studying at the library a lot anyway, and it's only a few hours of my time each week.

I just got back from a meeting with my counselor to discuss how many students I could manage this semester with my course load. We've decided that I can take on two this semester, and I've been assigned to the athletic department. Which means I'll be tutoring athletes who need to stay eligible in their sports. I'm not going to pretend that I know much about any sport, but I am warming up to football. Only because Noelle has dragged me to some games, and I consider some of them friends.

I pull into the apartment complex and into my parking spot. Noelle isn't home, based on her car not being in the spot next to mine. We're supposed to have dinner together tonight, but she must be running behind schedule. She is student teaching at one of the elementary schools in town and occasionally has to stay late.

I grab my phone out of the cupholder, then pick up my backpack from the passenger seat and step out of the car. I shoot her a text.

> Chelsea: Hey! What time do you think you'll be home?

> Noelle: Hey, Chels! I just got in my car and was getting ready to text you. Casey invited us over for dinner. Charlie is cooking tonight! If you would rather stay home, we totally can, but just wanted to put it out there.

I laugh. She's sweet for the invite, but I know she wants to see her boyfriend, Casey. Not that I don't think she wants to hang out with me too. It's that I know she'll end up at Casey's at some point anyway because they're wildly in love. And I don't mind going over there. His friends are fun, and his twin sister, Charlie, is a good cook, too, so it's really a win all around.

> Chelsea: Sure, no problem. Do you want me to meet you there? Do we need to bring anything?

> Noelle: Yes, meet me there. We don't need to bring anything, I think she has it covered. See you soon!

> Chelsea: Okay, sounds good!

Unlocking the door to my apartment, I walk in and drop my bag, keys, and phone on the kitchen table. I change clothes and even spritz on some fresh perfume.

Not gonna lie; I like having the place to myself. The silence can be deafening to someone who can't stand to sit in their own thoughts. For me, it's a comfort. It means nothing bad is about to happen. No drama, no fights. No hurt and no heartbreak.

My room is organized and clutter-free. As a kid, my house was the opposite. My parents were addicts, borderline hoarders, with piles of trash and empty bottles covering every surface. Aunt Laura's home was starkly different—minimalist and orderly. At first, the lack of chaos made me uneasy, but eventually, I found peace in it. I even crave it now. My psychology classes call it a trauma response—growing up in a house filled with garbage and gunfire rewired me to cling to control. Every folded shirt and cleared counter is my way of building safety. It's not just tidiness. It's survival.

But survival isn't the whole story. I'm not the awkward girl I was when I first got here. I'm confident, fun, and maybe a little too busy, but I like who I am.

I go to the fridge to grab a bottle of water, then back to the table and sit down. I want to get a few things marked off in my calendar. I have my schedule perfectly planned and my study notes color-coded. Before I leave, I need to send my boss an email with my availability.

Ten minutes later, my phone dings. It's Noelle, asking when I'll be there. I make a stop in the bathroom to take care of business. I wash my hands, then check myself in the mirror. My hair is almost black, and my curls can be unruly at times, but they're surprisingly in control today. I don't wear much makeup, if any, and today was a no-makeup day. I splash some water on my face, then swipe some mascara on my long lashes.

I shake my head and roll my eyes at the fact that I'm putting in extra effort to look good tonight.

Yes, my past was chaotic, and I may have some minor OCD tendencies. That said, I'm pretty confident and generally don't give much thought to what other people think of me. I've worked too hard to build my own confidence. There's one person who—against my better judgment—makes my heart race, and I might care a *little* about what he thinks of me. And I'm one hundred percent sure he'll be there tonight.

CHAPTER
TWO

BO

WE'VE JUST FINISHED PRACTICE, and I'm about to shower when Coach Pettys walks into the locker room and calls a meeting. We circle around him in the center of the room. Coach's hands are on his hips, and I can't tell if the smirk on his face is a good smirk or a *you guys are fucked* smirk.

"Okay, boys, I'm gonna get right to it. At the end of last year, right after our spring training season, we were approached by the Sports Network about participating in a docuseries for this season. It took some heavy paperwork, but the university approved it." He huffs a laugh, and my teammates clap, clearly excited.

Me? I have a feeling I know what's coming, and I'm not exactly excited about it. I suspect that the camera crews will want to follow me around specifically. It's not that I'm not used to the attention, but I really want to stay focused this season with minimal distractions. But with me being ranked the number one quarterback in college football, they will likely want to interview me a lot at the very least.

"So, with that being said, we have some changes we're going

to be making before the season really gets underway. Starting with a team curfew." Coach's assistant, Roger, hands him a paper. "For our away games, the schedule will pretty much stay the same. You will have your normal check-in time. Home games, we will now leave campus the night before and stay in a hotel. We will have a team dinner and an activity, likely a movie night, then a nine p.m. room check. That means, you will be in your assigned room, ready to sleep. Not chatting with your girlfriends all night, not playing games on your phone." He pauses and looks around the room. "You can thank your previous teammates, Schuster and Smith, for this addition to the schedule this season. With all eyes on us, we have to stay disciplined and represent the school positively."

Casey is standing to my left and nudges me with his elbow. "Did you know about this?"

I shake my head. "Not any more than you guys did."

"I mean, I get why they're doing it, and maybe I won't hate it. But I like my girl staying with me before games." Casey folds his arms across his chest.

"You like your girl staying with you any night, regardless of if we have a game or not." I laugh and shove him playfully.

"Truth. Dude, Beck would have hated this so hard. Or found a way to get my sister in the room." He laughs.

"Probably." I smirk. "Honestly though, I don't hate the idea of the curfew. I like quiet before games."

Casey starts to speak, but Coach snaps his attention to us and looks over his glasses at us and raises his eyebrows.

Then he continues talking. "As far as the production schedule, you will be notified in advance if they want to record any of you individually. Roger will hand out the packet for you all to review. Look it over carefully, memorize it. You can direct any questions to Roger, and if he doesn't know the answer, he'll find it for you." He takes off his glasses. "That's it for today. Hydrate, eat, and get some rest. We're going hard again tomorrow."

Coach looks over to me. "Callaway, meet me in my office after you shower."

"Yes, sir." I nod, then turn toward my stall.

Casey follows. "What's that about?"

I shake my head and shrug. "Not sure. Could be anything really."

He slaps my shoulder. "Better you than me, man. I'm gonna shower at home. I'll see you there." He grabs his gear and leaves the locker room.

I look over at Coach and see he's talking to a few of the other coaches, so I grab what I need and make my way to the shower.

Sitting in the coach's office feels like waiting for the school principal to come in and issue detention. My hands are a little sweaty, my knee is bouncing, and I keep checking the time on my watch. While I was in the shower, I thought about every possible scenario that might explain why I'm here.

Now, I'm a confident guy. I'm a leader on the field, and I like to think that carries into my personal life as well. Things like school, sports, and friendships have always come easily to me. Don't get me wrong; I work hard, and I stay focused. I'm a doer, not a sayer. Still, I'm not exactly sure why I'm here. Could be the show. Or it could be the psychology class that I'm surprisingly struggling with. I mean, I guess I can't say struggling, but I defi- nitely bombed the first test. In my defense though, I really don't think I should be in the class to begin with. It has absolutely nothing to do with my business major, but whatever.

I hear Coach talking in the hall. Then the door opens, and he shuts it behind him.

Shit.

"Callaway." He nods, then takes a seat at his desk. "I'll get right to it because my wife is expecting me home for dinner tonight since I haven't been home all week."

There's a folder sitting on top of a stack of papers, and he takes it and sets it in front of him, then puts on his glasses. "You know why you're here?"

"I have a few guesses, sir." I fold my hands together, elbows on my knees. "My psychology class? Or the show?"

He nods. "Yes to both. But let's do the class issue first. Son, how did you get a D on your first quiz in an introductory class? You're one of the smartest kids I know. This doesn't track."

I swallow a lump in my throat before I answer, "Well, sir, I'm not exactly sure why. Honestly, I'm still shocked my advisor missed putting this required class in my schedule freshman year. And I'm also confused about why I need it for my business degree."

"It doesn't matter why. What matters is that it's required, and you're barely passing, which is a big problem for me, son. I need you on that field for every game this season. I want that trophy again this year. And I know you want to go out strong—am I right?" He tilts his head and looks at me over his glasses.

"Yes, sir." I nod.

"Good. So, here's what we're gonna do. You'll be assigned to a tutor, and you'll establish a schedule with her around your practice schedule while also being mindful of her availability. Am I clear?" He opens the folder and starts scanning the paperwork.

"Yes, sir, absolutely respectful of her time." I sit back and grip the arms of the chair. "Is she a TA or something?"

He shakes his head. "I believe this is a paid job for her, so really, whether you show up or not, she'll get paid, but Bo, you'd better be there for every single second. If that grade isn't moved up to at least a B on your next paper, I'll have to pull you, and I really can't afford to do that. Understand?" He doesn't look at me, but he takes a sticky note off a pad and starts writing.

"I understand." I scoot forward in my seat to see what he's writing.

"I'd also gather that your father monitors your grades?" He picks up the note, folds it, and hands it to me.

"That he does, sir. I'll have to let him know about this and about my tutoring. It's always better if he hears it from me first." I chuckle uncomfortably and take the sticky note from him and put it in my pocket.

My dad is the Chief Justice of the Supreme Court in California, and he keeps tabs on me pretty closely for multiple reasons.

"I can imagine so, which brings me to the next topic. The Sports Network wants to shadow you. The docuseries is about the team primarily, but they are specifically asking to have access to you during the entire season. Now, I have sent over all the paperwork to your father to review, and he signed off on the accessibility to you from a legal standpoint. But as your coach, I want to tell you that if at any time you don't feel comfortable or you need a break from filming, just say the word. Again, I need you to be on top of your game, and I won't risk the distractions this might cause for you." He leans back in his seat, assessing me.

"Yes, sir. That shouldn't be a problem. Just tell me what they need from me, schedule-wise. Although I'd prefer they try to keep their filming at the field as much as possible. Not that my personal life is all that exciting, but still, I'd like to have some downtime to myself, and I definitely don't want them following me to tutoring."

He lightly smacks his hand on the table, signaling the end of our conversation. "I don't think that will be a problem. Call this girl as soon as possible and get your time coordinated. I want an update by Friday on when your first meeting is." He stands and walks around his desk.

I take that as my cue to also stand. "Yes, sir. I'll take care of it right away."

He opens the door and stands beside it, waiting for me to leave. "See you at practice tomorrow, Bo." He holds his hand out for me to shake.

"See you tomorrow, Coach." I release his hand and walk out the door.

I can hear one of my roommates still hanging around in the locker room, so I head in the direction of his loud voice.

"Sup, Callaway. I didn't realize you were still here. I thought you'd left with King." Silas finishes packing up his bag, zips it, and heads in my direction.

"Nah, I had a meeting with Coach real quick. You riding with me?" I don't really want to tell him I need tutoring right now, especially not in front of my other teammates.

"Yep, let's roll. I'm hungry, and I always love it when it's Charlie's night to cook." He laughs and rubs his stomach.

I hold out my fist for him to bump. "No doubt it'll be good. Her nights are by far my favorite."

We live in the same house with one of our other teammates, Casey King, and his twin sister, Charlie. We all take turns making dinner one night each week and eat together. It's a nice tradition they started a few years ago when Charlie moved in.

Silas and I make the walk to my SUV, chatting about practice and some of the new plays we'll be running this season. We've been practicing for a month now, but the season is just getting started, so new plays and adjustments are usually made once the coaches see how we work together as a team.

When I get to my car, I put my gear in the back seat, then get into the driver's seat. I pull out the note from my pocket so I don't forget about it and wash it. That would be bad. I open it to stick onto my phone and see the name written on it. She just so happens to be the girl I can't stop thinking about since I met her.

But she doesn't know it because I've never made a move. She kinda intimidates me, to be honest.

Silas hops in the front passenger seat after tossing his bag in the back seat. "What's that? You get a girl's number?" He smirks.

"Uh, yeah, something like that." I quickly put the note on my phone and set it in a small compartment on the left side of the wheel, out of view from Silas.

Our ride home takes minutes, and I pull up behind Casey's girlfriend, Noelle's, car on the street in front of the house. I pocket my phone, and then we both grab our bags from the back seat and make our way to the door, still talking about football.

Silas walks into the house first and announces our arrival. "Daddy's home!" He drops his bag by the door, right in my path.

A round of laughter rings out.

"Ew, Silas. Don't ever say that again!" Noelle calls out.

I move Silas's bag out of my way with my foot, then set my bag down next to his. When I walk around the corner and into the kitchen, I stop in my tracks.

She's here. The girl I can't stop thinking about. Chelsea Sullivan. My new tutor.

CHAPTER
THREE

BO

IT'S NOT uncommon for Chelsea to be here when Noelle is over, but I mean ... what are the chances? We talk on occasion, but usually within the group, never one-on-one. Now, I'm not an overly superstitious guy, but I feel like this could be a sign to take my shot.

Trying to act nonchalant and like her number isn't burning a hole through my pocket, I stroll into the kitchen. "What's up, ladies?"

I look around at each female in the room, smiling and nodding, then stop on Chelsea. She's smiling back at me, but I must stare a little too long because she breaks up the awkwardness.

"Uh, hi, Bo." She laughs and brushes a strand of hair behind her ear.

I look away first because I don't need to embarrass myself further. "Where's Casey?" I ask, looking at Noelle.

"He's on the phone with Beck in his room. I'm sure they're almost done." She tilts her head toward his room while she grabs some plates from the cupboard.

"Oh, awesome. I want to go say hello to the big shot too. It's not every day your buddy is recruited to the NFL. I want to see how things are going in Chicago."

I turn to look at Charlie. "When does he come home for a visit?"

She's standing at the stove, pulling out what looks to be roasted chicken and potatoes. "I think he's planning to come down for the first game, but he hasn't gotten his tickets yet. If he comes, he'll have to leave right after. They have their last preseason game that weekend."

"That's right. Okay, I'm gonna go say hello. How much longer until dinner?" I put my hand in my pocket over my phone.

"Probably about five minutes, but don't hang up. I want to say goodbye." She calls after me. "Silas, no! Do not pick at the chicken with your fingers. Go wash your hands."

I laugh, hearing her scold Silas. "Will do." I wave my hand over my shoulder.

When I reach Casey's room, I tap on the door.

"Come in," he shouts from the other side of the door. "Sup, man. Dinner ready?"

"Charlie said it'll be another five minutes. I just wanted to say hi to Beck." I nod toward the cell in his hand.

"Let me put it on speaker." Casey taps the speaker button on his phone. "You there, brother?"

"Yeah, I'm here," Beck says. "How's it going, Callaway?"

"It's going. Casey tell you about the new curfew and the docuseries?" I huff a laugh.

Beck chuckles. "He did. Glad it's you guys and not me."

"Dude, it's gonna suck. The curfew part of it. I have my routine at home." Casey groans.

"You mean, your routine at home, where you fuck your girl-friend all night?" Beck laughs.

"Well, I mean, yeah. But also, it's not just fucking. She's the love of my life." Casey puts his hand over his heart, smiling. "I like having her here when I wake up too."

"Right, we're all aware of that. Speaking of girlfriends, where is mine?" The cell rings with an incoming FaceTime call from him. "Switch it over so I can see my girl."

Beck's face appears on the screen. He's sitting on a couch, with the skyline of Chicago in the background. The lights of the skyscrapers are starting to turn on, making the city shine. Chicago is a fun city. It's not one of my top choices, but I like to try picturing myself in places my friends play.

"You look rough, brother." Casey winces. "Is that a shiner?"

"Nah, just a little scratch. I got nailed by Johanson in practice the other day. Fucker was trying to lay me out and nearly did, but I juked right before he got me hard. Still got me hard enough that I slid across the turf. My helmet scraped my face. Hurt like a motherfucker more than the hit did." He smirks and shakes his head.

Pete Johanson is a beast. He's a safety for Chicago—and not someone I ever want coming at me. Lucky for Beck, he's his teammate, and the only time he has to face him is in practice.

"Rub some dirt on it. You'll be fine." I wink at him and give him my signature smile. The real one, not the one I use for media.

Beck gives me the finger. "Go get my girl. Oh, and, Bo? Have fun with all those interviews for the show this season. I'm sure you'll have a great time, getting followed around." He laughs.

"Well, I mean, I'm not sure they'll follow me around all the time, but, yeah, not looking forward to it." I shake my head and put my hands on my hips.

"Dude, they're gonna follow you around." Casey smirks and nods.

"Still waiting to see my girl. I'll catch up with you guys later." He waves his hand to gesture for us to walk out of the room.

"Char! You're being *beck*oned. Get it? Why am I so funny?" Casey laughs as he walks out of the room.

I follow him, laughing and shaking my head. "You're such a dork, dude."

Noelle, of course, thinks he's funny. "Casey King, you are a dork, but you're mine." She giggles and wraps her arms around his shoulders once he hands his phone off to his sister.

I glance over at Chelsea and see her smiling and watching them, which makes me smile. Her smile lights up her whole face. It's the kind of smile where you can tell the person is really happy, that it's genuine.

Silas must have left the room while we were on with Beck, and he walks back into the kitchen. "We ready to eat? I'm starving." Grabbing one of the plates off the counter, he starts scooping some of the potatoes from a bowl onto his plate, then grabs some chicken and salad too.

"Sure, go right ahead, Silas. We aren't waiting for my sister, who cooked the meal." Casey chuckles.

"Oh, sorry. Should I put it back?" he asks us.

"NO!" we collectively shout.

Silas smiles, knowing that would be the answer. "I'm a growing boy. I need to eat. My stomach waits for no one."

Just as he sits, Charlie comes back into the room, face a little flushed. "Silas, go right ahead." She waves her hand toward his food.

"Sorry, Charlie. I was hungry, and I wasn't sure how much longer you would be on with Beck. I heard you on the phone with him when I passed your room. Sounded like it was gonna be a while." He tries to smother a laugh.

"I have no idea what you mean, eavesdropper." Charlie spins on her heel and walks over to the food.

"Uh-huh. Out of respect for you and your brother, I'll keep what I heard to myself." He can't hold his laugh in anymore.

"Nope. Stop." Casey plugs his ears.

"Okay, kids. Let's just get our food and eat. I want to hear more about the docuseries y'all are going to be a part of this season. That sounds like fun!" Chelsea says as she walks over to grab a plate.

Casey starts to tell them everything that we know. I still need to look through the paperwork and also call my dad at some point tonight, not only about the show, but also about my tutoring. He's not going to be happy about the tutoring part. I'm not so sure how he'll feel about the show.

"So, will they come here to the house, do you think, or just stay around the stadium and locker room? And do they travel with y'all?" Noelle asks.

"I hope they don't come to the house. My room is a mess at all times, and my mama would kill me if it was caught on camera." Silas shovels more food into his mouth.

"Gross, Silas. Don't talk with your mouth full," Charlie scolds him, then looks at her brother. "What do you think, Case? They won't come here, will they?"

He shakes his head. "I don't think so. I would guess there's something in the contract about players' privacy."

Chelsea raises her hand, and it's freaking adorable. "I can look at it if you want. I mean, I'm not a lawyer yet, but I can definitely understand legal contracts."

"Oh, that's a good idea, Case. Let her look at it." Noelle nods.

"Yeah, you can take a look, but you have to sign a blood oath that you won't share it with anyone." He looks at her and raises his brows, trying not to laugh.

Chelsea makes a cross over her heart. "I promise. Attorney-client privilege and all that." She giggles.

"You're hired!" Silas says, raising his hand.

"Oh my God, Bo. Are you allowed to participate?" Charlie asks.

I pause, my fork just in front of my mouth, ready for me to take a bite. "Uh, what do you mean? Of course I can."

"I just meant, like, with your dad in politics and stuff. What is it he does again? I didn't know if that would be something you could do or not. Have the exposure or whatever," she says.

"Well, I'm not sure if you know this, but I'm on TV every weekend during football season." I laugh and try to think of a way out of talking about my dad too much.

"Ha-ha. I know, but it just popped into my mind. Never mind. It's none of my business." She waves her hand and continues eating.

"No, it's your business. You are my friend and roommate, but honestly, I don't have much to tell. I'll talk to my parents later and fill them in on what's going on." I'd really like to end this conversation about my dad.

"What does your dad do, Bo?" Chelsea asks.

And now I have to give them something. Although Casey knows my dad is a judge. He's not saying anything, but he's watching me to see what I'll share.

"He's a judge."

"That's right! I couldn't remember for some reason. You don't really talk about your parents much," Charlie says.

Chelsea is looking at me, head tilted to the side. "Oh, wow. That's really cool. Here in Oklahoma?"

I shake my head. "No, I'm from California." That's all I want to say about it, so I need to redirect the questioning. "So, Chelsea, what kind of law do you want to practice?"

She finishes chewing and takes a drink of her water. "Family law. Mostly children's rights type of stuff."

"I think that would be hard. I would want to save everyone," Charlie chimes in.

"Same! We'd have a house full of kids, Case." Noelle leans her head on Casey's shoulder.

"Well, most kids aren't that lucky, so that's why I want to be their voice when they don't have one." Chelsea gives a soft smile and looks down at her plate. It feels like she wants to talk about her interest in law as much as I want to talk about my dad's career.

I want to ask her more questions, but I want to be the only one to know the answers. What she likes, doesn't like. She fascinates me, and I want to know all about her. I want to know *her*. And lucky for me, I'll get my chance.

After dinner, Silas went to his room to play video games, and Charlie went to her room to call Beck again. I know it's hard on them, being apart this year. So, I'm sitting on the oversize chair we have in the family room, watching *SportsCenter* with Casey, Noelle, and Chelsea. Well, Casey and I are watching, and the girls are talking about something else.

I keep sneaking glances at Chelsea though. She's in leggings and a T-shirt that shows a sliver of her stomach. Her long, dark hair looks a little wild, and her legs are curled under her while she speaks animatedly to Noelle. But it's her eyes that mesmerize me. They're green, and they practically sparkle when she smiles.

Chelsea Sullivan might just be the most beautiful woman I've ever seen.

She catches me looking at her and smiles softly. When she looks back at Noelle, she leans in for a hug. And I'm jealous.

"I'd better get going. I have some work to do before I get to bed tonight. You're staying here, right?" she asks Noelle.

"Yes, I'm staying here tonight, unless you want me to come with you." Noelle stands when Chelsea stands from the couch.

"Don't be silly. Stay. I'm good, I promise." She walks toward the door and slips her shoes on.

Seeing this as my chance to talk to her alone for the first time tonight, I get up from the chair before she can leave. "I'll walk you to your car."

She stops for a second and looks at me. "Oh, okay, thanks."

I don't bother looking at Casey and Noelle. I'm sure they're wondering why I'm walking her out. "No problem."

I open the door for her, and she walks out before me.

We're halfway down the walkway when she speaks. "You don't have to walk me to my car. It's literally right in front of the house." She looks up at me.

"No problem at all. But I do have a reason to." I glance at her, smirking.

"Oh, yeah? What's the reason?" She turns to face me when we reach her car.

I clear my throat. "Well, it looks like we'll be spending more time together, so I wanted to talk to you about it so we could coordinate our schedules."

She looks confused. "What do you mean? Because I come over?"

"Not that. Um, it looks like you're my tutor." I hold out my hands.

"Your tutor? For what?" she asks, shaking her head.

"Well, long story, but my advisor made a mistake, and I guess I needed to take a psychology class my freshman year, but didn't. So, now, I'm in the class, and it's not exactly in my comfort zone, so I pretty much bombed the first quiz." I put my hands in my pockets and look down.

"Oh. Wow, okay. Not what I was expecting." She laughs.

"What were you expecting?" I ask, hoping maybe she was wanting me to ask her out. Because I want to do that too.

"I'm not sure, but I'm just surprised you need tutoring. You seem like you have your shit together, and I know y'all need to keep your grades up to play." She shrugs and looks down at her shuffling feet.

"Yes, we do, which is exactly why I need your help." I bend down to try and catch her eye.

"Just because you want me to be your tutor doesn't mean I automatically am."

"Oh. You're right. Coach gave me your number so I assumed—"

"I have to accept you as someone I'm willing to work with."

The side of my mouth tips up at the challenge. I kind of like the hard-to-get attitude, even if it's as my tutor. I give her the California charm. "Well, to start, I'm great company."

She raises a brow. "You think so, huh?"

"I'm charming, courteous, and an excellent conversationalist."

Her lips twitch like she's holding back a smile. "That's three. Got anything else on your résumé?"

"Plenty. I'm punctual, I listen well, I smell amazing, and I'm very easy on the eyes." I flash her my most practiced grin.

That finally earns me a laugh. "You smell amazing?"

"Don't take my word for it." I lean just a little closer. "Go ahead. Check for yourself."

She shoves my shoulder with a laugh, cheeks pink. "You're ridiculous."

"And fun. Don't forget fun. I'm basically the full package."

"Full package?" She folds her arms, smirking. "You realize you're trying to sell yourself for a study session, right?"

"Hey, if I'm this good at convincing you to tutor me, just imagine how great I'll be at acing psychology."

Chelsea looks up and meets my gaze. "All right, Bo Callaway, I'll help you get your grade up." She laughs, then turns to walk to the driver's side of the car, and I follow. "Do you have your phone on you?"

I pull my phone out of my pocket, pushing the Post-it Note with her number off it first. I don't know why I don't want her to know I have it. But for some reason, I want her to give it to me. "Yep."

She tells me her number, and I tap it into my phone while she speaks.

"Got it. Thank you." I drop my phone back into my pocket.

Nodding, she opens her car door. "Text me so I have your number. When I get home, I'll send you some dates and times, and we'll schedule the first session. Does that work?"

I grab the top of the door and hold it open while she gets into the car. "Sounds good. Thank you, Chelsea." I bend down so she doesn't have to look up.

"No problem. That's what I get paid for." She giggles. "I'm guessing the guys don't know about it, and that's why you didn't bring it up earlier?"

"Yeah," I sigh. "I'm not embarrassed or anything. I just want to take care of it privately, if that makes sense."

She looks at me for a long second and nods. "I get that. The need for privacy. I won't say anything to anyone."

"Thanks, Chelsea. Don't forget to text me your availability tonight. Coach wants me to get started as soon as possible so I'm ready for the next test." I mean, it's not a lie, but also, I want to talk to her some more.

"I won't forget."

She reaches for the handle to pull the door closed, but I wave her off and close the door for her.

When she starts the car, I step away so she can pull out of the spot on the street. She smiles at me as she passes, and I raise my hand to wave goodbye.

Once her taillights are gone from my view, I text her a simple, 'Hi, it's Bo,' then walk back into the house. Casey and Noelle must have gone to bed, which I'm kind of grateful for. I don't really want to answer questions.

I lock the door to the house since it seems everyone is in for the night. Then I grab a water bottle from the refrigerator before going to my room. I pull my phone out of my pocket to check the time to see if it's a good time to call my dad. The sooner I can get this over with, the better. I push on his Contact, and he answers on the second ring.

"Hello, son. I figured you might be calling me today." He chuckles.

"Hey, Dad." I close my bedroom door and then lie down on my bed. "You did, did you?" I smile.

I get along with both of my parents and my two sisters, Savannah and Caroline, who are still in high school, and generally, their approval makes my life … easier. I've been in some sort of spotlight my entire life, between football and my dad's career. But also, my dad's family is wealthy and fairly well known in California, regardless of his status as a Supreme Court judge.

"I assume you knew about the show before today, right?" he asks.

"We knew at the end of last year that it was a possibility, but since we didn't hear anything, I thought maybe it was dead in the water. You found out before me, I take it?" I shake my head even though he can't see me.

He lets out a deep laugh. "I did. But you know that's part of the process. It's a pretty standard media agreement. You know by now what you can and can't say regarding the family, so I'm not worried about that. According to the contract, you should be able to have some privacy, but, Bo, they are going to be on you the whole time. You understand that, right? This is a big year for you, and you have a lot of eyes watching."

As if I don't know. I can handle the pressure pretty well, but when he puts it like this … yeah, it becomes real.

"I know. I'm not worried about it. Hopefully, it will be fun, but for my sake and my roommates', I don't want them here at the house."

"The house is off-limits, so you should be okay. I think you or one of your roommates has to agree to them coming into the house. Just make sure no one allows it." He laughs.

"Yeah, no. Casey's pretty private, as is his sister, and Silas already said he doesn't want them here because his room is messy." We both laugh, and then I clear my throat. "There is something else I need to talk to you about."

"Okay ... what's going on?" he asks.

"I know you'll get notified, but I wanted to be the one to tell you that I need to work with a tutor to get my psychology grade up. We had one quiz that I didn't do well on, so Coach has set me up with a tutor so I don't lose my eligibility." I pause. "I'm not worried about it, and Coach isn't either. Plus, I know my tutor, so it should be fine."

My dad sighs. "Bo, really? Psychology?"

"I know. I'm still annoyed that I have to take it at all." I sit up in the bed and swing my legs to the side.

"Right. Makes no sense, but you do what you have to. Regardless of where you get drafted, you know we want you to finish your degree," he says pointedly.

"Yes, I know, and I want to. My football career won't last forever." As much as I hate to think it, it's true.

"No distractions this year, Bo. You hear me?" I can hear him moving papers around. "I have to run. Call your mother later to say hello. She misses you."

"Will do. Talk to you later, Dad."

"Love you, son," he says before he hangs up, not waiting for my response.

That went better than I'd thought it would. I've always had good grades, and my parents expect it of me and my sisters. Not doing well in school is just flat-out unacceptable. So, I think that's why his lack of lecture surprises me.

I stand up from my bed and walk out of my room. Now that the call is done, I'm anxious to hear from Chelsea. Walking into the kitchen, I go into the pantry and grab my secret stash of Twizzlers. I don't eat a lot of processed sugar, but Twizzlers are something I could never give up.

After pulling off five ropes, I put the bag back in my secret spot and walk back to my room, eating the whole bunch as I go. With my free hand, I grab my bag off the floor and set it on my bed. I need to pull out my practice gear before it stinks up my bag for days.

I finish my Twizzlers, then unzip my bag, taking everything out I need to wash. I set my phone on the bed beside my bag so I can see when Chelsea texts. I'm not usually the kind of guy who waits for a girl to make the first move. When I want to talk to someone, I call or text. But there's something about Chelsea that makes me want to let her set the pace.

Maybe it's because she's not like anyone else. She doesn't fake laugh at my jokes just to boost my ego. She smirks, then fires back with one of her own, which is usually sharper than mine. I've watched her stop in the middle of a crowded hallway to help a freshman who dropped an armful of books. I've seen her turn down a party invite without hesitation because she had a test the next morning. And the way her whole face lights up when she laughs? That's the kind of thing you don't forget, no matter how much you try.

Plus, there's something reserved about her. Like she has a little secret, and I'm intrigued as all hell to learn what it is she hides behind that smile.

I look down at my phone again before I leave my room to go start a load of laundry. If she doesn't text tonight before my alarm goes off to signal my bedtime, I'll text her first thing in the morning. Or maybe not first thing because I'm not sure if she's an early riser, like me, so maybe by, like, nine a.m. Totally reasonable.

CHAPTER
FOUR

CHELSEA

MY WHOLE WAY home from dinner last night, I thought about Bo. When he had said he was walking me out, my mind ran through a few different scenarios, one of which was that he was going to ask me out. To my surprise, I was disappointed he hadn't because, throughout the night, I'd caught him looking at me. But not in a creepy way. In a *I like you* kind of way.

When I got home, I took my shower and got myself ready for bed. Before turning in, I texted Bo the days and times I blocked for tutoring and waited for a reply to see if they worked with his class and practice schedules. He didn't reply right away, so I turned in for the night, but when I woke up this morning, there was a text from him, saying he would meet me tomorrow mid-morning at the library, which was my first available time slot. I wasn't sure if it could work with his schedule between classes and football, but he didn't ask for a different date, so I assumed the timing worked for him.

I'm on my way to class with a lot on my mind. I still need to finish a few law school applications. However, I'm still unde-cided about where I want to apply, aside from Walker and Penn.

My cell phone rings just as I'm pulling into the commuter parking lot. When I put my car in park, I pull my phone out of my bag and see that it's my aunt calling. My sister's eighteenth birthday is coming up, and I know they both want me to come home to celebrate it.

"Hello, you've reached Chelsea Sullivan. I can't come to the phone right now, but if you leave me a message, I'll probably text you back." I can't hold in my laugh.

My aunt and I are really close, although it took a little bit of time for that to happen.

"Hello, Chelsea Sullivan. This is your favorite aunt calling." We both laugh now. "Did I get you at a bad time? I don't have your new schedule in front of me."

"No, I'm good for a few minutes. I just pulled into school. I have about ten minutes before class, so you'll be walking with me."

I turn off my car, grab my backpack, and get out. I lock the door with my key fob over my shoulder as I walk. I switch my phone to my other hand so I can put the other strap of my backpack over my shoulder.

"Okay, I'll be quick. Are you going to be able to come home for Torie's birthday? It would mean a lot to her," she says quickly. "I love that you took extra classes this summer, but Florida misses you … and so do we."

I gnaw at my bottom lip. "I know. I'm trying to figure it out. Let me get through the day and double-check my schedule. I just talked to her the other day, and I really want to see her for her big day. She said you're taking her to the Bahamas with a few friends for graduation?" I ask.

She sighs. "Yes, that's what she wants to do. I would much prefer a one-on-one trip, like you and I had for your graduation, but you know Tor; she is a social butterfly and wants all her *besties* to come. I just hope Eve's mom, Julie, doesn't want to join us. She gets on my nerves."

"Eww, yeah, she's not fun. What's the plan for her birthday?

Are we just doing the three of us, or is she having a bunch of people there? I just need to be socially prepared." I laugh.

"Well, it depends on what day you come in and how long you get to stay. Dinner with the three of us for sure." I hear her moving around her office.

She's a pediatrician, and she must be between patients. I can see her office in my mind. Probably still featuring my and Torie's artwork from school and pictures of the three of us.

"I just got to my building, so let me get back to you later on whether or not I can come in early, but it's not likely." I see a few people from my class walk by and into the building. "I'd better run. Class is about to start."

"Okay, sweet girl. I'll talk to you later. Have a good day. I love you!" Her voice pitches at the *I love you*.

"Love you more. Talk to you later," I say and start to take the phone away from my ear to disconnect.

"Oh, wait, Chels! We need to talk about that letter sooner rather than later. Sorry ..." She stalls.

The letter.

It's been something Aunt Laura has brought up a few times over the last month. It was sent to the house, and she forwarded it to me. It's sitting in my desk drawer, unopened and staring at me whenever I go to grab a pen.

"I mean, I would rather not. But we'll talk about it later. I don't want it on my mind today. I have a lot to do," I say, aggravated. Not at her, just at the mention of the letter since it's from my dad.

"I know. I'm sorry. It just popped in my mind. Love you." She makes a kissing sound.

"Love you too. I'll call you guys later." I disconnect and pull the door open to head into my class.

Funny enough, it's a Developmental and Child Psychology class. I'm sure they could do a whole case study on me and my sister. It'd probably be enough material for an entire semester.

We're actually both as mentally healthy as anyone could be, considering our history. Torie was pretty little when my aunt got us; she really doesn't have many memories of what it was like with my parents before my mom died. Luckily.

I, on the other hand, remember a lot. And most of it wasn't good. Especially the memories from that night my mother was killed. I've been through years of therapy, and I've dealt with the trauma of it all, not that I don't get bad dreams here and there, but I know how to process it in a way that isn't harmful to me or sets me back in any way.

Thinking about what could have happened to us if we hadn't had our aunt … I can't even imagine how we would have turned out or if we would have been able to stay together at all. After my mom's murder, the Florida Department of Children and Family immediately took custody of us and, within twenty-four hours, had a shelter hearing before a judge. At the shelter hearing, my aunt—the only surviving blood relative we had, who we didn't even know—was granted emergency placement. Most cases aren't as easy as ours was in terms of placement.

After social evaluations and more hearings, the court granted my aunt a long-term guardianship plan. She legally adopted us nine months later.

And that's why I want to go into family law, advocating for children. We were fortunate that she wanted us without a doubt in her mind. At least, that's what she's always told us. She's never made us feel like we weren't wanted or loved. Sure, it was difficult in the beginning, especially with me becoming a teenager not long after she got us. Dealing with all the counseling and the hormones on top of it … bless her for not giving up on me. She has been a mother, in every sense of the word, to us both, and I wouldn't be where I am today without her.

After class, I decide to stop at the coffee shop in the campus common area. When I walk into the building, I look to my right and spot Bo sitting on one of the couches in the lounge area, looking like the snack he is, wearing gray sweatpants and a Walker University Football T-shirt with his number on it. I internally debate on whether or not I should go say hello or if it would be weird. I mean, he's my friend, sort of, and I'll be tutoring him, so I probably should.

Why am I acting like this? I literally never get flustered with guys. My thoughts make me laugh, which draws his attention. I'm looking right at him and laughing. Great.

He smiles and waves at me. "Hey, Chelsea. What's so funny?"

Now it really would be weird if I didn't go over and say hi, so I stroll over to him. "Hey." I smile and shift my bag on my shoulder. "Oh, nothing. Just funny running into you here."

He nods. "I mean, not that funny, considering I go to school here too." He laughs. "You between classes or done for the day?"

"Just finished one class, and I have one more before I'm done. But then I need to meet the other student I'm tutoring." I take a seat on the chair next to the couch.

He puts his hand on his heart. "You mean I'm not your only one? I'm crushed," he says, laughing.

I smile at him and feel my cheeks heat. "I have another. I'm sorry, but you'll have to share me." I shrug.

"I don't like to share. Is it another athlete?"

"Soccer," I state.

"Damn. Those guys are fit and definitely have a good time. I bet he tries to sweep you off your feet."

"Well, it's a *she*, not a *he*. Not my type, although she could be a new bestie. You never know."

His shoulders relax as he sits back. "But I'll be your best student." He winks at me and smirks.

"Oh, yeah? You take direction well then? Like to be told what to do?" I smile, testing him a little to gauge his response to my blatant innuendo.

He barks out a laugh. "In certain situations, yeah, maybe. I guess we'll have to see how it goes." He leans back in his chair and tilts his head, his brow raised as he studies me. "So, what brought you to Oklahoma? Doesn't seem like the kind of state a girl from the Sunshine State would want to go."

"Says the West Coast guy."

"Exactly. But I'm here for football. Because no one just wakes up and says, *You know where I want to be? Oklahoma.*"

I smirk. "Maybe I did."

He chuckles. "Nah. You're too smart for that."

I swirl one of my curls between my fingers, keeping my tone light. "Let's just say … it was time for a change. Walker was far enough away, and that was enough."

"That's all you're giving me?"

"That's all there is," I answer easily, though I can see the way he's still searching my face, like he's trying to pry more out of me.

"You're tough," he says finally, grinning. "Most people like talking about themselves."

"I'm not most people."

"No kidding." He shakes his head but smiles like he's enjoying the challenge. "All right. I'll let you keep your secrets— for now."

I lift my brows, playful but firm. "Smart choice."

We stare at each other for a minute, smiles on both of our faces. I sit back in my chair, crossing my legs to mirror his casual sprawl.

"So, besides football and being a mediocre student, what else should I know about you?"

He smirks. "Mediocre? Harsh. You've never even seen me study."

"Exactly," I shoot back. "The fact that I had to be recruited to keep you eligible speaks for itself."

"Fair," he concedes with a laugh. "Okay, let's see ... I like wings, video games, and long walks on the beach ... at least, that's what it says on my dating profile." He winks, and I know he's kidding.

"Any special talents?"

"I could answer that in more than one way, but I'll keep this PG." He taps his chin like he's thinking hard. "I make the best chicken wings you'll ever eat."

I arch a brow. "You cook?"

"*Cook* might be a strong word," he admits with a grin. "But I grill like a champ. You haven't been here when it's my night to cook. My roommates beg me to do it every time there's a game."

"Impressive. Wings and video games. Truly a renaissance man."

He points at me. "Don't forget the long walks on the beach. That's key."

I laugh. "Except there are no beaches in Oklahoma."

"Minor detail." He bends closer to me, smirking. "You're not supposed to poke holes in my profile. You're supposed to be impressed."

"Oh, I'm very impressed," I say, deadpan. "You're basically every girl's dream guy."

"Exactly." He sits back, smug, though his eyes are glinting with amusement. "And you? What's on your profile? Got any hobbies?"

I tilt my head, smiling like I might answer. "Wouldn't you like to know?"

He groans, dragging a hand over his face. "You're gonna make me work for every scrap, aren't you?"

"Pretty much." I'm enjoying the little spark of frustration in his eyes. "Fine. I'll give you a hint. I like organizing."

"Organizing?" His brows shoot up. "Like … closets? Calendars? Color-coded chaos?"

I shrug, keeping my tone light. "Exactly that. Drawers, closets, planners … I like putting things in order. It's kind of my thing."

"You don't watch those organization porn videos on TikTok, do you?"

I lean forward and drop my voice to show I'm serious when I say, "All. Night. Long."

He laughs, shaking his head. "Okay, I have to admit, that's way more specific than I expected. And somehow … kinda cute."

"You might be the first one to ever believe so," I tease.

He laughs again, clearly entertained. "Unbelievable. Organized chaos … meets mystery girl."

"Exactly," I reply, flashing him a small smile.

We stare at each other, smiling. There's a sizzle in the air between us that seems to have ignited over simple banter.

This kind of feeling isn't something I'm used to. Magnetic men aren't usually my type. I like them mellow and easy to get over when the relationship ends.

Bo, though, is a different breed of man. He's the kind that can pull you in with chiseled good looks and then trap you with his wit and humor. That is a dangerous combination.

My phone buzzes from my bag, breaking my attention from him. I pull it out and see a text from Noelle.

"Oh, I'm very impressed," I say, deadpan. "You're basically every girl's dream guy."

"Exactly." He sits back, smug, though his eyes are glinting with amusement. "And you? What's on your profile? Got any hobbies?"

I tilt my head, smiling like I might answer. "Wouldn't you like to know?"

He groans, dragging a hand over his face. "You're gonna make me work for every scrap, aren't you?"

"Pretty much." I'm enjoying the little spark of frustration in his eyes. "Fine. I'll give you a hint. I like organizing."

"Organizing?" His brows shoot up. "Like ... closets? Calendars? Color-coded chaos?"

I shrug, keeping my tone light. "Exactly that. Drawers, closets, planners ... I like putting things in order. It's kind of my thing."

"You don't watch those organization porn videos on TikTok, do you?"

I lean forward and drop my voice to show I'm serious when I say, "All. Night. Long."

He laughs, shaking his head. "Okay, I have to admit, that's way more specific than I expected. And somehow ... kinda cute."

"You might be the first one to ever believe so," I tease.

He laughs again, clearly entertained. "Unbelievable. Organized chaos ... meets mystery girl."

"Exactly," I reply, flashing him a small smile.

We stare at each other, smiling. There's a sizzle in the air between us that seems to have ignited over simple banter.

This kind of feeling isn't something I'm used to. Magnetic men aren't usually my type. I like them mellow and easy to get over when the relationship ends.

Bo, though, is a different breed of man. He's the kind that can pull you in with chiseled good looks and then trap you with his wit and humor. That is a dangerous combination.

My phone buzzes from my bag, breaking my attention from him. I pull it out and see a text from Noelle.

Noelle: I have some bad news.

"Oh no." I huff.

"What's wrong?" Bo asks.

"I'm not sure. I just got a text from Noelle, saying she has some bad news. I mean, it could be anything from her breaking a nail or something serious." I snicker.

Chelsea: What's wrong?

Noelle: So you know the guys that live above us?

Chelsea: Yesss...

Noelle: Apparently, they have a cockroach issue, and the entire building needs to be fumigated.

"Fuck," I whisper.

"What is it?" Bo prods.

I groan. "The guys who live above us have a roach issue. I guess they have to fog the whole building, which is really inconvenient."

Chelsea: Awesome. I assume you'll go stay with Casey, right?

Noelle: Yes, and I don't mean to overstep, but I asked him if you could stay there too. Charlie was with us and said you can bunk with her or something. Or she said she can give you her room and go stay with Arbor and Lily.

Chelsea: I don't want to take her room. I mean, it doesn't matter to me about sharing a room. Whatever is easiest. Can you tell Casey and Charlie I said thank you?

Noelle: Absolutely. I guess we need to get our stuff today. They're starting tomorrow.

Chelsea: Okay, I have tutoring until four, but I'll run home after. Should I just meet you at the apartment or Casey's?

"Can I help with anything?" Bo asks.

I shake my head and look at him. "No. I mean, I guess you already are. I'll be staying at your house for a few days. Casey offered to let me stay there while the apartment building is getting debugged."

A slow smile spreads across his face. "Tutoring and a roomie, huh?"

"Looks like it." I turn my attention back to my phone.

Noelle: I won't get home from school around then either, so I'll meet you there, and we can go over to the house together. Does that work for you?

Chelsea: Sounds good. See you later.

I check the time, then close out my screen and put my phone back in my bag. "I need to run. I need a caffeine fix before my next class. So, I guess I'll see you later." I stand.

Bo stands with me and slings his backpack over his shoulder. "I'd better get going too. I need to get to the field soon. I could use an energy drink or something. I'm starting to drag."

I bite the inside of my lip to keep from smiling and start walking toward the coffee shop.

"What do you like to drink? Are you a sugary coffee drinker?" he asks.

I shake my head. "Not too sugary. I want more coffee than sweetener or syrups. I usually go for a chai or a macchiato with a dash of caramel in it. Or sometimes, when I'm feeling a little quirky, I'll branch out and do a matcha."

"Is that the green one?"

"Yeah."

"Does it taste like grass? I imagine it tasting … earthy." He laughs.

I look up at him and smile. "Not really. At least I don't think so. Why don't you go crazy and try one today?"

"Maybe I will," he says.

We reach the shop and step up to the counter.

"This is my treat," he says.

"You don't have to do that." I wave him off.

"Nope. I insist." He puts his hand on my lower back, which shoots tingles straight up my spine, and guides me forward.

I place my order for a vanilla chai and give them my name, and he orders the matcha and an energy drink and gives them his name.

"Double fisting, eh?" I look at him.

"The energy drink is my backup plan in case I don't like the matcha." He chuckles.

The barista gives him the total, and Bo pulls out his phone from his pocket to tap the payment. Once he's paid, he drops his phone back in his pocket, and we move down the line, his hand on my lower back again. When we reach the end of the line, his hand stays in place, and I don't say anything.

I'm not sure if this is like an automatic reaction for him or if he intends to touch me. I don't hate it—that's for sure. I can feel the warmth of his hand through my clothes. It's calming, but also … those tingles are back.

"Chelsea," the barista calls out.

"That would be you." Bo slides his hand up my back, then drops his hand.

I take my drink off the counter and turn to him. "Thanks for the chai. I appreciate it, even though you totally didn't have to."

"It's not a problem, and it's absolutely my pleasure to serve you, Chelsea." He places his hand on my shoulder and squeezes gently.

Our gazes are locked, and we're both smiling.

"Bo!" the barista calls out.

Without breaking his stare, he reaches over and grabs his two drinks and tips his head in the direction of the exit.

I turn on my heel and start walking, feeling his stare on me. I've always thought he was good-looking, but it seems like his hotness is all up in my face now. Possibly because I've spent more time around him over the last year, and lucky me ... I'm about to spend more time with him.

When we get outside the doorway of the coffee shop, he comes up next to me so we're walking side by side. "What class are you in now?" he asks.

I push the door to the outside open, and he reaches over me to hold it open.

"Environmental Law and Crime." I wiggle my eyebrows.

"Wow, okay. That sounds intense." He chuckles. "You excited about that?"

I smile up at him as we walk toward the building where my class is located. "Actually, yes."

"Good. It definitely makes the class go faster when it's something you like." He takes a sip of the matcha and scrunches up his nose.

"Don't like it?" I ask him, giggling.

He turns his head side to side. "Actually, it's not too bad. A little sweet, but not too sweet. Has a grassy flavor. Kind of like drinking a shot of wheat grass with milk in it."

"I don't think I've ever had wheat grass, so I can't tell you if you're right or wrong." I shrug.

"You're not missing anything. I drink it occasionally because it's good for you, but it's not a preferred beverage." He snickers.

"I'll take your word for it." I tilt my head toward the building in front of us. "This is me. I guess I'll see you tonight."

He smiles a wicked smile and nods. "Looking forward to it. Have a good class." He starts walking backward.

Smiling, I shake my head and turn to open the door.

Those eyes, that smile, and that body of his could make a girl lose her mind. Except for me, of course. Because I know better. At least that's what I'm going to tell myself since he and I will be sleeping under the same roof.

CHAPTER
FIVE

BO

WHEN I SAW Chelsea walk into the commons today, she nearly took my breath away. It reminded me of the first time I'd met her. It was last year, move-in day for her and Noelle into their apartment. I got out of Casey's truck, and when I saw her, I'd nearly stopped in my tracks.

Like then, today, she was wearing cutoff jean shorts, a baggy T-shirt, and a pair of Vans on her feet. The only difference today was that her long, wavy hair was down instead of in a ponytail. She's absolutely beautiful, and there's no pretense with her. And her confidence makes her even more stunning.

The change between now and then is, I'm not as tongue-tied around her. And if I'm not mistaken, she was flirting with me earlier. To be honest, I'm not really sure why I haven't taken a chance with her before now. Sure, I've been hyper-focused on football and getting to the next level, but I'm not a saint, and I've had some mutual fun with some lovely ladies around campus. Just haven't found anyone really worth pursuing until her. But with her having to stay with us temporarily and getting assigned as my tutor ... I feel like it's a sign.

My stop at the coffee shop put me about five minutes behind schedule, but it was absolutely worth spending a few extra minutes with her. Standing at the crosswalk, waiting for the light to change, I take another sip of the matcha and decide it's just not for me, so I toss it in the garbage can next to the light post.

The light changes, and I start walking toward the field house, sucking down my energy drink quickly because once I get into the building, I need to hightail it to the locker room, where I'm supposed to be for my first interview for the first episode of the docuseries. I'm used to the media attention at this point, and I'll try to use this opportunity to show the NFL teams that I'm ready for the next step, but now I'm just anxious to get home and see Chelsea again.

I pull the handle on the door just as Ace and Aston Griffith walk out.

"Sup, fellas." I nod at them.

Their older brother, Archie, and I played together my first year here. He's a beast, and he now plays for the Cowboys. These two are twins, but couldn't be more different personality-wise. Aston is much calmer in person, but a terror on the field. Ace is a complete joker on and off the field. Both of them are amazing ballers though.

"What up, Callaway?" Ace holds out his fist for a bump.

"Bo." Aston nods.

"Where are you two going? We have practice in an hour." I stand with my back to the door, holding it open.

"We'll be back before it starts. Ace wanted to try out the cryo chamber, even though I told him he should do it after practice, but he thinks he knows best about everything, so here we are." Aston rolls his eyes.

"Oh, yeah. How'd you like it, Ace?" I ask him, smiling.

"Shrank my balls, dude. Not a fan of that, but I'm definitely doing it again after practice sometime." He chuckles.

I look at Aston, who is shaking his head.

"I gotta head in. I'll see you boys in an hour." I turn to walk into the building.

"Later," they both call out.

I walk down through the hall of champions toward the locker room. Trophies, various awards, and thousands of photos line the walls—all of Walker University's greats, including photos from our championship win from two seasons ago, my freshman year.

Pushing the door open to the locker room, I see the camera crews already set up, and Casey is there, talking to Coach Pettys. He was getting interviewed today as well. He'll be a number one recruit as a wide receiver this year for sure, so he'll have a good amount of eyes on him.

I walk toward them to say hello. And I'm not really sure what the process is, so I want to ask Casey how it went for him.

"Hey, Coach. King," I nod at Coach and fist-bump Casey.

"Hey, Bo. How's it going?" Coach smiles and tilts his head to the side.

"Going good. Do I need to change?" I realize I might be underdressed in my sweatpants and T-shirt, but Casey's fit is about the same as mine.

"Nah, you're fine. They know they're filming athletes." Coach chuckles.

"Right. I just wasn't sure if I should maybe put different pants on or something." I honestly didn't think about what I was wearing when I left the house today.

"Do you have other clothes here?" he asks.

"I mean, nothing a whole lot different than what I have on, I guess." I shrug.

"Dude, you're fine. You'll be sitting in the chair the whole time anyway. It's not a big deal." Casey ruffles my hair. "You might want to run a comb through that mop though."

"Dick," I mutter.

"Bo, I'm not sticking around, if that's okay. I have a few

things I need to take care of before practice." Coach places his hand on my shoulder.

"Yeah, I'm good." I nod.

"I'll keep an eye on him, Coach. I'll make sure he doesn't discuss the playbook or anything." Casey wraps an arm around my shoulders.

"Whatever." I laugh and push his arm off of me.

"You'll have fun." Coach chuckles. "Emily, from our media department, will keep an eye on you in case you need anything or feel uncomfortable with any questions." He turns and walks away.

I head over to my stall to fix my hair that Casey messed up, and he follows.

"Bo?" A woman in a pantsuit and pin-straight hair approaches me. "I'm Emily, one of the producers from the Sports Network. I'll be working with you on *Gridiron Stallions*. We're excited to be highlighting the team and following you throughout the season."

"I'm honored you chose our program."

"Between us, you were a big reason why we did. There were a lot of teams being considered. Hopefully, we'll be able to end the series with a big announcement, like maybe where you're going next year."

I clap my hands and nod. "Yeah, I'd like to know the answer to that myself, but I need to get through this season first."

"Right. We'll need you in five. Can you be ready?"

"Yes, ma'am." I nod.

"Ew, don't call me ma'am. I'm, like, two years older than you," she says as she walks away.

Casey and I look at each other and laugh.

"Oh, so, hey, Noelle and Chelsea's apartment building needs to get fumigated, so they're staying with us for a few days. Is that cool with you?" he asks.

I nod, maybe a little too eagerly. "Yeah, man. Not a problem with me. Totally sucks about the building though."

"Right? So gross. I guess it was the guys upstairs having the problem, and then the super decided it was best to treat the whole building, which is smart. Noelle would flip if they got roaches in their apartment." He grimaces.

"I don't think anyone wants to have roaches. Pretty disgusting." I shake my head.

"Exactly." He puts his hand on my shoulder. "So, I wonder what they'll ask you about."

I pull a deep breath in and exhale. "I'm assuming about the upcoming season, no?"

"Yeah, I just wonder if they'll ask us all the same questions or if they'll be different for each player." He drops his hand and starts walking toward the center of the locker room and the cameras.

I check my hair in the mirror inside my locker and swipe my hand through it quickly to smooth it back the best I can. My phone buzzes in my pocket, so I take it out and see a text from my dad, telling me to have fun with the interview and keep my answers geared around the season. As if I don't know what I'm doing. I give the text a thumbs-up and set my cell on the shelf in my stall. If it buzzes when I'm getting interviewed, it will distract me.

When I walk over to the makeshift set, the producer gestures to the chair in front of the cameras. "Hey, Bo. I'm Kyler Bozeman, the producer for the show." He has an iPad in one hand and holds his other hand out to me, and I shake it. "I'll go over the whole process with you, then answer any questions you might have. Sound good?"

"Yep, sounds good to me." I look over at Casey, who's still standing nearby. "You sticking around for this?"

"Nah, I just want to make sure my QB is all set." He winks at me.

"Okay, Bo, so you'll stay in that seat for the interview today. We'll ask you questions, which will be edited out so the viewer won't hear the questions, and you'll answer. Don't say my name in response to any of my questions either. Ideally, we want it to be as conversational as possible and less interview-style. Does that make sense?" Kyler asks.

"Understood. I'll do my best to be as natural as possible and not sound robotic." I chuckle. "I'm used to pressers, so I should be fine."

"I'm gonna head out, Callaway. See you on the field in a bit."

I hold my hand out to Casey for a bump.

"Later, man." I nod at him as he turns to walk out.

Kyler is standing closer to me now, then calls over a girl who is holding a comb and what looks like powder that girls put on their face. "Hair is fine. Brush the nose and forehead."

I've never worn any kind of makeup a day in my life. "Is that necessary?" I ask him.

"It's just to take the shine off the skin. Once we set the lighting, sometimes, the face can look a little glossy. You don't need much." He turns and walks back over to a high chair and sits down. He sets his iPad on his lap and taps on it a few times.

The girl with the makeup walks away, and I shift in my chair until I'm comfortable. I don't want to come across stiff or awkward on camera. I run my hand through my hair again, brushing it back.

"Let's get the mics adjusted and get moving. We have forty minutes to get Bo done before his practice. Then we'll wrap today." Kyler nods to someone near the big light next to his chair.

I watch as the guy sets a long pole up with the mic attached. He settles it between me and Kyler.

"Check, check," Kyler says, and another guy standing off to the side in front of a computer monitor gives him a thumbs-up.

Lights dim in the room, making the red lights above our lockers and the W on the ceiling glow bright. There's a soft light shining near me, but not directly on me. I feel like I'm under a spotlight in a way.

The same guy who adjusted the mic holds a board like you

see in the movies. It has my name on it. "Bo Callaway. First interview." He claps the top piece to the body of the board.

"Introduce yourself first, say where you're from, then roll into answering the question." He looks at me, and I nod in understanding. "Bo, you were the number one recruit in the country coming out of your senior year in high school. Tell us why you chose to come to Walker University instead of, let's say, Ohio State, who recruited you heavily. Or staying in California and playing for USC or UCLA." Kyler nods at me to start.

"Bo Callaway, San Francisco, California. Number six. Quarterback for the Walker University Stallions." I shift in my seat and fold my hands in my lap. "Walker was always my top choice. If you want to be legendary, you come to Walker." I unfold my hands and lift them up slightly. "I mean, the football program's history speaks for itself. There's just a standard of excellence that is expected; it's the culture. When you come into the building and you see all the history lining the halls, no other program in the country compares. You want to be part of that history, be remembered."

"When you came to Walker, did you know you would be taking over the starting position from Liam Pitz?" he asks pointedly.

"Liam Pitz is an amazing quarterback and my friend. I don't see the need to discuss that on camera. It has nothing to do with the upcoming season. Move on to the next question, please." The question annoys me because what I said is true. Liam is my friend, and honestly, I had to prove myself the same as he did that season.

"Fair." He shifts his head to the side and looks back at his iPad. "Can you tell us about your relationship with Coach Pettys?"

"When I met Coach Pettys, I knew we would be a good fit. Not only has he had an amazing career, but his coaching style matches what I need to inspire me to be the best quarterback I can be. Not only do I admire him as my coach, but also as a man." I smile. "He believes in and cares about every athlete on the team. I can't imagine playing for anyone else."

Kyler asks me some more questions about the upcoming season, about teams I'm looking forward to playing, but thankfully and surprisingly, he stays away from asking personal questions. As we're finishing up, he explains that they'll be following me around campus from time to time and definitely around the team facilities. None of that surprises me, as it was all listed in the packets we were given. Am I looking forward to it? Not really, but also, I know there will be a lot of eyes on me this season, and I need to represent my team positively. I can talk football all day though, so as long as they stay in that lane, we'll be just fine.

A few hours later, I open the door to my house and hear laughter. Charlie, Noelle, and Chelsea are sitting on the couches, watching some reality show with people on a yacht. I don't think they've noticed me yet, so I just stand there quietly, listening to them.

"Oh my God, he totally slept with Kate. How have they been able to keep it quiet this long?" Charlie slaps her hand on her leg.

"Seriously, Sean is a total player. He slept with Mallory last season," Chelsea says.

"Yuck. How do they not have a gazillion STDs on those

yachts? They all slept with each other at some point or another."
Noelle turns to look at Charlie and sees me. "Oh, hi, Bo! Where's
Casey?"

"Hello, ladies. How's everyone doing?" I smile and look at
Chelsea.

She tucks a piece of her hair behind her ear, smiling.

Charlie turns to face me, still sitting on the couch. "Hey, Bo. If
you're hungry, I made some extra grilled chicken and veggies,
even though it's not my night to cook for everyone." She winks
at me.

"You're the best, Charlie. I'm starving." I pat my stomach.
"Did you all eat? Should I save some for Casey and Silas too?" I
ask, walking toward the kitchen.

"We ate already, but I'm sure my brother and Silas will need
to eat when they get home, unless they grab something at the
field," Charlie calls out.

"Okay, thanks." I grab a plate from the cabinet and set it on
the counter, then walk to the fridge and pull the chicken and
veggies out.

While I eat, I listen to the girls talking and laughing, and it
makes me smile. They're funny, talking about their predictions
for the show and making guesses on who will hook up. But what
I hear next stops me in my tracks.

"Speaking of hookups, Chelsea, whatever happened to that
guy you were hanging out with occasionally last year? He was
kind of cute," Noelle asks her.

*What guy? I don't remember any guys hanging around. She defi-
nitely didn't bring anyone over here.*

Chelsea lets out a laugh. "Oh, Patrick? He was just someone
to mess around with. Nothing serious at all."

"Patrick, that's right. I couldn't think of his name for some
reason," Noelle says.

"Yeah, he wasn't all that memorable in any area, if you know
what I mean," Chelsea says, and they all laugh.

"Oh, there's a really hot guy in my Art Therapy class. I could get his number for you. He seems like your type," Charlie says.

"What's my type?" Chelsea asks her with a giggle.

"Like, studious? I don't know." Charlie starts to laugh. "Just seems like someone I could see you with. Definitely not my type, but he is cute."

"Thanks, Charlie, but I'll pass. The last guy I hooked up with who was 'studious' got a little too serious, too fast. It has been a while for me though," she says with a sigh.

I mean, I volunteer.

They move on to talk about the show again, and I finish eating, still listening in. They're funny together.

Once I'm done, I clean up my dishes. Then I grab my bag from near the doorway and head toward my room. I'd love to hang out with Chelsea, but she seems like she's having fun with the girls, so I don't want to intrude. As I pass by them, I can't help but look over at her. We make eye contact, and I smile at her, and she smiles back.

When I get to my room, I set my bag down near my dresser and pull out clean boxers and shorts and set them on my bed. I need to jump in the shower since I didn't shower at the field today. In all honesty, I wanted to get home to see if Chelsea was here yet.

I walk across the hall and into the bathroom and take one of the fastest showers of my life. I step out of the shower and grab my towel, rubbing it over my head, then wrap it around my waist. I swipe some deodorant on, run my comb through my hair, grab my dirty clothes, and step out into the hall, the towel hanging from my hips.

Walking to my room, I catch someone staring at me from the opposite end.

Not just anyone.

Chelsea. She must have been heading from the living room into the kitchen, but now she's standing there, her pretty mouth slightly parted, staring at me with her eyes wide. Her eyes roam from my chest and take a detour south until she gives a little squeak and then blinks as if she wasn't just checking me out.

I wink at her, then walk into my room, tossing my dirty clothes in my hamper in the corner. I played it cool in the hallway, but internally, I'm fucking reeling. The cutest girl in all of Walker was definitely checking me out. No doubt.

After running the towel over my body one time, I throw it into the corner, right into the middle of the basket. I pull my boxers up my legs, then my shorts. I should probably put a shirt on before I walk back out there, but ... I think I'll test the waters with Chelsea a little.

I need to know if I affect her like she does me.

CHAPTER
SIX

CHELSEA

BO CALLAWAY IS a true work of art.

His body is made of marble, I swear. He's long and lean, with just a little muscle bulk. I've been to this house a dozen times and never caught any of the guys in a state of undress. Of course it had to be Bo. I already think he's crazy attractive with clothes on. Without them, he's mind-numbingly hot.

I probably looked like a deer in headlights.

I had gotten up to get a drink during an ad break of our show when I heard the door open from the hallway and instinctively turned to look. When I saw Bo standing there, shirtless, a towel hanging low on his waist, I felt like I couldn't move. And when I say low, I mean I could see a nicely trimmed happy trail leading to what I have no doubt is a beautiful package.

Yes, I'm envisioning the man naked.

Now, I know not all men who are pretty like Bo have beautiful dicks, but let's be so for real. I'm sure he does. And a girl like me, who loves a good hookup without all the fuss, wouldn't mind finding out. Like right now. Would it be weird for me to

stroll back on down that hallway and walk into his room and rip
that towel off?

Calm it, Chelsea. You want a hookup, not a sexual rebellion.

My internal debate pauses when I see him come out of his
room, wearing gym shorts, also riding low, but not as low as the
towel. I nearly drop the grape Powerade I grabbed from the
fridge.

"Hey," he says as he comes into the kitchen.

I'm still standing near the fridge, and he stops in front of me.

"Hi," I say with a slight stutter. Good Lord, what is wrong
with me? He's struck me stupid with all those abs on display.

"Can I reach around you to grab a drink?" he says, smirking.
There's a literal twinkle in his blue eyes.

"That it is, but I don't want to hit you with the door." He
chuckles, then stretches his arm over my head, grabbing the top
of the fridge.

"Oh, right. Sorry!" I duck under his outstretched arm,
laughing.

He opens the door and also grabs a grape one too. "Not a
problem. You girls still watching the show?" he asks.

I nod as I take a drink. "Yes, I think there's a little time left.
Did you want to watch something? And did I take one of your
drinks?"

He shakes his head. "No, you're good. We all chip in for
groceries. Grape is just my favorite." He lifts up his bottle and
taps it to mine. "Twinsies."

Did he just say twinsies? How cute is he?

"Grape is also my favorite. Blue is the runner-up. Red is a no
go. Plus, it stains." I turn and walk back toward the couch, and
Bo follows me.

"Agreed. I do like the white one too. I think it's like a cherry
flavor or something." He takes a seat on the oversize chair, and I
sit back down on my space on the couch, which is closest to the
chair.

"Yeah, that one isn't bad either," I agree.

"I like that the color hides the truth. You don't know what's inside until you take the risk and try it. Kind of like people."

"And who said you're not good at psychology?" I tease.

The show starts back up just as Casey and Silas walk in the door.

"Hello, ladies." Silas nods and smiles. "What do we got going on here?"

"*Below Deck*. Shh," Charlie says.

Silas chuckles. "Sorry. I'll leave you to it," he says as he walks toward his room.

"Hi, pretty girl." Casey bends over and kisses Noelle, then moves to her neck for more kisses.

I'm used to seeing them like this, and I'm so happy for them, yet I've never wanted what they have. At least not until now. Something tugs in my chest, an ache that feels both sharp and sweet. I want that—arms pulling me close, lips brushing against the curve of my neck, a love that belongs to me.

"Hey." She giggles. "What took you so long?" She sniffs him. "You showered at the field?"

"I knew we were on our own tonight, so I grabbed some food at the field, and then I got to talking to some of the guys. Sorry I'm late. And, yes, I showered at the field." Casey drops another kiss on her head, then walks toward his room with his bag in his hand. "Be right back."

Noelle gets up to follow him, and Charlie groans.

"I'm not waiting for you, Noelle! Chelsea and I are gonna keep watching with or without you."

"I'll be right back. Don't start it back up without me." She points at Charlie.

I look over at Charlie, and she rolls her eyes, making me laugh.

"Be right back, my ass. I swear if she's in there for more than a few minutes, we're starting without her. I need to get up early tomorrow, and I still need to call Beck too."

"I can stay out here on the couch if you want some privacy

with Beck. I totally don't mind. You guys are doing me a huge favor by letting me stay with y'all," I tell her.

"No, no! You can crash with me. I probably won't be on long with him. He's had a long day with meetings and practice." She waves and shakes her head.

I swallow and double down on my insistence that I stay on the couch so Charlie can have her room to herself. "Okay, but it's fine, really. This couch is huge." I pat the cushion behind me while looking around the room.

"I'll hang out with you while you wait," Bo chimes in, making me turn to look at him. His eyes are trained on mine with a furrow to his brow, like he's been watching my every action. "Or you can stay in my room. I don't mind."

Charlie gasps, making me look at her. "Bo Callaway! Are you trying to get my friend in bed with you?" She laughs.

I laugh awkwardly. "That's not what he means, Charlie."

I turn to look at Bo. His expression is sincere, and if I didn't know better, I'd think he could read my mind. I shake my head. "I will not take your bed. You need a good sleep, I'm sure."

"I sleep like the dead, so it doesn't really matter where my head lands." He sits up, setting his elbows on his knees. His tone is casual, but those eyes—those molten eyes that are looking my way—seem serious, almost protective. "I can get my pillow and stuff now, so you can get to bed whenever you want."

"Bo, seriously, I'm not taking your bed." I shake my head.

"I have to get up early anyway, so it just makes more sense for me to sleep out here so we're not all walking through here while you're trying to sleep."

He stands and starts to walk, but I reach out and grab his hand, making him stop.

What feels like a static shock shoots from my hand up my arm. I look up at his face to see if he could feel it too. He's looking down at my hand holding his, and he wraps his fingers around mine and squeezes gently.

"I, um … I promise I'm good," I practically whisper.

He pulls me up to stand. I drop my phone that was on my lap to the couch, and he tugs me to walk behind him.

"Is your bag in Charlie's room?"

"Yeah," I mumble. Not hating that he's still holding my hand.

I can feel Charlie's eyes on me, so I look over my shoulder and see that I'm right. She's got a smirk on her face, and she wiggles her eyebrows.

Bo opens her door and releases my hand to grab my bag.

"How did you know that was my bag?" I place my hand on my hip.

"Well, it's not pink, and I live with Charlie and know her bag because of her traveling back and forth to see Beck." He chuckles.

"Oh, right. Ha!" I reach out to take my bag from him, but he grabs my hand again.

We walk down the hall to his room, and he releases my hand and sets my bag on his bed. I look around, and everything is perfectly neat and in its place.

There's a dresser that has some photos of him from games, it looks like. A few pictures of what I'm guessing is his family. The older man in them looks just like Bo with grayish hair. The older woman is stunning, and the two girls in the photo are also beautiful. I see the resemblance with Bo and them.

They look like a nice, happy family on the beach. Everyone is dressed in white and blue, looking like a Ralph Lauren ad. They're picturesque.

The only picture I have of my family, we all look like we're annoyed, except for Torie, who has the cutest cheesy grin despite my parents' scowling faces.

"That's my family." He lifts up the picture and brings it over to me. "Dad, Mom, and my two sisters, Savannah and Caroline."

"Very … Southern." I look up from the picture to him.

He laughs and sets the picture back on the dresser. "Yeah, my mom is from the South."

"You have a beautiful family." I smile at him.

He looks at me like he's trying to figure something out. "Thank you. I like them."

"Well, that's good!" We both laugh. "Bo, I feel bad taking your room. We barely know each other, and I'm taking over your space."

"I wouldn't say we hardly know each other. We've been friends now for, like, a year, right?" He walks a little closer to me.

"Friends. Yes, of course." I nod, smirking.

We stand there, staring at each other for a beat, and then we hear Noelle call to me, breaking the moment.

"Chels! Let's go. We're turning the show back on."

"Coming," I call out.

I start to turn to walk out, but Bo places a hand on my shoulder.

"Hey." His hand slides down my arm. "I like having you in my space."

Now, I'm not the kind of girl who blushes, but I can feel the heat in my face, and I can't help but smile. "I like being in your space, Bo Callaway." It's a flutter of honesty that comes out before I realize what I'm saying.

He smiles and nods as I walk out. I look back over my shoulder and return his smile, and he turns and grabs a pillow off the bed.

When we get back to the family room, Casey, Noelle, and Charlie are all sitting on the couch, and Silas came back out of his room and is lying down on the floor, sprawled out for some reason.

"You okay there, Silas?" I ask him.

"Yep. I just need to stretch out my back."

He pulls his long, thick legs into his chest and holds them there. He's surprisingly flexible for as big as he is. I mean, they all seem big to me since I'm short. Bo and Casey are tall and definitely fit, but Silas is huge.

Bo sits back down in the chair, and I take my spot again on

the couch after picking up my phone and setting it on the arm of the couch.

"Okay, I'm back, let's do this." I clap.

As we watch the show, the guys all have commentary about the drama. Casey and Silas more so than Bo, but he adds comments here and there. And I hear him laugh a few times too. We lose Silas at some point. He's now snoring away, still on the floor.

After the show ends, Casey takes the remote from his sister and puts on ESPN.

"Hey, I didn't say you could change the channel yet. I wanted to watch one more episode." She slaps him playfully on the shoulder, and he ducks into Noelle, who giggles.

"Show's over, Char. Go call Beck or something." He points toward her room.

"Rude. Why are you trying to get rid of me?" She fake pouts.

"I could never get rid of you. From the time of our conception, I haven't been able to get rid of you." He starts laughing when she shoves him a little harder this time.

"You're so lucky I'm your sister and that I love you. You wouldn't be the same without me." She crosses her arms and narrows her eyes at him.

He wraps his arm around her and pulls her into his armpit. "I am the luckiest, I agree."

She pinches his side, and he lets her go.

"Oww! What was that for?"

"You literally put my head in your armpit. That's disgusting!" She starts to stand, but stops. "Oh, I wanted you to tell me how your interview went today."

"Me too! I totally forgot today was your day," Noelle chimes in.

Casey nods and shifts on the couch and puts his arm around Noelle. "It was good. Pretty easy since I'm a natural on camera." He chuckles.

"Right, right. You're a pro." Charlie rolls her eyes. "But, like, what did they ask you?"

"Mostly about the upcoming season. They did try to get me to say if I had any ideas on where I wanted to go, but I evaded the question and tried to keep it focused on this season." He shifts to look at Charlie. "They did ask me about Beck and if I missed playing with my best friend, which, of course, I said yes. They asked about your and Beck's engagement, and I said I was happy for you guys, then steered the questions back to the season."

"Well, that sounds like fun. Will you be one of the ones they interview throughout the season regularly?" Charlie asks him.

"Probably, but I haven't gotten a schedule or anything. Did you get one, Bo?" Casey looks over at Bo.

I look over at Bo, and he glances at me briefly. Then he lifts his arm and wraps it around the back of his neck. He brushes his hand from the back to the front, then back through his hair before squeezing his neck.

"No, I didn't get a schedule. They just told me that they would follow me around some, but mostly around the field. I would guess we'll find out in advance if they want us, but I'm not sure."

"What did they ask you today?" Charlie asks him.

"Nothing too interesting. They asked me why I came to Walker and a few questions about the season. That's about it." He shrugs.

I see Charlie's phone light up, and she picks it up.

"I'm gonna go talk to my fiancé. I'll see you all in the morning." She stands and walks toward her room.

"I think I'm gonna head to bed too. I'm tired. The kids were wild today for some reason." Noelle stands and holds her hand out to Casey, and she pulls him off the couch.

He hands Bo the remote.

"Yo, Silas." Casey nudges his leg. "Go to bed, bro."

Silas groans but rolls to his side and stands up. "Night, y'all."

"Night," Noelle says, then looks at me. "Are you good? Do you need anything?"

"I can get her anything she needs," Bo says.

She smiles at him, then at me. "Okay, well, let me know if you need anything. Night."

"Night, guys," Casey says with a wave as he walks out, pulling Noelle behind him.

Bo stands and comes over to sit next to me on the couch. "Do you want to watch something else, or are you going to bed too?"

I pick up my phone and look at the time, noticing a missed call from my sister. It's not that late, but I should probably go to bed soon and try to call my sister back. "I'll go to bed soon, so you can watch this. I don't mind. I've spent the last year learning all the football things, so it's a good idea for me to continue my sports education." I smile at him.

"Oh, yeah? Well, that's good, considering some of your friends play football." He winks at me. "I'm not staying up too late either. My bed time is ten thirty."

"Ten thirty? Are you an old man?" I laugh.

"Hey now, don't knock an early bedtime." He puts his arm on the back of the couch, practically touching my shoulder. "During the season, I try to stay on a pretty strict schedule with sleep. Recovery time is important for your body."

"Recovery time?" I ask, shifting to face him.

"Yeah, you know, because we put so much stress on our bodies with training?" He tilts his head to the side, looking at me.

I nod. "Right ... as I imagine all athletes do."

"Exactly. So, we need the muscle recovery time so we don't get hurt, but also so we can be at peak performance."

"Got it. That makes sense. And I would imagine you take some pretty big hits, huh?"

He chuckles. "I do. Seeing a two-hundred-and-thirty-pound linebacker coming at you isn't all that fun."

"I wouldn't think so, no." We both smile. "Well, how about I let you get your rest because not only do you need to be prepared on the field, but we have our first study session tomorrow, and I'm not gonna let you slack off just because we're friends."

"No slacking, I promise. I'm a good student." He gives me a flirty smile.

"Mmhmm." I nod, smiling. "Okay, well, I'll see you tomorrow." I stand, my phone in my hand. "Good night, Bo. Thanks for letting me sleep in your bed."

"Anytime, Chelsea." A slow smile stretches across his face.

I turn and walk toward his bedroom, feeling his eyes on me until I know he can't see me anymore. When I get to his room, I turn on the light, close the door behind me, then sit on the bed and text my sister to see if she's still awake since it's an hour later in Florida.

> Chelsea: You awake?

Torie: Yes, but I'm in bed.

> Chelsea: Okay, just call me tomorrow when you get home from school. I'll be in class, then work until around four p.m.

Torie: I'll call you then. I just wanted to see if you had made plans to come home yet for my birthday next weekend.

> Chelsea: I'm planning to. Let me just check flights tomorrow and see what I can find.

Torie: Try to come on Friday morning if you can!

> Chelsea: I'll see what I can do.

I smile, thinking about how excited she is about her birthday. All I've ever wanted is for her to be happy, to not have the same memories I have, and live her life with only what she knows now. My aunt gave us a great life, and all her birthdays should be celebrated.

Which is why I'm going to have to bite the bullet and travel to Florida to see her.

Torie: Love you, Chels.

Chelsea: Love you most.

I reach over and pull my charger out of my bag. I stand up and look around the room for an outlet to plug it in. I find one behind the nightstand next to the bed. After I plug it in, I grab my makeup bag that has my face wash and toothbrush.

When I open the door, Bo is coming out of the bathroom across the hall.

"Hey. I put some towels on the counter for you. There's a washcloth, hand towel, and a bigger towel for when you want to shower." He leans against the doorframe and crosses his arms, which makes his biceps look even bigger than they already are.

"Thank you. That's perfect." I walk across the hall and stand with him in the doorway, our bodies close. I look up at his face, then trail my gaze down to his tanned chest, then to his stomach and further to his dick. I could be wrong, but I swear I see it twitch in his shorts.

He leans down slightly, forcing my eyes to look back up at him.

"You okay? Looks like you have something on your mind," he asks.

"Who doesn't? Between school, work … or for you, sports … there's a million things on our plates, right?"

"The joy of being a college student. You're gonna be helping me out a lot with tutoring, but you know if there's anything I can do to help you, all you have to do is ask."

He's doing it again. In the living room earlier, I felt like he knew I was uncomfortable with the sleeping arrangements and came to my rescue. Now, it's as if he can read my mind.

Has he always been this way and I'm just now realizing it, or is this new and we suddenly have a connection that sparked somewhere in the last forty-eight hours?

"Night, Bo." I look at his face again. So handsome. So astute.

I kinda want to kiss him.

He sucks in a deep breath and looks toward the bedroom. "I'm gonna grab my stuff out of my room while you're in here, so I don't bother you in the morning. Night, Chelsea," he says, brushing against me as he leaves.

I run a hand across the back of my neck and try to cool my body temperature. Something has gotten into me lately. And by something, I mean Bo.

After I finish in the bathroom, I go back to his room and change into a T-shirt and shorts for bed. I flip off the light and walk to the bed, pulling the covers back and crawling in. His bedding smells just like him, and I want to be wrapped in it. I drift off to sleep, thinking about his eyes and the way they looked at me in the doorway. Like he liked what he saw too.

CHAPTER
SEVEN

BO

GETTING to sleep last night took a little longer than it usually does. It's a funny thing—attraction. I've always been attracted to Chelsea, and maybe it's because she's been around us more over this past year that I feel more comfortable taking my shot with her now. Because here's the thing with a girl like her: you don't just mess around with her. She's the kind of girl who gets in your veins and you crave her.

The timing of this is kind of funny though. This season is important not only for the team, but also for me individually. I have a lot to prove and many important decisions to make about my future. So, starting something with Chelsea could be distracting, but also, I'm not sure I care. A distraction like her ... totally worth it. The tutoring just gives me another reason to get to spend time with her.

I just finished my last class for the day and check my watch to see I have just enough time to stop and get her a chai before I meet her for our first study session. Did I memorize her coffee order? You bet I did.

After grabbing our drinks and a few cookies, I make my way

across the quad to the library. Our campus library is large, but she texted me earlier to meet her in one of the study rooms on the second floor, so I head toward the staircase and take two steps at a time to the top, steadying the tray of drinks in my hand.

I find her in the room farthest from the stairs and away from some of the other study group tables. I'm glad for the privacy the room offers because I don't really want to be interrupted by people wanting to talk football with me. It would have been ideal to meet off campus, honestly, but because it's a job for her, I guess she needs to do it at the library so she can report her time accurately.

Chelsea's sitting at the table, head down, writing something on a list. I tap on the door before I walk in so I don't startle her.

"Hey," I say as I open the door.

She looks up at me. Her gaze sparkles when she sees me, and her chest rises with a quick inhale. "Hey, Bo. How's it going?"

"Good. You?" I ask her, then set the tray on the table. "I brought you a vanilla chai and a few cookies."

She sets her pen down and reaches over for the drink, watching me. "That's so nice of you. Thank you."

"Not a problem." I pull out the chair across from her, set my backpack on the table, and sit down and fold my hands in front of me. "So, how are we doing this? Do I just go over my homework with you and we talk about it? I've never had tutoring before, so I'm not really sure what to do here." I open my hands and gesture to her notebook.

She smiles softly, looking at me thoughtfully. "Yeah, we'll review your notes from class, and I'll come up with some questions that could potentially be on your next quiz. I already have your syllabus from the professor and her notes from class this week, so I've started writing some questions for you." She taps her pen on her notebook. "But before we get started, I have to ask."

"Okay ... ask me anything." I smile back at her.

"Columbus, huh?" She leans forward and crosses her arms on the table.

I groan and tip my head back. "Yep."

"How has that never been brought up before? Does anyone know that's your name?" A small giggle-snort comes out.

"Hey, are you making fun of my name?" I tease.

"Absolutely not. I was just surprised when I saw the name on your class roster. I can't believe that's never come up on TV before either." She smirks.

"Honestly, I don't know how more people don't know, but I've never introduced myself to anyone, ever, with my full name. And when I started school, my parents must have told my teachers to call me Bo because no one ever calls me Columbus, except for my mom's family." I shake my head but smile. It's not that I'm embarrassed. Because I'm not. It's just different, and it doesn't roll off the tongue as easily as Bo does.

"So, is it a family name then?" She watches me.

"Yeah, it's my great-grandfather and grandfather's name. I'm the only grandson, so here we are. Actually, I'm the only boy on both sides of the family."

"That's a lot of expectation to live up to on its own, I would imagine. And you're the oldest in your family?" She takes a sip of her coffee, then picks up a cookie and breaks off a piece.

"I'm the oldest, yes. And the expectation right now is that I pass this class so I can have a future," I joke. Sort of. I don't mind talking about myself, but I also don't want to run out of time to go over what we need to do.

"Right. Sorry. Okay, back to it. Do you handwrite your class notes or do you use an app?" She brushes off the cookie crumbs on her hand with the other.

I grimace. "I usually record them, and then it, like, transcribes them for me to review. Honestly, I haven't looked at my notes for that class yet. Sorry."

"That's no problem. We'll go over it together, but just so

we're clear, I'm not doing the work for you." She picks up her pen and points it at me.

I place my hand on my chest. "I would never ask you to. I'm not afraid of putting in the work." I wink at her.

"Good to know." She smiles, then clears her throat. "Okay, so let's get to it. You only have an hour and a half before you need to leave for practice, right?"

I look at my watch, then pull out my phone from my backpack to set my timer so I know when we need to start wrapping up. Because the truth is, I could sit here all day and hang out with her and lose track of time completely. "Yeah, do you think we'll have time to get through all of it?"

"Oh, yeah. There's not a ton to go over here. I really just want to see where you are in terms of understanding the material." She flips through a few pages of her notebook. "Do you think it's just a lack of interest in the class?"

"Maybe. I'm not really sure." I shrug and pull out my notebook and pen. "I've just never really been into overanalyzing feelings and whatnot."

"That's not uncommon for men actually. And specifically, athletes, so I thought about that a little and came up with an idea. We'll incorporate sports into the lessons so it's more relatable to you. Because it's not really *all* about feelings; it's more about how to process and understand the information that your brain is receiving and the factors that influence it. Does that make sense?" She studies my face.

I nod. "Yeah, that makes total sense. I guess I didn't really think about it from that perspective. I hear psychology and automatically think that we're going to dig into feelings and emotions. And it's not that I minimize my or others' feelings. I just have always been able to compartmentalize it a little easier than some, I guess."

"Interesting. Well, I'm curious about how your mind works, so let's get started."

She takes a drink of her chai, and then we do just that.

An hour later, we've finished going through my notes and hers, but neither of us seems to be in a hurry to leave. And I want to get to know her better.

"So, Chelsea, tell me more about you. I know you're from Florida. Were you born and raised there?" I ask.

She nods somewhat cautiously. "I am, and, yes, I was born and raised there too."

"What part of Florida? I've only been there a few times, so I don't really know anywhere, except Miami, Tampa, and Jacksonville."

"I'm from Naples, on the southwest coast." She's pretty short on her responses, not giving me a lot, but she doesn't seem mad that I'm asking.

"I haven't been there. Is it nice?" I reach over and take the last little piece from the second cookie.

"Ah, yeah, it's nice. Hot, humid, beachy. Typical Florida. A lot of wealthy people live there. It's referred to as the Beverly Hills of the East Coast or something." She lifts one shoulder and smirks.

"The humidity in Florida is a killer. So, what does your dad do?"

I'm curious only because Chelsea doesn't come across as a spoiled rich kid. But when I look at her, she seems uncomfortable, shifting in her seat.

"Um, I was raised by my aunt. She's a pediatrician. We're not *rich*, rich like some of the kids I went to school with, but she has a very successful practice. She's the best pediatrician in Florida, in my opinion, not that I'm biased or anything." She tilts her head, smiling.

As much as I want to ask more about why she was raised by her aunt, I won't. Today. I remember a woman and a younger girl with her when she moved into the apartment last year, but I assumed it was her mom because we weren't introduced. "What's your major?"

"I'm prelaw. Walker has one of the best programs for prelaw studies."

"That's cool. I didn't know that about the prelaw program." I nod. "You have a sister, right? Your aunt and sister … they were here when you and Noelle moved in last year?"

She smiles genuinely then and nods. "I have a little sister, who I guess isn't so little anymore. She's turning eighteen next week."

"Eighteen, huh? Big birthday."

I watch as she starts to pack up her bag, but halfway through, she pauses, her hand resting on the zipper. She exhales through her nose, eyes flicking down, like she's debating whether to tell me something. Finally, she looks back up.

"It is. I'm going to go home this weekend to celebrate. I'll be back early on Sunday though, so it's a quick trip."

"So, you'll miss our first game of the season?" I'm disappointed she won't be there. I don't have the right to be disappointed, but I am nonetheless. "That's a bummer."

"Yeah, I know. I don't have student tickets anyway, so I probably wouldn't have gone. No offense." She lifts her shoulder.

"None taken. But whenever you want to come to a game, say the word. I can get you tickets. I'm sure you could go with Charlie and Noelle too, right?"

"Okay, thanks. Yeah, I went with them a few times last year." She nods.

"I remember. You had a cute little beanie with one of those

balls on the top." I want to make it clear to her that I notice her—have noticed her.

"That's right; I did." She clears her throat. "So, your sisters—how old are they?"

I pick up my phone and find the latest picture they sent me of them together and turn it toward her. "I know you saw that picture of us on my dresser, but that was a few years ago, right before I came to Walker. This is them now. Savannah turned eighteen in July, and Caroline turns sixteen in November."

She's looking at my phone screen. "They're beautiful, Bo. Are y'all close?"

"Yeah, I guess. We text each other, but I don't really talk to them on the phone much. They're busy with their own schedules, too, so they don't come out to many games. And my parents don't get out here much either." I really wanted to know more about her and talk less about my family.

"Yeah, you'll have to tell me more about your dad sometime. I'm curious about his path to becoming a judge. I think our time is just about up."

She starts to stand just as my alarm chimes on my phone, so I slip my phone in the pocket of my jeans and pack up my bag quickly.

"Wait, I'll walk out with you." I zip it and put it over my shoulder, then reach for hers to carry too. "Here, let me carry your bag."

"Ha! You don't have to do that. I'm very capable of carrying my bag around." She looks up at me and smiles.

"I don't doubt that you are, but I would like to carry it for you." I reach out again, and she lets me take it off her shoulder.

She places her hand on my forearm. "Hey, thanks again for the coffee and cookies. And for carrying my bag for me. You're a good guy, Columbus Callaway." Her smile stretches across her face.

"Shhh ... seriously, don't tell anyone my full name." I bend down close to her ear, half whispering, even though we're still in the study room alone.

She turns her head, and our lips are just a breath apart.

She crosses her heart with her finger. "Your secret is safe with me."

"Thank you. So, where are you heading next?" A slow smile spreads across my face, and I hold the door open for her.

"I'm done for the day, so I'm going home. Or I guess your house, since we aren't allowed back into our building yet. I need to work on my applications for law school and sort all that out." She looks at me as we walk down the stairs and lifts her eyebrows. "Sounds like a good time, right?"

"Probably more fun than dodging linemen." I chuckle.

"Agreed. So, I guess I'll see you later?"

When we exit the building, she reaches for her bag on my shoulder, so I slip it off and hand it to her, brushing her fingers with mine.

"Yep, I'll be home after practice. Did you sleep okay in my room? I forgot to ask."

She smiles and nods. "I did. Thank you. I still feel bad, taking over your room."

"Don't. I swear I'm good." My phone buzzes, and I pull it out of my pocket to check the time. "Shit, I'd better go. I'll see you later," I say, walking backward.

"See you later, Bo." She winks. Yes, winks at me.

I smile at her and turn. The smile stays on my face the whole way to the field.

Coach is standing outside his office as I walk into the locker room. "Hey, Bo. How you doing?"

I reach out to shake his hand. "Doing good, Coach."

He places one of his hands on my shoulder, my hand still in his other. "Did you take care of the tutoring?"

"I'm pretty sure you know I did, Coach." I chuckle because I know Coach knows everything about everyone. More than we probably realize.

He laughs and releases my hand and my shoulder. "You're right; I do. Have you started yet though?"

I nod. "Just coming from our first session."

I think I'll keep the fact that I know Chelsea to myself and definitely the fact that she's staying with me right now. I don't want them to assign me to someone else. I want to spend as much time with her as I can.

"Good, good. I look forward to seeing your progress. Now, go get ready. We're on the field in fifteen." He turns to face one of the other coaches, who came up while we were talking.

"Yes, sir."

I spin on my heel and walk toward my stall. My practice gear is already hanging in it, ready for me to dress. I pull open the bottom drawer under the seat and drop my backpack in there. I forgot to run it to my car before I met up with Chelsea. Which also means I forgot my gym bag, which has my shorts in it.

I look around the room and see one of the equipment managers carrying water bottles to the cart. "Hey, man. Can you grab me some shorts? I forgot my bag in my car."

"Sure thing, Bo. Give me a few. Do you need anything else?" He sets the bottles on the cart and walks back toward the uniform closet, looking over his shoulder at me.

"Oh, yeah, a rash guard would be good."

After we won the championship, our alumni sponsors were incredibly generous, as were our athletic sponsors. We get everything from shoes, suits, workout gear, and team track suits. Before, we'd had a tight setup, but even more so now. Anything we want, we pretty much just say the word.

I see Silas on the other side of the room, lacing his cleats. Then Casey flies in through the door and sprints over to his locker near mine.

"Sup, man." He glances over at me.

"Hey. What are you rushing for? You still have, like, ten minutes to get ready." I start pulling off my shirt and jeans.

"I lost track of time, then had to run across campus to get

here. Literally ran." He starts laughing. "I nearly took out a few people on my way."

"Do I even want to ask why you lost track of time?" I ask while taking my pads off the hook and setting them on the bench.

"Probably not." He looks over at me with a grin.

"Here you go, Callaway." The equipment manager hands me my clothes.

"Thanks. Appreciate you." I bump fists with him.

"Why don't you have clothes?" Casey asks while stripping down.

I clear my throat. "I forgot to go to my car after class to get my bag."

He looks over at me, suspicious. "You forgot something?"

"Yep," I reply curtly.

"Uh-huh. Who is she?" He chuckles.

"Why would you assume it's a girl? You know I don't chase girls around." I huff.

I see him nod out of my peripheral vision.

"I guess you're right. But it's unlike you to forget to do something when it comes to football."

"Fine, I was studying with Chelsea." I slip on my rash guard.

"Chelsea? Noelle's Chelsea?" He pauses and looks at me.

"Do we know another Chelsea?"

He pulls his shorts on and looks at me.

"What?" I laugh awkwardly.

"You're more than just studying with her, aren't you? I suspected you liked her, but after last night and now this, I'm sure of it." He points at me, smiling.

I'm not even gonna try to pretend with him. He's one of my closest friends here.

"Nothing's happened. We're just friends. But, man to man, yeah, I'm really into her. I have been for a while, honestly."

"Yeah, I've seen the way you look at her. I just didn't know if it was general appreciation or if it was something more. But last night, when you offered her your bed, I wondered. Good for you, man. Just don't fuck around with her. I really like her, and she's, like, Noelle's best friend."

"King, when have I ever fucked around with someone? Emotionally. The girls, friends I've spent time with, understand what we are and aren't. And it's not like I'm some big player either."

He knows that, and he also knows I don't toy with people.

"True. You never bring them home though or spend time with them after a hookup. I just don't want Chelsea to be one of those kind of *friends* for you."

"Chelsea is different. Yes, she's obviously gorgeous and smart. But I like her—you know what I mean?" I slip on my pads, then my practice jersey.

"I do. She's a cool girl."

Both dressed at this point, we begin lacing up our cleats.

"Do you know much about her? She mentioned going home this weekend for her sister's birthday and said she was raised by her aunt. She didn't seem to want to elaborate on why, and I didn't press her. But I'm curious about her."

He shakes his head and stands. "Not really a lot. If Noelle knows anything, she's never mentioned it to me, but I've never had a reason to ask either." He takes his helmet off the hook in his stall, then slaps me on the arm as he passes. "Let's go, QB. You're gonna be late."

I shake my head and laugh. I'm never late; I'm usually the first one on the field. I grab my helmet and follow him. I need to clear my head and focus on what I'm here to do. Then I can get home and see her again.

CHAPTER
EIGHT

CHELSEA

THE LAST FEW days went by fast. School kept me busy, and then I had one more study session with Bo before I left for Florida. Staying at his house has been kind of fun actually. I like my own space, and I don't mind being alone in general, but having all of them around is nice. The eye candy on display is an extra bonus too. Bo specifically. I did feel bad about taking Bo's room though. He swore it wasn't a problem, but I felt even worse when I saw him stretching out his back last night. He said it was from practice, but I'm sure sleeping on the couch for days hadn't helped.

I'm at the airport, waiting for my flight to leave, and my phone buzzes. I look down to see a text from my aunt.

> Laura: I'll meet you in Arrivals. I can't wait to see you! Have a good flight.
>
> Chelsea: Sounds good. See you in a few hours.

Another text comes through, but it's from Bo this time. We

haven't texted each other since we made our plans for tutoring. But I can't lie and say I'm not happy about him texting me now.

> Bo: Did you make it to the airport?

> > Chelsea: Yep, I'm just waiting for my plane to get here.

> Bo: The waiting is the worst. I don't mind traveling, other than all the waiting.

> > Chelsea: I don't really mind the waiting. I love to people-watch. You can find out a lot about a person by observation.

> Bo: Oh, yeah? Have you ever observed me, Miss Future Attorney and Psychology Expert?

> > Chelsea: All the time. 😌

Am I flirting? Indeed I am. Over the last few days and in our study session yesterday, we've been flirting. I'm not sure why it took us so long to talk like this, to flirt—because I have no doubt he's just as into me as I am him. And it's not like I don't know him at all. We've spent a year in each other's circle. But something has changed.

I've dated a few guys since I've been at Walker, but nothing serious. Mostly for sex, to be completely honest. And it's been a while since I've gotten laid, which could be why I'm feeling the flirt more than I usually would. Nah ... Bo is just fun to be around and very nice to look at. It's not a hardship, flirting with him.

> Bo: Okay...and? What can you tell about me from observation?

> > Chelsea: First, let the record reflect that you're objectively hot.

Bo: Ha! Back at you. But what else?

Chelsea: You're patient, emotionally regulated —very prefrontal cortex of you. You have a way of stepping back, observing, instead of needing to be the loudest in the room. Honestly, if I were profiling you, I'd say you're the kind of guy who notices details most people miss.

Bo: So, you've been profiling me?

Chelsea: Oh, absolutely. And my professional conclusion? You're trouble. The best kind.

Bo: Hmm. That sounds pretty accurate. You're good at this. I do like to observe rather than be the one talking for sure.

There are exactly three people I care about deeply in this world, and their opinions matter to me. The rest of the noise I can shut out. But Bo is quickly becoming someone I want to really know me, too, and I care about what he thinks.

Chelsea: And...

Bo: And what?

Chelsea: What do you see when you observe me?

Bo: I actually think we're pretty similar in a lot of ways. I think you're also very thoughtful about how you react and respond to people. You're social, but don't want to be the center of attention. You are comfortable in your own skin. You're honest, but only offer your honesty if asked directly. You're funny, too, although I don't think you realize it. But you're mysterious. You have secrets, and I respect them. Maybe if I'm lucky, you'll let me be your vault.

His answers make me smile. He's spot-on for the most part. Being comfortable in my own skin has taken some work though.

Chelsea: I would say that's accurate too.

Bo: I know. 😉 And another thing I know by my observation of you is that you like me.

He's going for it now, I guess.

Chelsea: That would be correct. Just like I know you like me. By observation, of course.

Bo: Oh, I definitely like you. Why do you have to go to Florida again? Any chance you can miss your flight on purpose?

I giggle.

Chelsea: My little sister's birthday. But don't you have to go to a hotel or something tonight?

Bo: Yeah...to eliminate distractions.

Chelsea: Distractions being girls?

Bo: That and partying. You remember Smith and Schuster, right? Well, they got in trouble for being late and hungover a few times last season, so that's why we have to do this now. But also because the pressure is high this season for us to get another national title.

Chelsea: That makes sense. So do you just go to the hotel and go to bed?

Bo: Not right away, no. The schedule says we'll eat dinner, then we get to go see a movie at the movie theatre for a team activity. I'm guessing we'll get the theatre to ourselves, but I'm not really sure yet. Then after that, we have curfew at nine thirty.

Chelsea: Is it a lights-out-at-nine-thirty type of situation?

Bo: I don't really know. We've actually always had curfew, but the coaches just called us the night before and made sure we were home. So, I don't know if they're coming around each room or what. I'll let you know later.

Chelsea: Please do. I'm fascinated by this adult-curfew situation. If I had an athletic bone in my body, I would probably thrive on the structure of it all. I like knowing what to expect and what the expectations are up front.

My need for transparency is definitely related to my trauma. My parents were so unpredictable and volatile, which was literally the only thing I could count on. Their bad behavior.

Bo: So you don't like surprises?

Chelsea: Not really, no. Although, you bringing me chai this week for our tutoring sessions was a nice surprise.

Bo: Noted. I'm glad you liked it.

A high-pitched buzzing noise comes across the speaker. "Sorry about that, folks. Flight 841 to Fort Myers will be boarding in the next twenty minutes. If you're not already at the gate, please make your way to it. The plane has just arrived."

Chelsea: My plane just got here, so we'll be boarding soon. Have a good rest of your day!

Bo: Have a safe flight. Text me later if you can.

Chelsea: Okay, I will, but won't you be busy?

Bo: I'll answer.

I shake my head and smile.

Chelsea: Okay, but don't get in trouble. Walker University fans wouldn't be happy if their star wasn't on the field tomorrow .

Bo: Ha-ha. Talk to you later.

I drop my phone in the small pocket of my bag and make sure my earbuds are in there. My newest audiobook is already cued up for the trip, and I want to get it started as soon as we take off. Coincidentally, it's about a quarterback falling for his tutor.

Two and a half hours later, I land in Florida. When I step outside to look for my aunt in the line, the heat blasts me immediately. It gets hot in Oklahoma, but the humidity here is an absolute killer. And I forgot to put product in my hair this morning, so I can already feel my hair frizzing. Awesome.

I pull out my phone from my bag to call her, but I see her drive up in her Land Rover before I press Call. I hold up my hand, but she already sees me and is waving at me through the window. She has a huge smile on her face. Sometimes, I think about how wild it is that she and my dad are siblings. They couldn't be more different.

When she stops in front of me, I open the door and get into the passenger seat, putting my bag between my legs on the floor.

"You know you can put that in the back, right?" She gestures toward my bag.

"I know, but it's not that big, so I'm good." I lean over and give her a side hug. "Where's Torie?"

"She's at home, getting ready for dinner." She looks at me and rolls her eyes. "It's just the three of us for dinner, but we might see someone she knows while we're out, so she has to be prepared, I guess. God forbid she go out without makeup and hair."

"Right." Now it's my turn to roll my eyes. "So, where are we eating? I'm actually starving. I've hardly had much today."

"She wants to go to Del Mar tonight, then tomorrow …" She glances at me and grimaces.

"What?"

This can't be good if she's grimacing.

"We're all going on airboat rides," she says quickly.

"We're what now? Did you say we're going on airboat rides or just one ride?" I narrow my gaze at her.

"Technically, one ride, but two boats because of the amount of people we have in our party." She has a worried smile on her face.

"And?" I prod.

"So, I just need you to be the adult on one of the boats."

"Why though? Don't they only have to be sixteen to go alone?" I pull out my phone to double-check.

"Yes, but some of the parents want to make sure the girls are properly supervised." She shakes her head.

"Well, I mean, alligators are great for supervision. What is it they think their daughters will be doing that requires an adult?

These girls will all be running around college campuses in less than a year. They do realize that, right?"

"Chels, I know it's something your dad used to do with you, but while you have a negative association with the activity, Torie really wants to do it. She's really excited to go. I know you hate it, but I need you. And more importantly, your sister wants you there." She tilts her head and smiles.

"I mean, I don't think I have a choice, do I?" I laugh.

"You always have a choice—you know that. But your sister and I would like you to be there."

If I stayed away from everything that reminded me of my childhood, I'd never step inside this state—or about every fast-food chain in the country. And while I avoid a lot of things that bring back negative feelings, I can't deny that the most positive thing in my life is my relationship with my sister. If having me there is important to her, then I have to do it.

I take a deep breath and then put on a smile. "Okay, but you'll have to braid my hair tonight—tight. It will get so wild with the heat, water, and wind." I pull my hair up into a ponytail and take an elastic off my wrist to wrap it.

"I know you've been avoiding the topic, but we need to talk about the letter," she starts.

I turn my head toward the window. "To answer your question, no, I still haven't opened it, and I don't have any intentions of doing so right now."

"Chelsea …"

"Aunt Laura," I sing back to her. "This is Torie's weekend. Can we just shelve it for a few more days?"

She lets out a sigh. "Of course we can. I'm just so happy you're here, and I have all of next week to harass you about it," she says with a smile, and I groan, which she clearly ignores. "So, anything new with you at school? How are your classes going?" She merges onto the highway toward Naples.

"Classes are good; work is good. Oh, I forgot to tell you." I turn toward her in my seat. "Noelle and I are staying at her boyfriend's house because our apartment building had to get fumigated."

"Oh, gross!" She fake gags. "You know how I feel about bugs."

"I know. I don't even want to think about what was in the walls, honestly. We never had any issues in our apartment though."

"Doesn't Noelle's boyfriend play football or something?"

"Yes, he does, and so do his roommates."

"Oh, so I'm sure that's a real hardship, staying there." She laughs.

I laugh with her. "Definitely doesn't suck. Especially when they all walk around shirtless."

"I bet! I vaguely remember a few of them when we moved you in last year."

"Yeah, so Casey is Noelle's boyfriend. Then there's Silas, who was the really tall one, and Bo. He's the quarterback," I say, looking out the window.

"I've seen him on TV, I think. He's very good-looking."

"He is indeed. And nice." I look at my phone to check my texts just in case he texted me after we talked earlier, but nothing new is showing. "I'm actually tutoring him too."

"Oh, really? For what?" She tilts her head in question.

"He got a bad grade on the first test in a psychology class, which accounts for a large part of their overall grade. So, in order for him to stay eligible to play, they hired me to help him get the grade up."

"Well, if anyone can help him, you can. My smart girl." She reaches over and takes my hand.

It took me a while to get used to her hugging us or showing us any physical attention really. My parents hadn't been affectionate with us at all. But I don't mind it now.

"Yeah, and I kind of like him too. We've been flirting a lot. Which is funny because we've been around each other pretty regularly, but it's like a switch flipped, and now we're all flirty with each other."

I'm not sure why I'm telling her other than the fact that I haven't really told anyone about it yet. Noelle and I haven't gotten to spend a whole lot of time alone this week, so it wasn't easy to find a time to talk to her about it.

"Oh, to be young and flirty." She sighs. "Enjoy it all, kid."

"Yeah, I mean, it's just fun right now. I don't know if it'll turn into anything. We have very different paths. I'll be going off to law school, and he'll be heading to the NFL next year."

"You never know, Chels. Keep all possibilities open." She squeezes my hand, then releases it to turn the wheel, and we exit the highway.

"I wouldn't mind seeing him naked a few times. That's definitely a possibility I would like to keep open."

I bark out a laugh when I look over at my aunt and her wide eyes. I can tell she's trying to be cool about it though.

"I'm sure that would be a delight. But you don't need to tell me about it if it happens. Just promise me you'll practice safe sex if it comes to that."

"Absolutely. The pullout method is highly effective," I say sarcastically.

She looks over at me with her mouth agape. "Chelsea Sullivan."

I can't stop laughing at the shock on her face.

"I'm serious, Chelsea. Promise me."

Once I catch my breath, I reach over and touch her arm. "I promise. Don't worry; I have no intention of having babies anytime soon."

"But you do want babies? Someday, of course."

I pick at the seam of my purse. There's a small string sticking out—most people wouldn't even notice it—but I give it a tug, and it unravels a little more.

"Yeah, for sure. But I have a lot to do first. I would love to explore adoption too." I study her face because I've never mentioned adoption to her before.

She looks over at me for a second, but I don't miss the shine in her eyes. "Any child, whether biological or not, would be lucky to have you as a mother, Chelsea."

"Thank you. I had a good role model."

"Oh my God, stop. You're making me cry, and I can't see!" She wipes at her face.

I pull out a tissue from the small pack she always keeps in her glove box and hand it to her.

"Sorry." I laugh, then admit, "The great thing about adoption is, I can give a kid a better story than the one they started with. Love them, support them, let them know they're wanted. And maybe it's selfish, but I like the idea of choosing someone—and being chosen back—without the whole mess of finding a guy first. And honestly, why settle down when casually dating is so much fun?"

"Ahh. The old fear of commitment."

"I don't have any *fear*. I just don't see the need to be in a fiery, passionate, dramatic, all-consuming romance."

"You know, Chels, it's okay to have more than a fling with someone. Not every relationship is like the one your parents had." She glances over at me.

"Oh, I know." I shrug it off like what she's saying isn't hitting home in some way. "I just don't want to get invested in someone when I'm leaving and he's leaving too."

"I get it; I just want to see you consider it, is all. Love can be a very wonderful thing," she says wistfully.

"Since I've never been in love, I can't say that I know that to be true, but I'll take your word for it." I look over at her. "How is it you know so much about love anyway? I've never seen you with a man."

"I've dated, and I've had serious relationships in the past, before you girls came to me. I just haven't had much time in the last ten years to get into anything. You girls needed me more than I needed a relationship."

"You should take your own advice then. It might do you good to get dicked down too, Aunt Laura." I can't hold the laugh that I try hard to keep in.

"Good Lord." She shakes her head, but has a smile on her face. "And who says I haven't?"

I gasp. "Aunt Laura! Have you met a man? Do you have a ... loverrr?"

She wiggles her eyebrows. "A lady never kisses and tells."

"Well, you're no fun! Bravo though. You need to get some too."

"Chelsea, I mean it. You're not a kid anymore. I don't have to worry about you meeting the wrong boy and getting into trouble. You're a woman now, and it's time you started taking some chances. I spent my twenties buried in med school, doing everything I could to avoid the opposite sex. And while I want you to stay focused on law school, I also want you to have a little fun. Meet a cute guy. Go on dates. Let yourself be romanced. Don't wait until your forties to realize you deserve that."

I widen my eyes and grin. "Okay, who are you, and what have you done with my aunt Laura?"

She laughs as the light turns green.

"This new guy must really have you under his spell," I tease, smirking. "Either that or his dick is huge."

She bursts out laughing. "What in the world will I ever do with you?"

"Make me chaperone a bunch of teenage girls and then feed me to the alligators, apparently."

She glances at me, still chuckling, and shakes her head. "You're impossible."

"Admit it," I say, trying not to smile. "You love me."

"Oh, I do," she says warmly. "More than you know."

The rest of the short ride to our house, we talk about her and her job.

When we pull up to the house, my sister is standing outside, waiting for us. She's literally bouncing up and down. I look over at my aunt, and we both start laughing.

"Get ready for the weekend of Torie!" my aunt says.

I reach for the door handle with one hand and grab my bag with the other. "Can't wait!"

While we were at dinner, I got a text from Bo, asking if I got home safely. I told him we were out to dinner and I would text him when I got back to the house. Which I did, but they were at the movie, so he couldn't text back and forth.

So, I took my shower to get the travel crud off of me, had my aunt braid my hair, and then crawled in to my bed. I didn't really expect to hear from him again because of the curfew, but at nine forty-five, which is ten forty-five my time, my phone buzzes.

Bo: Are you still awake?

Chelsea: Yes, I just got into bed though.

Bo: Do you want to go to bed, or do you feel like talking?

Chelsea: I can talk, but don't you need to go to bed soon?

> Bo: Yeah, but I'd like to talk to you if you're not too tired.

I can't help but smile.

> Chelsea: Yeah, we can talk.

My phone rings a second later with a FaceTime call.

"Hi," I say, smiling wider. "You meant, like, actually talk and look at each other."

He chuckles. "Yeah, I meant actually talk with voices and faces." He's in his bed too. Shirtless. "Did you have a good time at dinner?"

"We did. We went to Torie's favorite restaurant, so she was happy. Even happier when we came home and had dessert. The girl loves birthday cake."

"That's good. I bet they were happy to have you home." He smiles.

"They are. It's good to see them. It's funny because I don't feel homesick when I'm gone, but when I'm here, I realize how much I miss them. Is that weird?" I purse my lips and tilt my head in question.

"No, I know what you mean. I feel the same when I go home, which isn't very often." He leans over and reaches for a bottle of water on the table next to the bed.

"Did you get your check-in from your coaches yet?"

He takes a drink and nods. "Yeah, right before I texted you. They gave me a room to myself tonight, which I don't mind because I get to talk to you now." He smirks.

"Ahh, well, getting special treatment is quite nice." I laugh.

He places his hand on his bare chest. "I'm not gonna complain."

"What time do you get up in the morning? Your game is at one, right?" I ask.

"Yeah, I'll probably get up around six, but we don't have to be downstairs for breakfast until eight. After breakfast, we head to the field and start preparing for the game."

"Oh, wow. I didn't realize you go that early to the field."

He nods. "Yep, even if we weren't at a hotel, we would still be required to be there a few hours before."

We talk a little more about the game-time process, which I find fascinating. The way they have to mentally prepare is something I guess I never really considered.

He yawns, which makes me look at the time.

"You should probably get to bed, huh?" I ask him.

He shakes his head. "Not yet. I want to talk to you, unless you want to go."

I smile. "I'm good. I just don't want to be blamed if you're tired tomorrow."

"Nah, I'll be fine. What are you doing tomorrow? Do you know yet?" He moves his arm behind his head, laying on it.

I roll my eyes and shake my head. "Yes, we're going on an airboat ride with my sister and her friends."

"No way! That's cool. I've never been on one." He laughs. "You don't look excited."

I sit up, leaning against the headboard, making my loose T-shirt slide off my shoulder, and prop my phone on my legs. "I mean, it's fun, but not something I ever wanted to do again."

"Why not?" He has an adorable, crooked smile on his face.

I glance toward the window, watching the palm trees blur together for a moment before I answer, "Mostly because I can't hear well for days after, even though they give you headphones. And my hair ..." I point to the two braids.

"You look really cute with the braids. I was going to say something when we got on actually." He bites his lip.

Why is that so hot?

"I like the shirt too, by the way." He grins.

"You do, huh?" I pull the shirt up my shoulder a little.

"Oh, don't do that. I want to picture you just like that as I fall asleep," he says in a gravelly voice.

"Are you flirting with me?" I tilt my head, smiling.

"Yes." His smirk is slow, deliberate.

"Good." I shift again and lie back down on my pillows, trying to ignore the flutter in my stomach.

His eyes are dark, intent, even on the screen. His lips part slightly, and his gaze lingers like he's memorizing me. There's a heat there that makes my pulse race—something intimate, something that feels like it's only for me. My chest tightens, and I know whatever he's about to say will make me forget everything else.

"Chelsea, I'm just gonna put it all out there. I want you."

I suck in a breath, not expecting him to say that.

"I mean …" He runs a hand over his jaw, the crooked smile on his face softening into something real. "I want to date you."

"So, you don't want me? You just want to date me?" I tease.

His eyes widen, and he shakes his head. "No! I mean, yes. I want to date you, but, yes, I most definitely want you too." He has a serious look on his face. "I really like you. I'm crazy attracted to you, but I really like you as a person too. And I'm hoping you feel the same."

"I feel the same." I can't lie.

His confidence in himself, him telling me all of this, is turning me on. Big time.

"Really?" A slow, sexy smile spreads on his face.

I smile and nod. "Yes, really."

I take a breath, letting my pulse settle, and admit quietly, "I've been thinking about you a lot lately."

"While my charming disposition is definitely what won you over, I know it's my body you want. Namely the abs," he jokes, but the flicker in his eyes tells me we both know there's truth under the teasing.

"The looks are … well, let's just say, you're more than easy on the eyes."

His expression shifts; playful melts into something darker. "Can I tell you something?" He looks at me with heat in his eyes. "The other night, when you went to bed, and we ran into each other in the hall?"

I swallow, the memory sending a shiver through me, and nod.

"I wanted to push you up against the wall and devour you. Then I wanted to carry you into my room and lay you out on my bed. Fuck." He tilts his head back, jaw tight, then looks at me again.

"If you had kissed me ..." I trail off, my voice low, teasing. "I don't know if we would have made it to the bedroom."

He grins, dark and knowing. "Damn. I should have kissed you, but I wasn't sure if you were as attracted to me as I was to you."

I smirk, leaning a little closer to the camera. "I could definitely tell by the bulge in your shorts that you were into me. And I wasn't turned off by it. In fact ... I was wondering exactly what you had going on underneath those shorts."

He bites his lip, a slow, dangerous smile spreading. "Is that so?"

I shrug, trying to look casual, but the heat crawling through me gives me away. "Maybe. But I think you already know the answer."

His voice drops slightly, rougher now, and I can almost feel the weight of him through the screen. "Knowing that you've been sleeping in my bed is making me lose my mind. I can't stop thinking about you."

"I can't stop thinking about you either," I say softly. My tone drops low, the kind of voice that hints at exactly how much I've been thinking about him.

I imagine running my hands over his hard chest, feeling every muscle, every divot of that perfectly sculpted body beneath my fingertips. My hands would glide lower to his thighs, tracing the strength there, so taut and powerful.

I imagine straddling him, hips pressing against him, mounting Bo and riding him, feeling every inch, making me shiver.

He must be imagining the same thing because he lets out a deep groan. "Fuck ... now I'm hard," he hisses.

"Because of me saying I can't stop thinking about you?" I smile, a little smug.

"Yes," he says bluntly, eyes dark and intent. "I want more than to kiss you, Chelsea. Like I said, I want to devour you."

I'm getting wet just at the sound of his voice and the picture he's painting of devouring me. I want him—desperately. On my lips. On my skin. On my clit.

I know if I asked him for phone sex right now, he'd be game. Bo is unabashedly honest, unapologetically himself, and up for anything.

He's also fire and intensity ... all the things that can lead to chaos if I'm not careful. But instead of fearing it, there's a pull I can't shake.

My aunt's words echo in my head. "... *it's time you started taking some chances.*"

As much as I want to hear the sound of his words all night and have him unravel me, I force myself to pause. At least for tonight.

"Well, you should probably go take care of that then. And I"—I roll over to turn off my light—"should go to sleep."

When I turn back to the camera, he moves his fingers over the screen in a telltale shape.

"Did you just take a screenshot of me?" I giggle.

"I did. So I can go take care of my hard-on." He winks at me, and a wave of heat runs right down my body to my center. "One more thing. Did you drive to the airport or get a ride?"

"I took an Uber. Why?"

"Perfect. I'll come pick you up on Sunday, and we can hang out." He says it like there's no alternative. And I like it.

I smile, and he smiles back.

"Okay, that works."

His smile grows wider. "Good. Looking forward to it. Night, Chelsea."

"Night, Bo." I smile and shake my head slightly, then end the call.

CHAPTER
NINE

BO

WE ARRIVE by buses at the stadium two hours before game time. Then we make our way down the Walk of Champions from the entrance of the field to the stadium gates. On our way in, I have my headphones on so I can keep the noise of the fans lining the walkway from distracting me. Casey's by my side, but I see him veer off to say hello to his parents, sister, and Noelle. I wave when they look my way, and I think Charlie wishes me luck, but I just nod and keep walking. I can't really talk to anyone before we play.

I like to be mentally prepared and usually walk through plays in my mind, and I can't do that if I lose my concentration. I don't even look at my phone until after the game. I always let my playlist run until it's time to get dressed. Even then, I'll set my headphones on the shelf and leave them running.

Once I get to my stall, I sit and start to take my dress shoes off. We're required to wear suits on game days, which I don't mind, but I can't wait to get these shoes off. Then I stand and pull out my warm-up gear from the top shelf of the locker and set it on the bench. I'm unbuttoning my shirt by the time Casey comes in.

Coach enters the locker room and whistles to get our attention. I remove one side of my headphones to listen.

"You all have about ten minutes to be ready for warm-ups. Get moving." He claps his hands a few times.

My teammates turn back to their lockers and start moving a little faster. I do too. I get my pants off then pull up my gym shorts. I grab my cleats and prop one foot on my bench and loosely tie the laces, then do the other foot.

I look over at Casey when I'm ready, and he nods. I still have one headphone off, which he knows means he can talk to me now.

"After we stretch, you wanna throw the ball around?" he asks.

"Yep. Let me get my arm and shoulder worked out and stretched first. I'm definitely in the mood to launch some rockets today, so I hope you're ready." I hold out my fist, and he bumps it with his.

"You know it. Let's do it."

Once on the field, I run through my stretches and drills until I feel loose. Phil Collins is in my ear, banging on the drums, singing about what's coming in the air tonight, and I'm feelin' it. I air-drum along with him a few times and sing a little too. Not too loud though. My voice is shit.

I see the coaches and some of the other guys start to head back into the locker room, so I toss the ball I'm holding to one of the equipment managers and jog toward the locker room. I look up at the Jumbotron and see myself, so I lift a hand and smile, which causes some cheering. I hold up my index finger just before I enter the tunnel and hear more cheering.

Being a leader on the field and really in the eyes of the nation can hold a lot of pressure. When I first came to Walker, it all felt pretty intense, but having Liam Pitz as a mentor helped me keep things in perspective and reminded me why I was here. And I remind myself of it every time I walk into the locker room. It's my job to get out on that field every weekend and have fun and win some football games. Plain and simple

It's about twenty minutes until game time, and we're all feeling the energy in the room. "Thunderstruck" is blasting through the speakers, and I nod my head along to the beat. Coach has already given us his speech, so it's my turn. I start clapping my hands to get their attention and walk into the center of the room.

"I want you guys to think about one thing today. Think about what you had to do to get here. The drive, the determination, the work ethic—all of it brought us to this day." I look around the room at my teammates. "And today is our fucking day!" I clap my hands. "This is our field! The eighty-five thousand fans sitting in the stands are ours!" I pace the circle, looking at each player as I pass. "They came here to see us win! This is our time! And this is our motherfuckin' house!"

The locker room erupts in noise. My teammates are jumping up and down, getting hyped.

"Who are we?" I yell.

"STALLIONS!"

"I said, who are we?" I hold my hand to my ear and bend forward.

"STALLIONS!"

"Whose house is this?" I hold up my hand.

"OUR HOUSE!"

"Let's go take what's ours, boys!" I clap my hands. "Bring it in."

Everyone huddles around me and each other.

"Stallions on three. One, two, three, STALLIONS!"

We break up and grab our helmets from our stalls, and run out to the tunnel leading to the field. Game day at Walker is unlike anything else I've ever seen on any other campus. Our stadium sells out for every game. The noise of our eighty-plus thousand fans, the band, the announcers over the loudspeakers —it's enough to get your blood pumping.

I make my way through my teammates until I reach the front, standing behind Coach. Casey comes to stand next to me, and then Silas stands on my other side.

"Let's go, QB1!" Silas hits my helmet.

I rock back and forth on my feet and roll my neck, ready to get out there. The horses that run out onto the field at the beginning of every game are in position. The banners on either side of us are flying. The smoke machines are already smoking. As soon as the band starts playing our fight song, we get the signal and run onto the field behind Coach. I put my helmet on as I run to the sideline.

"Testing," I say into the microphone inside my helmet.

"All clear, six," my offensive coordinator says in my ear.

The plays are called to me into my helmet from the coaches and offensive coordinators in the booth.

"Stay light on your feet today, Bo. They're gonna try to blitz every chance they get. Watch, look, and listen," one of them says.

"Got it." I take a ball from one of the trainers and start tossing it to one of the coaches to stay loose.

After throwing a few back and forth, I look up at the clock and see we only have a few minutes left until the game starts. I toss the ball one more time to the coach and jog down to the end zone. A few guys—including Casey, Silas, and the Griffith twins —join me. I take a knee and remove my helmet and set it next to me. I drop my head, close my eyes, and do what I need to do to get my mind right. Then I tap my chest with two fingers, kiss the tips, and raise them toward the sky, looking up.

Now ... I'm ready to win.

The first half of the game went by fast, with us scoring three easy touchdowns. One was a pass to Casey for a forty-five-yard touchdown. The next one was with one of our running backs who took over for Beck, Jake DiAngelo. The third one was to Ace Griffith, who is a tight end. He's got the size of his brother Archie, but Ace is faster on his feet.

It's the fourth quarter now. The Kansas Jayhawks came back from the half at full force, and they're hungry for a comeback. Their defense has been all over me, and we can't make any progress. We're at third down on their twenty-five.

"Okay, boys. Let's make something happen." I hear the call in my ear and repeat it to my team. "O Near Sixty-Two F Angle Ohio."

We all clap and line up on the line of scrimmage.

When I get into position behind our center, I scan the defense to look for any break or change in their formation. I glance over at Casey briefly to let him know he's getting the pass.

I call out my all-go call-sign signal. "Red thirty-two, red thirty-two, set, hut."

I catch the ball, and I have seconds to throw before a lineman tackles me. I see Casey juke and run his route, looking over his shoulder for the ball I send spiraling toward him. He catches it over his shoulder and brings it to his chest just as I get tackled, so I don't see where he landed.

The whistle blows, and a flag is thrown because of the late hit I took, which gives us an automatic first down, even though we got it with Casey's catch. We move to the two-yard line.

"We're going Mario on this one. Break." I clap, and we break.

Mario is our call sign for a tush push, which places my linemen behind me once the ball is snapped and they shove me through the Hawks' defense and into the end zone.

"Red thirty-two, red thirty-two, set, hut!"

When the ball snaps, I grab it easily from my center, and my teammates shove me through their line for the touchdown. I hear the whistle blow, and the crowd erupts.

Once my teammates pull me out of the pile, we run over to the cheering sideline.

Coach Pettys grabs my helmet as I come to stand next to him. "Helluva game, kid!" He smacks my helmet and laughs.

Our kicker and special teams go out to the field, and we secure our win.

I run out onto the field as the clock winds down and shake their quarterback's hand, along with a few other guys I've gotten to know over the years.

Then our media manager comes over to me and takes my elbow. "Bo, we need you over here." She leads me over toward the camera crew near the tunnel.

"Congratulations on your win, Bo. You had an amazing fourteen out of seventeen passes completed in the fourth. What was clicking for you that late in the game?" the reporter, Holly, asks me, microphone in hand.

"Thanks. Yeah, I just felt like everything was working for us, and I hit a good stride to finish it out." I lean down when she starts to speak again because I can hardly hear her over the crowd noise.

"You have a lot of pressure this year to get another title. How are you managing it?" she asks.

"I'm just taking it one game at a time, Holly." I give her my best media smile and nod.

"Thanks, Bo." She shakes my hand and drops the microphone, and the cameraman turns the camera off of us. "I look forward to watching the rest of your season."

"Appreciate you, Holly. See you soon." I give her a two-finger wave as I walk away and into the tunnel.

When I get into the locker room, everyone is celebrating the win, and music is blasting through the speakers.

Our media manager comes over to me at my locker. "You have ten minutes to get undressed and into the press room."

"Got it." I nod and start to pull off my pads.

Coach Pettys comes in and gives his speech. He hands the game ball to Casey. He had seventy-two yards today and two touchdowns. If Casey averages the same yardage in each game, he'll be a first-round draft pick for sure.

I set my pads on the ground in front of my stall and then grab my phone from the top shelf. I haven't looked at it since early this morning. There's a new text from my dad and one from Chelsea. I look at hers first.

Chelsea: Congrats on your win!

Bo: Did you catch any of the game?

Chelsea: I didn't, sorry! We just got back from the airboat ride. I'll watch some of the highlights though.

Bo: My number is six in case you forgot.

Chelsea: Oh, I know. Star of Walker University.

> Bo: Ha! Casey was the star today. Wait till you see some of those clips.

> Chelsea: Awesome! I bet Noelle is excited. I'll text her.

> Bo: I have to run to press now, but talk later?

> Chelsea: I'll be here.

My name is called before I can reply, so I set my phone back on the shelf. I really need to change my shirt at the very least. I'm soaked. Sarah, one of our trainers, walks by, and I reach out to her.

"Hey, Sarah. Can you see about getting me a fresh T-shirt quickly?"

"Sure thing. Give me a sec." She hurries away and comes back a few minutes later and tosses me a fresh T-shirt.

"Thanks. You're the best." I wink at her, which only makes her roll her eyes, making me laugh.

I pull my phone out again and look at my dad's text. He's been blowing up my phone with texts lately about staying focused on my future and not getting distracted. It's strange in a way. He's never been this persistent before.

> Dad: Great game today, son.

> Dad: I know you're busy, Bo, but it's important that I speak with you as soon as possible. This isn't negotiable.

If he had left it at the first text, I probably would have at least replied with a thank-you. But I'm not in the mood for a lecture about staying focused after a win like this, so I'll pass.

I put my phone back on the shelf and shake off thoughts of my father, refocusing on what I need to do next.

When I walk into the press room, I see the reporters all holding their phones in their hands, notepads on their laps.

I take a seat at the table and adjust the microphone. "Hey, everyone."

Murmured hellos are returned.

"Let's get this started so I can go catch my shower. I stink." I run a hand through my sweat-soaked hair. "All right, who's up first?"

CHAPTER
TEN

CHELSEA

MY FLIGHT LANDED twenty minutes ago, but it took forever for us to disembark. I didn't check any luggage, so I make my way to Arrivals to wait for Bo. We talked again last night after his game, and I gave him my flight details. But I haven't stopped thinking about our conversation the night before his game. Thinking about him jerking off to my picture … turns me on. I was hoping for more flirting when I talked to him last night, but he was so tired; he practically fell asleep while we were talking. Plus, I had to get up early to make my flight back here, so our conversation was short.

As the escalator goes down, I pull out my phone from my bag and send a quick text to my aunt to let her know I got home safely. Then I text Bo to let him know I'm on my way down. When I get near the bottom, I look up and see Bo standing there. His hands are in his jean pockets, and he's wearing a tight black T-shirt and a baseball hat with the Walker logo on it. When he sees me, a smile breaks across his face.

Good Lord is he gorgeous.

He removes one hand from his pocket and waves, then walks toward me. When I reach him, he pulls me in for a hug.

"Hey. Did you have a good flight?"

"Yeah, it was uneventful, thankfully. Thanks for coming to get me." I pull back from him.

He reaches for the bag on my shoulder and slides it off my arm before hoisting it onto his. "Of course. I couldn't wait to see you." He looks down at me and smiles.

"I'm happy to see you too."

He shifts my bag to his other shoulder and then reaches for my hand. The feeling of my hand in his should feel foreign to me, but it doesn't. His hand is big and warm, and I can feel the rough calluses on his palm, but mostly, it just feels comfortable. Like it's something we've always done.

"Are you hungry? We could stop and get something to eat on our way back, or we can eat at the house."

We walk out of the doors and toward the parking garage.

"I'm a little hungry, but I can wait until we get to your house. Honestly, I wouldn't mind a shower. I always feel gross after traveling." I scrunch my nose.

"All right, to the house it is. I'm sure we have stuff to eat, and if not, we can order food in. I can take care of that while you shower or something."

He releases my hand and puts his on the small of my back when we reach his SUV. Then he opens the door for me and closes it when I'm in.

He rounds the back of the car, opens the back door, and sets my bag on the floor behind the driver's side, then gets in. This is the first time I've been in his car. It smells like him, and it's sleek with black leather seats and trim.

It's not the first time I've been near him, and yet this time, it feels like we're on top of each other—in the best possible way. The energy in the car is thick, almost electric. Whatever we are, whatever this is, our relationship has shifted into something new. It's still easy and playful, but there's this heat now—this low, constant hum of awareness between us. I'm torn between asking him about his day, telling him something funny from the weekend, or just making him pull over so we can have a ridiculously heavy make-out session on the side of the road.

Once we're on the road, he reaches over and takes my hand in his, pausing my internal dispute. "So, tell me about the airboat ride. I was crashing hard last night. I'm sorry you didn't get to tell me about it."

"It was good. My sister had a blast, so that's all that matters."

And it really was okay. Torie and her friends loved riding through the swamp and catching sight of some pretty big gators.

I tell him more about it, and then he tells me more about his game yesterday.

Before we know it, we're back at his house.

We walk into the house, and Bo has my bag over his shoulder.

"I'll go put this in my room and get you a towel for your shower. Help yourself to anything you find in the kitchen," he says over his shoulder.

I take off my shoes and set them by the door, then walk into the kitchen and open the fridge to see what they have, but I'm still not very hungry, so I just grab a bottle of water and lean against the counter. The house is quiet, and I didn't see Casey's or Noelle's cars outside, and I don't hear Silas or Charlie, so I wonder if we're alone. We haven't been here alone together. It makes me feel a little anxious, but also … excited. Not that I expect anything to happen between us.

Bo walks over toward the door and takes his shoes off, then comes into the kitchen.

Okay, so as it turns out, the horny part of me is winning over the conversational one because looking at him in his tight-fitted shirt, which showcases his gorgeous body, is making me salivate … and not for food.

"Find anything in here to eat?" he asks.

I let out a shaky breath, completely surprised by my behavior. I don't get shy around guys. If I want to hook up, I do. When I'm ready to walk away, I do.

Bo is just a guy.

So, why does he make my heart race like this?

"I think I can wait awhile. I'll probably just go take my shower, if that's okay?" I push off the counter and move to walk by him when he reaches for me.

"You okay?" He takes my hand in his and rubs his thumb over the top of it.

"Oh, yeah, I'm good. I'm a little tired, I guess. It was a busy weekend." Maybe he senses my anxiousness, so I try to seem more relaxed than the butterflies floating around in my belly. I place my other hand on top of his. "Can I get a towel?"

"I set one on my bed for you." He studies my face for a minute. "Let me know if you need anything else."

As we look at each other, I think about what my aunt said to me this weekend about opening myself up to someone. For me, I think a lot of my reluctance or … I guess I'll just admit it … my fear about letting myself be vulnerable or falling hard for someone is because my parents' relationship was so volatile. They were fire and passion and drama and violence. They didn't set a good example, so I don't really know what a healthy relationship between a man and a woman looks like in real life. My parents were so consumed and obsessed—with each other and their addictions—that they couldn't care about anything else. And I've never wanted to feel that … out of control.

But standing here, looking at this beautiful man, I make the decision that I want to try to let this, *us*, happen.

I release his hand, and in a bold move, I lean up and kiss his cheek. My lips linger seconds as I take in the salt of his skin and the wildly sexy smell of his sandalwood bodywash.

"Thank you," I say as I pull back and lick my lips.

As I walk away, I can feel his eyes on me.

I grab some clothes and the towel from his room and then take a quick shower. I put on my favorite pair of loose cotton pants, a bra, and a nearly threadbare T-shirt. It's one of my favorites, and I'll keep it until it falls apart. My hair is wet, so I twist it into a knot at the top of my head.

When I'm done, I walk into his room and see him lying on his bed. He changed into gym shorts and took his hat off. It's insane how I find him in a pair of mesh shorts so damn delectable. His feet are bare and crossed at the ankles. The TV is playing an NFL game.

He looks up, and his eyes widen as he takes in my T-shirt, which is quite thin, and there's a solid chance my nipples are showing through. He takes a deep inhale.

I nod toward the screen. "Did you just get this TV? It wasn't in here before."

"I had it in my closet, but never set it up. I don't know why I didn't think about it until now. I should have connected it before the first night you stayed in here. Sorry about that." He swings his legs to the side, and his feet touch the carpet.

"Oh, no worries. I didn't really need one." I'm still standing near the doorway, holding my things. I see he moved my bag to the floor in front of the dresser, so I walk over, bend down, and start to put my dirty clothes into my bag.

"You can leave your shower stuff in the bathroom. Noelle has some of her things in there. It doesn't bother us. And you can wash your clothes from your trip." He stands and walks toward me.

"Okay, I probably will, but I don't want to deal with it today," I say as I stand. "Did you eat something, or do you want to watch the game for a bit first?"

A curl falls out of my bun, and he reaches out to tuck it behind my ear, then rests his hand on my shoulder.

"Not yet. I'll wait for you to eat, so just tell me when you get hungry."

"Okay," I say a little breathlessly.

There's definitely tension in the air, heightened by the fact that I know we're alone.

"Chelsea"—he leans in and traces a path down my arm to my hip—"do you know how bad I've wanted to kiss you since that first night in the hall?" He squeezes my hip. "Will you let me kiss you, Chelsea?" He presses in closer. "I can't walk away again without tasting you." He brings his hand up to my neck and wraps it around. "Just one kiss."

"Yes." The word is barely out of my mouth before his lips are on mine. But it's not a rushed kiss. It's slow and deliberate. Savoring.

I need more.

I lift up on my toes and wrap my arms around his shoulders and pull him in closer. When I part my mouth for him, the kiss deepens, his tongue stroking mine, like he's memorizing my taste, making heat simmer low in my belly.

His other hand cups my cheek, then slides into my hair. Our tongues tangle, and when I suck on his, he lets out a deep groan and slides his hand from my neck down to my ass, pulling me into him even closer. I can feel the ridge of his hard-on through his shorts against my stomach, which only makes me feel like I'm on the edge of losing control and fucking him right now against this dresser.

A door opens, but I barely notice. But then I hear voices. Bo must hear them, too, because he slows the kiss, but doesn't pull away. He kisses me softly once, twice, then rests his head against my forehead, our breaths quick.

"Holy shit, Chelsea. We need to do that again."

A laugh rumbles in my chest, and I try to keep it in since we know someone is home. And I really don't want to draw any attention to us.

"I agree. We definitely need to do that again. Like, as soon as possible."

"As much as I want to close my door and stay in here all night, we'd better go say hello to whoever it is." He pulls his head away from mine and drops his hand from my neck and waist, walks over to his closet, grabs a hoodie, and wraps it around me.

"No one else gets to see those perfect tits but me," he says, smirking.

I feel heat in my cheeks as he zips me up, then takes my hand in his.

We walk out hand in hand, but I let go before we see Casey and Noelle in the kitchen. It looks like they had the same idea we did because Noelle has her legs wrapped around Casey's waist and they're kissing.

Bo turns his head and looks back at me, smirking, then turns to face them again. "Hey, guys. What's up?"

Noelle pulls away from their kiss and looks over Casey's shoulder and sees us. "Oh, hi, guys! Chels, you're back!" She unwraps her body from Casey's and comes over to hug me. "How was it?"

"Hot." I hug her back and laugh. "But Torie had fun and was happy I came, so it was worth it."

"Oh good. I can't believe she's eighteen. She still seemed so young when I first met her." Noelle pulls away and walks back toward the kitchen.

"Hey, Chels," Casey says with a wave.

I nod and smile in response. "What are you guys up to?" I see a few grocery bags on the counter that weren't there before.

"We ran some errands and stopped to get some food from the store. Did you guys eat yet?" Noelle walks over to the bags and starts to empty them.

"Not yet. I wasn't hungry, but I could eat something small now. What are you guys having?" I walk over and help her.

"I was just going to make some snacks for now while we watch the game. Beck's game starts in, like, thirty minutes." She nods toward the TV.

"Do you need any help, pretty girl? I'm going to get the TV on." Casey walks over to her and kisses her cheek.

"I'm good. I'll call you if I need you." She turns to kiss him. "Thank you though."

"You coming with me, Callaway, or helping the girls?" Casey asks with a smirk.

Bo looks over at me, like he doesn't want to walk away from me just quite yet. "I'll come with you."

I look back at Noelle when he walks away. "That's where Charlie is? Beck's game?" I put a block of cheese in the fridge.

"Yeah, she left Saturday morning. It was a little up in the air until then on whether or not she would be able to get up there." She sets some ground sausage next to the stove.

"What are you making with all the cheese?" I ask her as I take out more cheese from the bag, a jar of salsa, and some tortilla chips.

"I'm going to make taco dip, but I have to try to do it as healthy as possible for the guys. And it's not easy. I had to replace the Velveeta with real cheese." She laughs. "I have some veggies and some hummus we can get out too."

"Okay, I'll get some of that stuff ready while you make the dip."

She hands me a cutting board, and I get started.

After we're done, we join the guys and watch the game. Noelle cuddles up to Casey on the couch. I sit on the opposite end, closest to the chair that Bo is sitting in.

"Hey, come sit with me." He holds out his hand to me.

It is a large chair, and we could both fit in it, even with as big as he is. But ... our friends are here. I know they won't care, but this feels like a big deal for me. I look at Noelle and Casey, and they're watching the game. And they're not the type of people who would make us feel uncomfortable. Silas ... might say something, but he's not here. So, I take Bo's hand, and he pulls me into the chair with him, right on his lap.

I glance over at Noelle, who looks at me and just smiles.

Bo shifts a little in the chair and turns us slightly so we can both see the TV. Beck is on the field right now, and it's pretty crazy to me that these guys are my friends. Never could I have imagined that I would be mixed in with a bunch of athletes like this, let alone professional and almost-professional athletes.

It's like a whole new world to me, so I still have questions, which Bo patiently answers. The way he explains things is somewhat mesmerizing. He's passionate about the sport for sure, but I feel like he really wants me to understand it too.

The game goes by quickly, we've had our snacks, and Bo ended up making some of his "famous" wings, which were pretty good. Silas came home during the game and joined us. Then we watch Beck in an interview after the game is over, and Casey FaceTimes with Charlie, who's waiting for Beck to come out. She'll be flying home in the morning.

I let out a yawn, and Bo pulls me in closer to his chest.

"You getting tired?" he says softly in my ear.

"Yeah, a little, but I'm not sure I could go to bed yet." I turn my head to the side to see his face.

"Do you want to go watch something in my room?" The hand he has on my thigh starts inching up higher. "I'm dying to kiss you again."

I suck in a deep breath because, well, I want the same thing. Sitting in his lap for most of the game did nothing to stop me from thinking about our kiss earlier. "Okay, yeah, let's go watch a movie or something. Unless there's another game you want to watch. I don't mind either way."

He stands with me in his arms and starts walking toward his room. "Night, everyone," Bo says as we walk out.

I look over at Noelle, and she has a knowing smile on her face.

She mouths, *We need to talk,* but replies out loud, "Good night."

Then Casey says good night.

Silas murmurs something that I think is, "When did that happen?"

When we get to the room, Bo lays me on the bed, then turns

back to close the door. "So, what do you want to watch?" he asks as he comes over to the bed.

I scoot up to a sitting position against the pillows. "It really doesn't matter to me."

He climbs into the bed next to me, takes the remote off the nightstand, and turns on the TV. There's another football game playing; this time, it looks like the Cowboys.

"Archie's game is on, so we can watch that for a while until we decide. Does that work?" He sets the remote back on the nightstand, then turns his body toward mine.

"Yeah," I say in a breathy voice I almost don't recognize.

He reaches his hand out to cup my face, his thumb stroking my cheek.

I'm looking between his mouth and his eyes, and I'm not sure which one of us moves first, but the next thing I know, our mouths are fused together. This kiss, it isn't slow like our first kiss. It's urgent, wet, and I can't get close enough to him.

I shift my body so I'm lying flat on the pillow, and he positions himself over me, but not on top of me. I wrap my arms around his shoulders. His face is above mine when he pulls away, breathless.

"Fuck," he says before leaning back in to kiss me.

I'm so lost in our kiss; I'm not sure how much time passes. I'm consumed by it, by him. My hands start to roam from his shoulders to his neck and into his hair, pulling him in closer to me. I slant my head to deepen the kiss, and his groan vibrates against my lips, making me shiver. I could explain that my response to him is because I haven't had sex in a while, but I think it's just him. He turns me on like I've never been before.

And this isn't a hookup. This is more. I can feel it in the way he looks at me, the way he kisses me, the way he pays attention to everything I say. All of those things just turn me on even more, to be honest. His insanely hot body could be part of it too. And I would be stupid not to take my time tracing every slice of muscle on this man's body. With my tongue.

Moving my hands from his head, I reach down and grab the hem of his T-shirt and tug it up, breaking our kiss to pull it over his head. I smooth my hands over the muscles on his chest and sigh. "Bo Callaway, you are not real. This body of yours is insane."

When my fingers trace the ridges of his stomach, he sucks in a breath. "I'm taking that as a compliment based on the way you're touching me, but I'm also very glad you think so." His hands move to the hem of my shirt. "May I?"

"Yes, take it off."

I move my arms above my head so he can slide my shirt over it. Then he tosses it to the floor, and reaches around me to unclasp my bra. I pull the straps down my arms and drop it on the floor.

"Chelsea, I just want you to know, I don't expect anything to happen tonight. I'm very happy with kissing and touching you." He looks down at me, sincerity in his eyes. "Not to say that I don't want to fuck you till the sun comes up, but I can be patient."

His honesty makes me laugh.

"How about we see how this goes and just do what feels right instead of overthinking it? I just want you to touch me, and I want to touch you. Whatever happens, happens."

"I can do that."

He leans down to kiss me again, his tongue tracing the seam of my mouth. I open for him, meeting his tongue with my own that leaves me breathless. Our tongues slide together as our hands start to explore.

His large palm covers my breast, squeezing it. Then he breaks the kiss and bends his head to take my nipple into his mouth and sucks, making me moan and my hips rise.

My hands hold his head as he nips and sucks each nipple. Turning my body even more into his, I drape a leg over his hip, and he grabs the back of my thigh. I move one hand from his head and slide it down his chest, his abs, then to the waistband of his shorts.

He pulls away from my chest and brings his face back to mine. His chest is rising and falling as I stroke the skin just above the elastic. "You're killing me."

Instead of responding, I slip my hand past the band, noticing he's also not wearing underwear, and run it down the thick, hard length of his cock. It twitches under my touch, and I wrap my hand around it—well, try to wrap my hand around it. He's big— like really big. When I start pumping his cock, he kisses me deeply and slower this time. Like he's mimicking the movement of my hand on him.

I'm so turned on now that I can feel the wetness between my legs. I need him to touch me, so I take his hand that's holding my thigh and bring it to my center. He takes my direction and pushes his hand into my pants. Finding I'm not wearing under-wear, he pulls back from our kiss.

"Bare and wet." Then he runs his finger through my wetness, stopping at my clit.

I can't help but move my hips as he slides his finger back and forth through my heat.

"Just like that." I pull him back in to kiss me and suck on his tongue, making him groan.

My other hand continues to stroke his cock, and I feel the pre-cum leaking from the head, so I smear it around the large tip and glide it down his length as he starts to thrust his hips.

His fingers move faster as my hips roll with each stroke, creating a friction that is bringing me closer and closer to orgasm. The first pulses hit slowly, and I have no doubt Bo can feel it when his finger pushes inside me. He pumps his finger in and out as my orgasm washes over me. Our mouths still fused together.

His dick jerks in my hand, and then I feel his cum dripping down his length as he reaches his own orgasm. I squeeze him gently and run my hand up and over the head, then remove my hand from his shorts.

As my orgasm fades, he pulls his fingers out of me, but continues to slowly stroke my clit. The sensation is almost too much for me, but I don't want him to stop either.

He breaks our kiss and looks down at me. "You're amazing. And next time, I want to watch you when you come all over my hand." He pulls his hand out of my pants and sticks his finger that was inside me into his mouth and hums. "So sweet."

My gaze is locked on his finger in his mouth. "Yes, to all of that," I manage to say.

He removes his finger, sucking on it as he pulls it out, then kisses me again slowly, tongue swirling around mine. Almost like he wants me to taste myself on his tongue.

When he untangles his tongue from mine, my hand, the one not covered in his cum, brushes through his hair. He tilts his head, resting it in my hand, then pulls his head far enough away to kiss my palm.

Then Bo kneels on the bed, looking down at his shorts. "I don't think I've come in my pants since my sophomore year of high school."

I can't help the laugh that bubbles out. "Yeah, you might want to change out of those." I reach out and pull on the band.

He places his hand over mine, wide smile on his face. "You should probably do the same." He winks at me, then gets off the bed. "I'll be right back."

When he leaves, I get up and strip out of my pants, using one hand, and then I find a new pair to sleep in. I'll still need to make a run to the bathroom to clean up a little. My one hand is still wet from his cum.

He comes back in a few minutes later, wet and wrapped in a towel. "Sorry, I had to rinse off real quick."

As I walk by him, I tilt my head up and pucker my lips for a kiss. "I'll be right back."

He leans down and kisses me softly. Then I go to the bathroom, where I clean my hand first, use the restroom, and wash my hands again before opening the door. When I cross through the hall to go back to his room, I notice all the lights are off in the house, so everyone must have gone to bed. I didn't even think about it in the moment, but I wonder if anyone heard us. Not that I really care, I suppose.

I open the bedroom door and find Bo on the bed, and he's under the covers. After I close the door, I walk over to the other side of the bed, and he lifts the covers for me to get in.

How sweet is he?

"You know, I've never slept with someone before. Like, fall-asleep sleep." I lie down and adjust the covers, but turn toward him.

He lifts his eyebrows. "Never?"

I shake my head. "Nope. I've never wanted to." I place my hand on his bare chest. "Until now."

He places his hand over mine and moves them both over his heart. His arm stretches out, and he slides it under my head. "Come here."

I scoot over to him, and he wraps the arm under me over my shoulder, tucking me into him. I tilt my chin and kiss his stubbled jaw. Then he leans his head down to kiss my lips.

As I settle into his arms, the sound of his heartbeat is the last thing I remember before I fall asleep.

CHAPTER
ELEVEN

CHELSEA

IT'S BEEN two days since the night we messed around. I have talked to Bo every day, but I haven't seen him since. And I'm back at my own apartment now, which I'm slightly disappointed about. I was starting to get used to having other people around, and being able to see Bo sleeping in his bed was a bonus too.

He's been busy the last few days with football stuff, and he had to do some more interviews for the docuseries. And I've been working on getting everything turned in for my law school applications. I get to see him at our study session today though, and I can't wait.

I'm walking to the library now. Luckily, I've been able to reserve the study area we've been using. I take the flight of stairs to the second level and head into the room. I'm just pulling my notebook out of my messenger bag when Bo walks in and sets his backpack on the table. He looks amazing in jeans and a tight black T-shirt.

"Hey."

One thing I've noticed in the time we've been spending

together and talking is just how deep his voice is. The timbre hits just right.

"Hi." I look at him and smile. "How's your day going?" I untie the hoodie around my waist, drape it on the back of my seat, sit down, and pull out the syllabus.

"Better now that I get to see you." He walks around the table to me, tilts my chin up, and leans down to kiss me, lingering for a minute before pulling away. He goes back to his side of the table, opens his bag, and starts taking out his notebook, phone, and tablet.

"Aren't you sweet?" I tease. "So, you have a quiz this week that we should study for today."

"Yep, I do. I feel pretty good about it though. The last few weeks have really helped." He takes a seat and pulls his chair in closer to the table.

"Good. I'm glad." And I am.

I really like to help people. It's not that Bo isn't capable of learning the material. I think, with him, it's more of a lack of interest in the subject maybe. Honestly, he just needs to pass the class. So, as long as I help him do that, I've done my job.

"Okay, let's get started."

"All right, let's get the school stuff out of the way so we can talk. I want to hear about your day." He pulls up his notes on his tablet and glances up at me, the corners of his mouth lifting.

"Not much to tell. I had class and met with my advisor this morning. Now I'm here with you." I shrug. "My life is pretty predictable. I like a solid routine, you know?"

"I do know. I'm the same," he says, watching me.

"Your old-man schedule, you mean?" I can't help but laugh.

He puts his hand on his chest. "Hey, don't knock it. I personally enjoy eating dinner early, and getting solid sleep is the best. I'm tellin' ya. Those old folks have had the right idea all along."

"I believe you. I just can't shut my head off as early as you do. I need to watch a show, scroll on my phone—although I need to stop doing that. It interferes with your sleep pattern or something."

"Yep. That's what our nutritionist tells us too. We need the sleep and downtime for recovery, but also for cognitive awareness. All that said, I do like being able to talk to you at night before bed. That's been really nice the last few days." He reaches across the table and hooks my index finger with his. "I also miss having you at the house and in my bed."

"You do, huh?" I tilt my head, studying his eyes.

Bo Callaway is the kind of guy who speaks from the heart, and you can read the truth in his eyes.

"I do. Have you missed me?" His mouth tips up on one side.

I'm not one to play games, so I tell him the truth. "I have. I was getting used to being in your bed. You've got a good mattress."

"So, you just miss my mattress?"

I pull in a deep breath because I know things are about to change between us. I can feel it. And I want it. I want to just be around him, to have his hands on me, his mouth on mine. "I've missed you."

He takes my hand in his and brushes his thumb over the top of my hand. "I want to see you tonight. Can you come over, or can I come to yours?"

"Um, yeah, either one works."

My guess is that Noelle will be at his place again with Casey, so that means we would have my apartment to ourselves. Not that I expect anything to happen, although I wouldn't mind. It would be good for us to hang out without everyone else hanging around too.

"I can make something for dinner at my place if you want. Noelle will probably be at yours again."

"Yeah, I'd like that." We sit, staring at each other in silence, both smiling. "Do you like to cook?"

I nod. "I do. I mean, I'm no Top Chef or anything, but I can make a few things. I guess I should ask if you have any food restrictions." I lift my shoulder.

"Not really. I try to avoid a lot of fatty foods though. I eat a lot of protein and veggies. But honestly, don't worry about me. I'll eat whatever you make. Can I bring anything?" He releases my hand and sits back in his seat.

"I should be good. I have to stop at the store on my way home anyway, so I can grab anything else I might need then." My phone buzzes with a text from my aunt, and I glance at it quickly, but close it out. I do notice the time though, and we're running behind. "You'll have to go to practice soon, so we should get started."

"Okay, let's do this."

Forty minutes later, we start to pack up.

I look up and ask him, "I think you're ready for tomorrow, don't you?"

"Yeah, I think so. I've gone over it on my own and now with you. So, unless she changes everything she's testing us on, I should be good."

I chuckle lowly.

"Thank you for helping me with this. I mean, I know it's your job, but you've been great, explaining things in a way that make sense to me."

"Happy to help, and, yes, it is my job, but I like working with people." I stand and grab my hoodie from the back of the chair.

"Well, you're good at it. If the lawyer stuff doesn't work out, you'd be an amazing teacher." He slings his backpack over his shoulder and walks toward the door.

"I feel like I'm pretty set on the law stuff, but thanks. I'll consider it for a fallback career just in case." I bring the strap of my bag over my head so it's crossing my chest.

Bo pulls the door open and holds it as I walk through, his hand touching my lower back.

"Oh, you know what? I need to go grab a book for one of my classes. You want to just text me when you're done with practice or something?"

"I'll walk with you. I have a little more time today. I already did my interview yesterday, so I just need to run to my SUV and grab my bag and drop my backpack off on the way."

"You don't have to come with me. I know where it is in the library, but it might take a minute to find it in the row." I adjust my bag so I can grab the paper with the name of the book on it.

Bo nudges my shoulder with his arm lightly. "I want to. Unless you want me to go. Is it some secret-society kind of book or something?"

"Ha, no. It's a biography that I'm referencing for a case study that I'm working on for one of my classes." I look at the numbers at the top of the stacks, trying to find the right one. When I spot it, I turn down the row.

I scan the shelves, looking for the book I need, but I can feel Bo close behind me. I stop and trace the numbers along the book spines until I see the one I need. Bo is standing close enough to me now that I can feel the heat of his body at my back.

"Did you find what you need?" he says softly in my ear, making me shiver.

The timbre of his voice is so fucking sexy. I could probably get myself off with his voice alone. No lie.

"Yeah, it's right here." I turn, and our chests brush against each other.

He lifts his arm and braces his hand on the shelf next to my head. His other hand comes to my hip. "I can't stop thinking about the other night."

"Me neither." I'm not the type of girl to blush, but I can feel the heat in my cheeks. Not from embarrassment, but from getting turned on just by his proximity. Right here. In the library. Where I work.

Ah, fuck it.

I take hold of his shirt and fist it in my hand, pulling him into me and bringing his lips to mine. When I slide my tongue into his mouth, we both moan. He drops his hand from the shelf behind me and wraps his arm around my waist, tugging me in closer to his body, and I can feel his hard-on through his jeans against my belly.

"Fuck yes." He kisses my forehead, then kisses me again on the lips. "We'd better get going. I can't be held accountable for my actions if we keep standing here, kissing. I'm about to blow in my jeans. From a kiss." He shakes his head, laughing, but he doesn't seem to be embarrassed.

"That might be hard to explain to your teammates in the locker room, I'm sure." I giggle. "Let's go."

I unwrap my arms and turn back around and grab the book I need. When I face him again, I see him adjusting his dick in his pants with a smirk on his face.

"Better?"

"As good as it's gonna get," he grumbles, but he's smiling.

We walk down the row and then down the stairs. I have to check out the book, so I walk toward the counter, and he stays with me. Once my book is checked out, we start to walk out, and a few people congratulate him on Saturday's game as they pass.

He reaches for my hand, but I pull away. I don't want my supervisor to see us holding hands if she happens to walk by. It's not in the actual rule book that you can't date a student you're tutoring, but it doesn't really look good either.

"You don't want to hold my hand?" He's looking at me, but doesn't look upset. "Are you embarrassed of me?"

"No, it's not that. I just don't want my supervisor to see us." I shrug.

"Ah, gotcha." He leans down close to my ear. "But when we're not in the library, will you let me hold your hand?"

He's so cute for asking. And I can tell he's being sincere. Like he doesn't want to do anything that would make me uncomfortable. Which just makes me like him even more. Because public displays of affection—or, hell, even just hugging my aunt, sister, or Noelle—haven't always been a natural thing for me. And I like that he can sense that about me.

I smile up at him. "Yes, Bo, I'll let you hold my hand outside of the library."

"Yes." He makes a fist and pumps his arm into his body.

"Oh my God, Bo." I can't help the loud laugh that squeaks out. "You're a dork."

He looks down and has a huge smile on his face, his eyes literally sparkling. "I wanna be your dork."

When we get to the doors, he holds one open for me. Then, as soon as we walk out of the building, he reaches for my hand.

I entwine my fingers with his, our hands between us. Like we've done this a million times before. Which, for me, is different, but I like it.

Bo's phone chimes, signaling it's time for him to head to practice. "Where are you parked?" he asks me.

"I'm on the other side of campus. You go. I'm fine."

I try to let go of his hand, but he pulls it up to his mouth and kisses my fingers.

"Get home safe. I'll call you when I get out of practice, okay?" He releases me and starts walking backward.

"Yes, sounds good. Now get to practice before you're late."

"Bye, Chelsea." He winks, then turns and jogs toward the stadium.

"Bye, Bo," I whisper to myself.

This could be a whole lotta fun or a whole lotta trouble.

CHAPTER
TWELVE

BO

THE WAY I run into the locker room once practice is over turns some heads for sure. I barely speak to anyone when I shower and throw on a T-shirt and sweatpants.

As I'm rushing out the door to my car with my phone in hand, ready to call Chelsea, Casey calls out to me, "Yo, Callaway! Where you running to like your ass is on fire?"

A few of the guys standing around laugh and chime in.

"Only one thing other than football that can make a man run like that. Pussy!" Trevor Diaz, one of our linemen, shouts.

I roll my eyes and shake my head, but keep walking. I hold up my middle finger as I walk out the door. Seconds later, my phone buzzes, and I look at it to see a text from Casey.

Casey: Seriously, where are you going?

Bo: Dinner

Casey: At home?

Bo: No

Casey: Bro, just tell me.

Bo: Chelsea's

Casey: Duuuude. Good for you, man. Don't forget to wrap it up. You don't want to pull an Archie.

I roll my eyes but laugh. Archie has a great life and loves his wife and daughter. Not that I would want that right now, but he regrets nothing.

When I get to my SUV, I toss my duffel bag in the back seat next to my backpack that I dropped off earlier. Just as I'm getting into the driver's seat, my phone rings. It's my dad. If I don't answer now, he'll probably try calling again later, and I really don't want to talk to him while I'm hanging out with her.

"Hey, Dad. What's up?"

"Bo. How was practice?" he asks, and it surprises me because he never calls to ask about practice.

"It was good. Thanks." Silence stretches. "Is everything okay?"

He sighs. "Do you have a girlfriend?"

I bark out a laugh. "What? Why?"

"I have a photo here of you kissing a girl's hand outside of the library, and it definitely looks like you're more than friends, Bo."

What the actual fuck? That was hours ago, and he already knows?

"Who took a picture of me? What, do you have spies on campus?" I say, even though it sounds preposterous.

My dad's a judge, not the CIA.

"There are a lot of people on campus in my Rolodex."

"Dad, no one uses the term *Rolodex*—"

"Bo, straighten up. I thought we agreed on no distractions. This is a big year for the two of us."

"Us? Last I checked, *I* was the one up for the draft. You have a big announcement or something?"

It's not a secret among the inner workings of our family that my dad's ultimate goal is to be a judge on the United States Supreme Court. A pipe dream for most, but for Callaways, things like becoming a professional football player or serving on the highest court in the land can easily become reality.

Keep your nose clean and your family tight and work harder than anyone else has been drilled into me since I was a child.

"Maybe. I need to have a discussion with you about a few things but ..." I hear his exasperated tone and can picture him running his hand over the back of his neck. "Just remember, it's your last year at Walker, and you need to keep your reputation squeaky clean."

"For the NFL?"

Dad pauses, and I hear the hesitation in his tone. "For ... a lot of things."

"Why would it be a problem if she was my girlfriend?"

I'm confused by this entire conversation. My dad has never asked or cared about what I do with girls. Likely because I've always been so focused on football, but still.

"I'm concerned that you're starting off on the wrong foot as it is, what with needing tutoring. And let's be honest—you might have won the game, but there's clearly some work to do. You need to be a leader on that field."

What the fuck?

"Right. Got it. No distractions here." I huff. "The girl I was pictured with—by the way, how did you see it? I was at practice for two hours and saw her right before. Are you having me followed or something? Is this some security detail type of situation?"

It'd better not be. I do not want to be followed around by some bodyguard. I'm fine with the crew here, filming, but when I'm off the field and out of this building, that's my time.

"That's not the point, Bo. I just want to make sure you're working toward the finish line here." He evades the question.

"The girl is my tutor, but also my friend. I've talked about her before. She's Casey's girlfriend, Noelle's roommate. But, yes, I do also like her. Not that it's really any of your business or anyone else's." I push start on my car, and the engine rumbles.

"I vaguely remember you mentioning something about her. What's her name again?"

"Why, so you can look her up?" I shake my head even though I know he can't see me.

"Name?" he asks again.

I know he can find out if I don't tell him anyway.

"Chelsea Sullivan." I can picture it clear as day. My dad is probably writing down her name and passing it over to his assistant to look her up.

"That name sounds familiar to me, but I can't place it." He harrumphs, and I can hear him tapping his pen on his desk.

"I doubt you would know her. She's from the East Coast." I'm trying not to sound defensive because I have no reason to be. But I don't need him digging around my life and scaring her off either. She seems like a pretty private person, and being around me will be challenging on its own.

"And? Your mother is also from the southern East Coast."

"Dad, let it go. Let me see how it goes, and if it looks like it's going somewhere, I'll want you guys to meet her anyway. You'd actually really like her. She's prelaw and very focused on getting into law school."

"Even more reason for you not to start something with this girl." He takes in a deep breath, then blows it out. "If she's going to law school, she doesn't need distractions either."

"Dad, we're not getting married today. Chill. We're hanging out."

"Bo, I'm not asking. I'm telling you. Whatever it is you think you have going with this girl, end it. Now. Do not disappoint me." He disconnects without saying goodbye.

I look down at my phone to see he really did hang up on me after issuing an order, like I'm a child. But as bothered as I am by my dad right now, I'm also really angry that someone is snapping pictures of me on campus. Sure, it's happened before, and I don't pay much attention to it. But it's not just me.

I pull out of the parking lot behind the stadium and call Chelsea. I want to hear her voice right now more than anything.

"Hi," she answers, and just the sound of her voice is like a warm blanket.

The question is, do I tell Chelsea about my conversation with my dad, or do I take care of it on my own? I don't want to lose what we have going because of it. She'd probably freak. She might have been raised by her aunt, but I bet her parents were average, normal people who didn't let future aspirations control their every move. I love my family, but I understand they could come off as upper crust for other people.

I've finally had my chance with her and made my move, and I don't want to jeopardize something before we know exactly where it's going.

"Hey, I just finished with practice. Do you want me to come over now?" *Please say yes.* "Or do you need some time?"

"Oh, no, you can come over. I'm done with the prep. I was just waiting for you before I put it in the oven because it doesn't take long."

"And you're sure I can't bring anything?" I'm nearing the grocery store, so I want to stop now if she needs something.

"Nope, I have everything I need."

"Okay then. I'll see you in about five minutes." I turn down the road that leads to her apartment.

"See you soon." Her voice pitches slightly, and it's fucking cute.

"Bye, Chelsea." I end the call.

I'm not gonna let this call with my dad ruin my night. He means well since he's seen reputations of good men go down because of bad choices and families torn apart because of sour relationships. He's worked too hard to get to where he is. Judge Callaway has an immaculate reputation, and it will stay that way.

Ending things with Chelsea because of his doubts when we're just getting started, ain't gonna happen. Fuck that.

Plus, once Dad gets to know her, he'll realize how amazing she is. Smart as hell, a future lawyer. A hard worker, has a loving family, and an awesome personality that keeps me on my toes.

Yeah, I've got it bad, and I'm not ashamed of it.

Within minutes, I'm pulling into a parking spot in front of her building. I don't need to bring my duffel bag inside, but I do want to take my backpack since I have an iPad in it. I get out of my car and reach into the back for my backpack. When I turn, I see Chelsea standing outside the door of her apartment. I wave to her, and she waves back and smiles at me.

I don't expect anything from her tonight, but I definitely want to mess around some more. Preferably with less clothes and not coming in my pants again. And glancing at what she's wearing, I'd say we're already making progress. She's got on a tank top that's hugging her chest so tight that I can see her already-peaked nipples through it. And the shorts … they're pretty fucking short. I notice a tattoo on her left bicep that I've never seen before that I definitely want to look at closer.

As I approach, her smile grows wider. "Hi," she says, leaning up to kiss me.

"Hi. I like this kind of hello."

I lean in and kiss her again. Her lips are soft, warm, a little hesitant at first—until I press closer and feel her melt against me. My hand slides to the back of her neck, fingers threading through her hair, guiding her deeper into the kiss. She exhales, and that tiny sound wrecks me.

She presses her hand on my chest. "Agreed, but let's not get carried away for the whole complex to see." She turns on her heel and walks into her apartment. "Do you mind that the windows are open? I feel like I need a few more days of fresh air in here."

I follow her in. "That's fine with me. You know you can still come stay at our house."

"Thanks. It's been days since the all clear, so it's fine, but I'm anxious to do a deep clean, and I have to wait another twenty-four hours." We walk into the kitchen. "So, I made lemon herb chicken breasts with couscous and snap peas. It should be ready soon." She leans up against the counter.

"It smells amazing in here. Thank you for inviting me over for dinner." I move in closer and reach for her hand. It's like I can't stop myself from wanting to touch her. And, fuck, after one kiss, I'm addicted to her.

"Noelle is always with Casey, so it just leaves me alone, and it's no fun, cooking for one. Every decent recipe is for servings of four, so I'm left with an insane amount of leftovers."

"You can always send them my way. I eat like a horse."

"Aside from your famous wings, do you make anything else?"

"No. I just know how to make those."

She places a hand on her hip. "Let me guess ... your mom and sisters do all the cooking while the prince gets waited on."

I cringe a little before I correct her. "We had a chef."

Her jaw drops as she gapes at my response. "You really are a golden boy."

"I wouldn't mind learning to cook. I think I'd like to serve you."

Her hand rises to her chest, and she crosses her arms. "Bo Callaway, you're being devilishly charming, again."

"Told you it was one of my best features. I can be an angel too."

I raise my brows and hold my hand out to her. She walks toward me, and I pull her into me. Her soft skin is like silk under my calloused hands. She looks down at me with her bright eyes and holds my stare.

"I can't figure out which part of you I adore more. The angel that rests on this shoulder," she breathes as she runs a finger down the side of my neck and traces the path over my shoulder.

It's a simple action yet so damn erotic. It's like I've never been touched by a girl before.

"Or the devil that says naughty things," she adds and then makes the same soft tracing motion on the other side.

"You're not so innocent yourself," I tease. "No girl who can touch a man and make him want to drop to his knees is that angelic."

She grabs the waistband of my sweatpants, which I'm sure are doing nothing to hide my growing dick, and her fingers curl over the elastic band. My cock twitches at the feel of her fingers on my skin. When she pulls on the band, my dick does a full salute, peeking out completely now, and she glances down.

"You bring out the best in me, I guess." She smiles, and I damn near lose it.

"Chelsea …" I say in a deep, gravelly voice. "I'm about five seconds from losing control here." I take my free hand and wrap it around the back of her neck.

"Chelsea …" I say in a deep, gravelly voice. "I'm about five seconds from losing control here." I take my free hand and wrap it around the back of her neck.

"Mr. Quarterback, about to lose control, huh? I think I like the idea of that." She releases the hand that's holding mine and slides it around my waist to my ass. "Kiss me, Bo."

I take her face in both hands now and tilt her chin up with my thumbs. I don't wait even a second before I lean down and kiss her. But I want to take my time with this kiss because she's not the kind of girl you waste a second with. My tongue glides along hers, and she tastes sweet, like a lemon drop.

Her hand slips inside my sweats, and she takes ahold of my dick, slowly stroking up and down. She breaks the kiss with a whisper. "You know you're huge, right? I can barely fit my hand around you." Her hand curls around the head, smearing the pre-cum, then moves back down the shaft to the base.

I feel like I'm about to either pass out or blow; I'm so turned on right now. And the compliment about my dick size ... yeah ... that made me even harder.

"Chelsea, if you keep stroking me like this, I'm going to come before we get to the good part."

"This isn't the good part, huh?" She smirks before leaning in to kiss me. Her hand that was in my hair now holds my head in place while she devours my mouth and pumps my cock with her other hand. She sucks on my tongue, making me groan.

I drop my hands to her waist and lift her up and set her on the counter, her legs opening so I fit between them. I glide my hands up her smooth legs, my fingers slipping just under the hem. My thumbs stroke the insides of her thighs, and goose bumps pop up, so I know my touch is affecting her.

"Are you wet for me?" I trail my gaze from her face down to her pussy.

Her hand pulls out of my sweats. She lays her arms, relaxed, on my shoulders, and one of her hands runs up my neck and into my hair again. She pulls me toward her, opening her legs wider, heat clear in her green eyes as she nods. "Are you just gonna stand there, staring at me, or are you gonna do something about it?"

"You're making it really hard for me to be good right now and take this slow."

She leans in and nips my neck just below my ear. "I don't want you to be good. I want you to fuck me."

"Oh, I'm gonna fuck you. But I want to take my time with this pussy. I want to taste you, tease you, make you beg for it." I move my hands to the waistband of her shorts. "May I?"

She nods, cheeks pink, smirk in place. Her hands move to her sides. Using her arms to support her, she pushes her hips up slightly.

Grabbing both sides of her shorts, I pull them and the scrap of lace under it off her legs. I slide my hands up her silky legs, sucking in a deep breath, gripping the top of her thighs, my thumbs resting near her bare pussy.

"Chelsea, you are perfect." Honest to God, I've never seen a woman more beautiful than she is.

"So are you." She leans forward and reaches for the hem of my shirt, pulling it up and off of me. Her hands skim down my chest and over my abs, making them contract. She traces both sides of my Adonis belt to the band of my pants. "Why is this so fucking hot?" She bites her bottom lip, watching her hands roam. She slides them into the sides of my sweats and around to grab hold of my ass.

I lean in to kiss her again, and this time, it's hot, wet, and urgent. I break away to catch my breath and pull down the strap of her tank top and move it down her shoulder to trail kisses along her neck and collarbone.

She pulls her hands out of my pants and raises her arms. "Take it off," she demands.

"Fuck yes."

She doesn't have to ask me twice. Taking the thin fabric in my hands, I pull it off slowly, watching her tits bounce a little as I lift it over them, then over her head before tossing it behind me. Her nipples are a dusty-rose color and perfectly peaked. I drop down to one of her breasts, sucking the nipple into my mouth.

Her fingers run through my hair and pull on it when I take her nipple between my teeth, adding just enough pressure to make her moan.

"That feels so good."

I take her other breast in my hand, squeezing it as I twirl my tongue around the other to ease the sting from my bite, then pull back to look her in the eye. "I want to make you feel everything." With my free hand, I tuck one of her curls behind her ear.

"Come here." Her hand that's wrapped around my neck guides me to her mouth. She traces my lips with her tongue, then slides it into my mouth, matching me stroke for stroke. Her other hand takes mine off her breast and moves it down to her center. "I want you here." She covers my hand with hers and pushes our middle fingers into her pussy.

"Oh shit." My cock jumps as we slide our fingers into her.

"Yes," she moans. "More." She pulls her hand away and reaches for my erection, nestled between us.

I pump my finger in and out, then add another to stretch her out. She's hot and tight, and there's no way I'll fit if I don't relax her a little more. "Feels like silk, baby. Open your legs wider for me."

She pulls her legs up and props her heels on the edge of the counter, completely spread wide. "Like this?" She smirks.

"Just like that." I lean forward and take her bottom lip and suck it between mine, then release it with a pop. "You look so pretty, spread out like this for me. Your pussy is dripping. All. For. Me."

I tilt my head and kiss her again, plunging my tongue deep inside her mouth. My hips start rocking in rhythm with my fingers pumping in and out of her.

She pulls back, breathing heavy. "For you. And before I come, I want you to get on your knees and taste me."

Goddamn.

When I start to feel her inner muscles contract, I pull my hand away and drop to my knees. With my thumbs, I spread her lips and swipe my tongue through her heat.

"Fuck yes. I want you to come on my tongue."

"Yes, please. Just like that." One of her hands is bracing her body, and the other hand moves to the top of my head. She grabs a handful of my hair, holding it. "Add your fingers and suck on my clit."

Jesus, this woman is gonna kill me. I fist my cock in one hand to ease some of the pressure while I slide two fingers into her with my other hand. I twirl my tongue around her clit, then wrap my lips around the nub and suck, making her hips lift from the counter. There's no doubt this countertop will need a thorough cleaning when I'm done with her. She's making a mess of it, and I love it.

"Bo," she gasps, and when I look up at her, she tilts her head back. "Fuck. I'm gonna come. Add another finger and swirl your tongue like you did before. I'm so close."

My pre-cum is leaking down my shaft, and I'm close to coming too. I have about a minute to decide if I'm coming in my hand or in her pussy. "Do you want to come like this or with my dick inside of you?" I still my hand inside of her.

She looks back at me, her chest rising up and down, and rolls her hips, fucking my hand. "I want your cock, but I'm not gonna last long." Her inner walls squeeze me. "I'm on the pill, and I was tested over the summer." Her fingers trace my face to my wet mouth. "I want you bare. Are you clean?"

"Yes, I'm clean," I choke out.

I've never had sex without a condom. But I might die if I don't get inside of her, so I'll question my recklessness later when the man downstairs isn't in control.

"Then get up here and fuck me, Bo." She sits up as I remove my hand.

Bringing my fingers up, I put them into my mouth and suck, and then I pull them out slowly. "Fuck, you taste good."

I wipe my thumb across her bottom lip, and her tongue peeks out, licking it.

I push my sweats down my legs and kick them to the side. Chelsea is looking at me like she wants to swallow me whole. And I fucking love it.

"Before we do this, I just want you to know that this isn't a onetime thing for me. I want you. Not just tonight. I want to know everything about you, see inside your mind, and I want to own your body. Will you let me?"

She blinks slowly and swallows. "I'll give you everything I can. I don't want anyone else but you, Bo," she says with a whisper. "Only you."

"I'll take it. In the meantime, I am yours. All of me." I grip the base of my cock and rub the head through her wetness and circle her clit. I look up at her and see her eyes locked on my dick. "You like that, baby?"

She nods. "I need you inside me."

"Yes, ma'am." I smirk at her, and she smiles back at me. Then I grab her legs under her knees and pull her closer to the edge of the counter. I push inside her heat slowly with short thrusts, letting her adjust to my size, both of us groaning loudly. "Oh fuck, you're so tight. I thought three fingers would be enough to get you ready for me."

"It stings but in a good way. Keep going. Deeper." She wraps her arms around my shoulders. "I need to feel you deeper."

I push in all the way into the hilt and stop. If I move, I'll definitely come, and I need her to come first. "Chels, you feel so good. Please tell me you're close. I can't be a one-pump loser."

She giggles, and it squeezes my cock, making my eyes roll back.

"I'm close, I promise. Now, fuck me." She tilts her hips, rocking against me.

So, I do. I pull out, not all the way, then slam back into her. Then I lean in and take her lips in a wet kiss. We kiss until we need to catch our breath, but my mouth hovers over hers, our tongues still seeking one another's. It's most definitely the hottest moment of my life. I can feel sweat forming on my brow, but there's no way in hell I'm stopping to wipe it off.

She pulls back and rests her forehead against mine. "I'm almost there. Harder." She's watching my dick move in and out of her. "Fuck, that's so hot. You have the most perfect dick."

"Fuck. Come, baby." I pump faster, deeper. "I'm gonna come."

She reaches between us, and I think she's going to play with her clit with her fingers, but she spreads them on either side of my dick and pushes the heel of her hand onto her clit instead. It's sensation overload for me, as I feel her inner walls contract around my dick, feel her fingers as I push in and out, and feel her rubbing against her clit. My balls tighten just as she starts to come.

"Bo! Oh my God, fuck yes." Her head tilts back, and I suck

her neck as I start to come. Her skin is damp and salty. And tastes divine.

She wraps her arms around my shoulders and pulls me in closer, hugging me. I can feel her heart beating against mine. I rest my head against hers, and a calmness I've never felt rushes over me.

Yes, I've been attracted to her, and I've wanted to get to know her, but this connection I feel with her makes me know without a doubt, as I stand here with her in my arms, that this is where I want to be forever. And there's no way in hell I'm letting her go. For anyone.

CHAPTER
THIRTEEN

CHELSEA

I CAN HONESTLY SAY that I have never in my life had sex like this. It's definitely not the ideal location in terms of comfort, but, holy shit, it was hot. My heart rate is finally slowing down, and I lift my head from Bo's shoulder. He pulls out and releases my legs, then moves his hands to my face, kissing me reverently.

The kiss starts to deepen again, but the timer on the oven buzzes, startling us.

He rests his forehead against mine. "We'd better get that before we burn the complex down, huh?" he says with a deep chuckle.

"Yeah, that would be bad, considering what we had to deal with last week. Can you pull that out of the oven while I go … clean up?" I run my hands over his shoulders and down his arms.

"I can do that." He lifts me by the waist and sets me on my feet.

My shorts, thong, and tank top are somewhere around here, but I don't bother looking for them because I can feel Bo's cum slipping out, which is equal parts hot and, well, sticky. I close the door to the bathroom, take care of business because no one likes a UTI, and wash my hands. When I look at myself in the mirror, I can't help but smile. My hair is coming out of my lose ponytail, my cheeks and chest are flush, and there's a faint bite mark on my neck.

I can hear him in the kitchen, so I dry my hands, then redo my ponytail quickly. When I open the door, the smell of our dinner permeates through the room. I'm not trying to brag or anything, but I'm a decent cook. I tried to pick something healthy this time since I know Bo has to watch what he eats.

The pan with our dinner on it is sitting on top of the oven, foil still covering it. Bo has his sweats back on, but no shirt, standing at the counter, where we just had sex, and he's cleaning it. I mean … how cute is he?

He looks up and sees me walking toward him, still naked. "Goddamn you are gorgeous."

He put my clothes on one of the stools at the bar, so I dress quickly. As I walk by him, I stop and lean up to kiss him. "You're gorgeous too." I nod to the counter. "Thanks for doing that."

"Of course." He tosses the paper towel in the garbage and washes his hands. The towel is hanging on the oven door that I'm standing in front of, so I scoot to the side so he can reach it. "It smells awesome." His stomach grumbles.

"Hungry?" I say with a giggle.

"Yeah, between practice and"—he wraps his arms around my waist from behind and rests his chin on my shoulder—"you, I'm starving."

I like being in his arms. He makes me feel safe, calm, and not at all anxious.

"I'm a little hungry myself." I reach into the cabinet in front of me and pull two plates from it.

"Can I do anything to help?" He kisses my shoulder and backs up so I can move to get the spatula from the cylinder.

"I think we're good. Just tell me how much you want, and then we can sit at the table to eat." I nod toward the table.

"You can load up my plate. I can eat all of this. Do you want something to drink?" He moves to the fridge and pulls it open. Like he's comfortable being here. And I like it.

"Sure, a bottle of water is good." I place two chicken breasts on his plate, then scoop some of the couscous and veggies onto the plate. I walk over to the table and set his plate down on a place mat in front of him. Then I plate my food and stop to grab us forks and knives before I sit down.

"Thank you, Chelsea. This looks amazing." He reaches for my hand, and I take it.

"You're welcome. I'm glad you're here. Now let's eat before you faint from starvation." I wink at him.

"I think I'll be fine, but I want to eat so I can get back to kissing on you." He releases my hand, picks up his fork and knife, then stabs into his chicken and cuts it up into neat squares, but looks up at me and smiles.

That smile of his does things to me. I feel a flutter in my belly when I think about what we just did, and I can't wait to do it again. "Yes, let's do more of that."

I cut into my own chicken and take a bite. He's watching me eat while he eats.

"So, Chelsea, tell. me about that tattoo I saw on your arm." He points his fork in my direction.

I turn my arm to the side to give him a better look. "This is Lady Justice." It's not huge, but it's big enough to cover my shoulder and halfway down my arm. "As soon as I turned eighteen, I went and got this tattoo. My aunt nearly killed me herself when she saw it. Not really because of it, but more so because of how big it was."

"Aha. That makes sense with you wanting to be a lawyer." He nods.

That's only a slice of why I got it, but I'm not ready to dive into my whole story. However, I can't help but hear my aunt's words in my head, telling me to be open to having someone to share things with. And I think Bo could be that person. Still, I don't think I can tell him everything right now.

"Yep. Plus, the sword looked badass, so it was a win all around." I smile at him.

We make small talk as we finish eating. He tells me more about the upcoming season and games he's looking forward to. I tell him a little about the classes I'm taking. We clean up the kitchen together, and then he leads me over to the couch.

I sit down, and he sits down close to me, stretching his arm along the back of the couch.

"Want to watch a movie or something?" I ask him as I pick up the remote. "Or are you gonna head home soon?"

He shifts and angles his body to look at me. "I would love to stay if you'll let me. I'm definitely not ready to go home yet." His fingers play with a few loose strands of my hair.

I set my hand closest to him on his thigh. "I would like that. So, should we watch something?"

"Would you be annoyed if I said I wanted to catch *Sports-Center*? I just like to see what they're saying." He lifts a shoulder.

"Yeah, totally fine with me." I hand him the remote. "Here, you can find it."

"Thanks. I still want to talk to you though. I want to know more about you and things you like." He finds the channel he wants, then sets the remote down on the coffee table in front of us.

"Okay, but you have to answer my questions too then." I hold out my hand. "Deal?"

Bo takes my hand in his. "Deal." He raises them and places a kiss on the back of my hand. "Let's start with the basics. What's your favorite color?"

"Umm ... probably orange." I tilt my head. "Yeah, orange."

"Orange? Really? I would not have guessed that. Why orange?" His thumb traces circles over the top of my hand.

I shrug. "I think because it reminds me of a sunset at home. I love when the yellows, pinks, blues, and the oranges of the sun all blend together when the sun goes down. It just feels magical, you know? Like you've made it through the day and it's time to just chill and get ready for a new one."

"I like that. We have some pretty great sunsets in California too. The Oklahoma sky isn't so bad either. But it's not the daylight or dusk I love. It's the dead of night. Did you ever notice how big the sky seems here?"

"Yeah, it's crazy, right? I thought it was just me. That was one of the first things I noticed when I moved here for school. I would sit outside my dorm room and just look up at the sky at night. It seems like the stars are never-ending. And so bright." I smile, thinking about how free I felt the first time I lay on the grass outside my dorm. The peace it brought me.

"I sit outside sometimes at night, looking at the stars. It almost feels like we're in a planetarium or something," he says, laughing.

I nod exaggeratedly. "It really does. That's a perfect comparison."

There's a flutter in my stomach—a deep, swoopy feeling that's somehow grounding and dizzying at the same time. It's ridiculous really. One minute, he's making me laugh, and the next, he says something about stars, and I swear my heart just ... flips. Like my body knows I'm falling before my brain's even caught up.

"Okay, so Chelsea from Florida has a tattoo and likes the color orange and the Oklahoma sky. What's your favorite candy?" He reaches over and pulls my legs over the top of his.

"I'm a chocolate girl. I can eat candy, but I prefer chocolate if I'm going to have sweets."

"What's your favorite chocolate then?" He rubs his hands up and down my legs.

"Probably Snickers or Twix. Snickers was my mom's favorite too." The words come out before I even process them. I never talk about my mom.

Aunt Laura's words play through my mind again about

being open to sharing with other people. It's just that no one really knows my story here and why I was raised by my aunt, and I like that. The anonymity from my old life.

"Was? Did she pass?" I can feel him searching my face. "You don't have to tell me if you don't want to. I just want to get to know you better, but I don't want you to feel uncomfortable either."

I pull a deep breath in and decide to give him some partial truths. "Yes, she died when I was twelve."

"I'm sorry, Chelsea. Did your dad pass away too?" The hand that's on the back of the couch moves to my shoulder, stroking it in a comforting way.

As much as I want to be able to talk about this with him, I just … can't. "He's just not in the picture." Which is true. "My aunt raised my sister and me, but you already know that."

He's looking at me like he can tell there is more to the story, but after a minute, he just smiles. "Right, yeah."

Time to switch directions before I say more than I want to. "So, Bo Callaway, what is your favorite color and candy?"

"Easy. Blue, although it's quickly changing to green. And Twizzlers are my favorite candy. I can eat an entire bag in one sitting, and I have no shame in that."

He places his hand on his chest. I put my hand over his and laugh.

"I'm not shaming you. I don't mind Twizzlers. But why is your favorite color changing?"

He moves his hand from his chest and slides it into my hair. "Because every time I see you and look into your eyes, I get lost in them."

"You get lost, huh?" I start to laugh. "That's a little extra."

"Yeah, I guess that sounds cheesy, but it's true. They're almost like a soft teal green or something. I've never seen anything like it. They're stunning."

I can feel my cheeks heat. "Thank you. I do like my eyes." I grab my ponytail. "But this, on the other hand, I could do without."

"Why don't you like your hair?" He pulls my hand away from the ponytail, laughing.

I shrug. "It's just thick and hard to manage sometimes. Although it's better here in Oklahoma than in Florida."

He looks like he's trying to hold in a laugh.

"Are you laughing at me?" I poke him in the side.

"No! I would never. I was just trying not to be a child and say, *That's what she* said."

"What?" Then it dawns on me. "Oh … thick and hard?" I laugh.

"Bingo! Sorry. I couldn't help it. I think I've been around my friends for too long."

I scoot into him closer so our bodies are touching. "You do have a good group of friends. Like, seriously, they're all good guys. I won't lie and say when I met y'all, I didn't think you were just a bunch of jocks. But I really like all of you."

"Ouch. But also, valid. That's why I love my friends. They're not full of themselves, and they're just honest and kind people, genuinely. You know?" He tilts his head to the side.

"For sure. They're good guys." I turn to look at the TV and see Bo on the screen. "Look! You're on TV!"

He nods, already watching. "Yeah, they're probably just talking about the game this weekend."

"It's an away game, right?"

He glances over at me. "Yep, we're going to Texas A&M. You gonna watch?"

"I'm sure I will. If Noelle and Charlie aren't going down there, I'll probably watch the game with them. What position do you play again?" I put my index finger on my chin.

He smirks. "I'll be the one throwing the ball."

"Ahh … the wide receiver?" I fake.

"Ha-ha, funny girl." He starts to tickle me.

"No! I'm so ticklish." I try to move his hands away, but he's too strong. "Uncle! Okay, okay." He stops, and I take his hands in mine. "Don't worry; I not only know what position you play, but I have your number too."

"You do, do you?" He lifts his eyebrows.

I nod dramatically, then hold an imaginary microphone in my hand. "Number six. Starting quarterback for the Walker University Stallions, Bo Callaway!" I drop my hands from my mouth. "Wait, or do they call you Columbus?" I know they don't, but I will never *not* bring this up.

"Very funny. You want to be tickled again?" He lifts me up and sets me on his lap, then places a kiss on my neck.

"Nah, I'm good." I wrap my arms around his shoulders. "Did you see everything you needed to see on the TV?"

He trails more kisses up my neck, nips my earlobe, then moves toward my lips. "I did." One of his hands is holding me around my waist, and the other starts making its way into my tank top. When he reaches my breast, he pinches my nipple between his thumb and index finger, making me gasp.

"Good. You should probably get to bed. You have a very busy day tomorrow. School, practice …" I drop my head to the side to give him more access to my neck.

"Don't forget; I have my test tomorrow too." He reminds me between kisses.

I turn my face toward his. "That's right; you do. So, we should definitely get you to bed." I kiss him on the lips slowly.

In one swift motion, he stands with me in his arms. "I agree. We should go to bed." He walks into the hallway. "Which one is yours?"

I point to my room. "That one." I can't help the smile spreading on my face.

When we reach my room, he strides toward the bed and lays me gently on top. "But first, I need to study a little more. My tutor likes to be thorough." He pulls my shorts off my body first, then strips off my tank top.

"You probably should. One more recap."

I scoot back further onto the bed and watch as he sets his phone on my nightstand and removes his sweatpants. He's hard again, and it's stirring heat low in my belly.

"Practice makes perfect and all that, right?" He climbs onto the bed, then trails kisses up my thigh as his hands hold my hips in place. "In fact, I think I'll start right here." He places a kiss right on top of my pussy.

When his tongue slides through my center, I let out a moan. "That seems like a good idea."

He hums in agreement and then continues to study. Every. Inch. Of. My. Body.

CHAPTER
FOURTEEN

BO

SEPTEMBER IS FLYING BY. We're on a hot streak of winning games, and I'm having the best season of my career. My psychology class? I'm acing it. It's because of my hot, amazing tutor.

After the night we slept together for the first time, I got a B on my test, which brought my grade up to secure my eligibility. I'm not sure I really need tutoring anymore, but Coach said I can continue for the whole semester, so I'm gonna take it. As much time I can spend with Chelsea, the better.

I attribute all the good things happening to her. She's my lucky charm. I even started calling her Lucky. At first, I don't think she liked it much, but now, she does. She just won't admit it.

We spend most nights together at her place or mine. Our friends didn't even blink when they saw us cuddling together on the couch one night. It was as if it had always been like this. And in a way, it does feel like Chelsea's been in my life longer than she has been. I'm loving every minute of being with her. And she seems to be happy too.

This weekend, we have a bye week, so as a group, Chelsea, Casey, Noelle, Charlie, Brooke, Silas, and I came to the Oklahoma State Fair. It was the girls' idea. They wanted to come see the rodeo.

I've never been to a rodeo. And I have to say, I'm already impressed. The arena is packed. Rows of seating circles the center of the arena, where I assume all the action takes place. There are banners and flags hanging from the ceiling, and there are chutes at one end, where I guess they hold the animals before they come out. It smells like a barn in here, which is to be expected, but not all that pleasant, if I'm being honest. There are cows walking around the ring, their handlers holding on to them by ropes. It looks like they're walking a giant dog.

"Here's our section," Charlie calls out and starts up the stairs, Brooke following behind her.

A little boy wearing a Walker T-shirt steps up to me before I can start up the stairs and asks me, Casey, and Silas for an autograph. He hands me the rodeo program and a pen. I sign it, then pass it to Casey to sign, and he hands it to Silas. His little eyes light up when Silas hands his paper back to him. It's fun to see fans like this in public, but I want to just be with my friends tonight and not worry about eyes on me.

As we climb up the stairs of the stands to find our seats, Chelsea is walking in front of me. It's taking all of my self-control not to throw her over my shoulder and find a dark corner somewhere. She looks so fucking hot right now in her skintight jeans, cowboy boots, pearl button-down shirt, and a cowboy hat that she borrowed from Charlie. Her hair spills down the back in gorgeous black waves.

I come up right behind her while we wait for Casey and Noelle to make their way down the packed row. I flip my baseball hat backward and lean into her, moving her hair off her neck, and drop a kiss just below her ear. "You're killing me in those jeans, Lucky. I can't wait to peel them off later."

She shivers and looks over her shoulder and winks at me.

"That sounds like fun, Callaway. But first, let's watch these cowboys try to tame these beasts! I'm so excited."

If I were a less confident man, I might be jealous. But I know she'll be coming home with me and in my bed tonight, so I just laugh. "Maybe I should try it sometime."

"Bo, no, absolutely not." She sits in her seat next to Noelle.

I sit down next to her and take her hand in mine. "Why? You don't think I can do it?"

"Oh, I'm sure you excel at everything you do." She kisses my cheek. "But your coach wouldn't be happy. And not to mention, you're way too tall to be a cowboy." She shakes her head.

"What do you mean, too tall? Is that a thing? Is there, like, a height restriction on cowboys?" I chuckle. "I don't think that's a thing, baby."

"Well, I don't really know, but I feel like you have all"—she waves her hand up and down my body—"this. Long limbs, muscles for days. I'm sure it wouldn't be easy."

I turn toward her and cup her face in my hand. "I think I know why you really wouldn't want me to do it."

Her eyes twinkle as she looks into my eyes. "Oh, yeah? Why's that?"

I lean in close to her face. "Because you would be too worried about me." I tuck a loose piece of her hair behind her ear. "Because you like me too much, and to even think about me getting hurt bothers you. It's okay, you can admit it." I place a soft kiss on her lips.

"Bo, I have to watch you get out on that football field every week. That's just as big of a risk as riding in the rodeo." She places her hand on top of mine and kisses me this time.

Noelle leans over. "She's right, you know. We have to watch you guys get out there every weekend, risking your safety. As much as it's a blast to watch you guys play, it's never easy, seeing any of you get taken to the ground." She winces.

Casey takes her hand and chimes in, "Aww, pretty girl. You

know I'm too fast to let anyone get to me." He kisses her on the cheek.

"Oh, really, Ironman? How's that bruise on your ribs healing?" She leans back and lifts her eyebrow at him.

"That was a shady hit. I'm fine. Besides, you kissed it and made it better." He grabs her by the neck and pulls her in for a kiss.

"Eww, that's gross, Case. I don't need to have that thought in my head." Charlie leans over and joins the conversation. "I guess this is my payback?"

"Actually, no. But it's not fun, is it?" Casey turns and wraps his arm around his sister's neck, tipping her cowboy hat forward.

She pushes it off, but laughs. "Whatever." She straightens her hat, then turns to talk to Brooke.

Chelsea squeezes my hand to get my attention. "To answer your question, yes, I do like you too much. I don't like seeing you get hurt." She swallows hard after she says it, like it was difficult for her to admit.

One thing I've noticed about her in the time we've spent together is that she doesn't like feeling vulnerable. She's cautious and likes to be in control, none of which I mind. I'm completely gone for this girl, and I will gladly drop to my knees anytime she demands. And I do.

The announcer comes on through the speaker system, announcing the next event before I can answer her, so I just kiss her again instead. While they announce the riders competing, Silas elbows me.

"Dude, I think I could do this. We had horses back home. I bet it's not that much different." He nods and has a smirk on his face. "I mean, I go up against three-hundred-pound linemen. I could handle a cow."

Chelsea leans around me, laughing. "Silas, those aren't cows. Those are angry bulls, not at all happy about having someone on their backs. I think it's a whole lot different."

"Eh, I think I could handle it." He waves it off.

Silas has become a good friend, and he's an interesting guy for sure. He's funny, but there is a serious side to him that we see at home more than in the locker room. He plays it off like he's a goofy guy with the girls around, but what they don't know is that Silas is actually insanely smart. He's an all-American scholar athlete.

"I think we could both do it, but my girl is right. Coach would have our asses." I hold out my fist for him to bump.

The rodeo starts, and the first rider lasts about three seconds before getting tossed. He bounces back up quickly, and the pickup men wrangle the bull back into the chute. It all happens so fast, and then the next guy flies out.

Charlie and Brooke are standing at this point, clapping and cheering for each rider. There is definitely an intensity to the sport that's unlike any other. Chelsea has her arm linked with mine, and her hand is resting on my thigh. She's watching each rider with awe, flinching when they get tossed.

"Scoot over, man. I'm going to hang with Charlie and Brooke." Silas stands to move by, and I'm too tall to shift my legs, so I stand too, letting him by.

Chelsea also stands and leans into me as he passes. "Do you notice how he's been staying around more when Brooke comes by the house or hangs out with us?"

I haven't really noticed, to be honest. I've been so wrapped up in her, football, school, and the filming of the docuseries. "Interesting. No, I haven't really, but they actually seem like a fit."

"I was thinking the same thing!" She leans up and kisses my cheek. "We should go eat after this. I had my eye on a funnel cake when we walked by the stand. It smelled so good. I might try a fried Twinkie too." She wiggles her eyebrows.

"Lucky, I'm sorry, but that just screams diabetes." I laugh when she mock pouts. "How about this: I'll buy you whatever sweets you want after we eat some real food?"

"Deal. But I'm not leaving without at least a funnel cake. It's calling to me." She winks, then turns her attention back to the arena.

Noelle has a pamphlet in one hand and grabs Chelsea's hand with her other. "Oh! They have a mechanical bull in one of the tents. We should do that!"

"Yes! That would be fun! But you go first." Chelsea laughs. "Just so I can scope it out before I do."

Noelle holds out her hand. "Deal. But you'll do it with me, right?"

Chelsea takes her hand. "Yes, I'll try it with you. Although I've never even ridden a horse. So, I'm sure I'll fall off before it even starts." She laughs.

"No, you'll probably nail it, and I'll look like the idiot. I don't care though. It looks fun." Noelle shrugs.

"I'll do it too," Brooke chimes in. "I've always wanted to try that. My friends and I went to a country bar a few weekends ago, and there was one there, but the line was too long, so we didn't bother."

Now that Chelsea mentioned Silas's attention on Brooke, I look at his face while she talks. He's got a little smirk going on while he listens to her. Maybe there is some interest there. I'll have to ask him later.

"Hey, the last rider is coming up. Let's watch, and then we can go look at this bull-riding thing." Casey says.

"I want to eat too!" Chelsea tells him. "I'm surprised you guys aren't hungry. You guys are constantly hungry."

"I ate a sandwich before we left, but I'm ready to eat again." He nods, then points at me. "Bo had two breakfasts today. One at the field after our workout and one when we got home before we left."

"It wasn't two breakfasts. That quesadilla I had before we left was just a snack." I pat my stomach. "I'm ready to eat again though. I went hard at the gym today."

"We can go in about"—Casey looks at his watch—"five

minutes or less, depending on how quickly this guy gets thrown off. Unless the girls want to stay for the barrel races. But those don't start for, like, forty-five minutes."

"I don't think I can wait that long to eat," Chelsea says.

"Me neither." Charlie joins in. "I'm getting hungry too, but I did want to see the barrel races. Those girls are badass."

"Maybe we can find another rodeo and go watch the girls some other time." She claps her hands. "Oh! Maybe when the guys are at an away game." Chelsea nods excitedly.

"Yes! I love that plan. I'm so glad you're in our mix of friends now, Chelsea. We needed another brain in here for all the good ideas." Charlie leans over and holds her hand out to Chelsea for a high five.

"Aww, thanks, Charlie. I'm glad to be part of the group too." She high-fives her and then turns to look at me, smiling.

"Hey, I have good ideas!" Brooke says.

"You do, babe. But Chelsea's, like, really smart." Charlie puts an arm around Brooke.

"And I'm not?" Brooke laughs, but she doesn't seem offended.

"You totally are. I'm just saying, it's good to have another brain in the mix. Whatever. You know what I mean. Let's watch this last guy and go."

They both laugh.

I wrap my arm around Chelsea and pull her in closer. "I'm glad you became part of the group too. Who knows if we would have met otherwise, you know?" I kiss her on the temple.

"I was thinking about that the other day. We were having a discussion in one of my classes about circumstance. There's a fancy name for it—apophenia. It's when people see meaning or patterns in random things that aren't really connected."

"So, you're saying, me running into you wasn't the universe working its magic? It was just … random chance?"

"Maybe. Or maybe apophenia's just the brain's way of explaining what the heart already knows." She pauses and pulls in a deep breath. "Like maybe I met Noelle during our freshman year so that it would lead me to you." She looks down, almost shyly.

"I couldn't agree more."

I cup her face and turn it toward mine and kiss her softly. It's meant to be a quick kiss, but the tenderness of the moment makes me linger on her lips for a beat longer than appropriate in public. And I couldn't care less.

We made our way to the food tent after leaving the arena, which also happens to have the mechanical bull. The mix of smells from all kinds of food permeates the air with a smoky, but sweet scent like funnel cakes. Casey, Silas, and I all got some barbeque while the girls got a variety, opting for more traditional fair food from what they tell me. Charlie and Brooke decided to split nachos and a big pretzel, and they each got a corndog. Noelle went the safe route with a slice of pizza. And my girl got a turkey leg that's possibly larger than her entire arm. With a side of fries.

There are rows of bench style seating in the food tent, and we find a spot near a stage area where a country band was playing, but they're packing up now. Our table is so full that it looks like a buffet. I look around at some of the other tables and see they resemble ours in terms of the amount of food. I guess eating at the fair is a big deal. I don't think I've ever seen so many options in one place.

"I can't believe that guy broke his arm!" Silas speaks loudly over the noise of the room. "That bull tossed his ass up into the air. Looked like a clean break, but that dude is cooked."

Brooke sits next to him and shivers. "I have seen you guys take some bad hits and even break some bones, but with all the padding, I've luckily never seen any limbs dangling. That poor guy."

"That dude will probably be back on a bull within a week. Those guys are nuts. Literally no fear." Casey shakes his head and chuckles.

"I would imagine you can't get on a bull if you are scared. Animals sense that kind of thing." Noelle lifts her brows at Casey.

"That's totally true. They can. I used to"—Chelsea pauses like she's thinking about something—"volunteer at a farm that worked with kids who had experienced trauma in their lives. It was incredible to see how they would respond to the kids when they first came in."

"I didn't know you did that. That's awesome." Noelle smiles at her.

Chelsea clears her throat. "Yeah, it wasn't always easy, but it was rewarding."

I watch her face closely to see if she'll continue, and when she doesn't, I try to ease the conversation to a place where she's not the center of attention. "Okay, but do you think that bull felt bad when the guy got hurt?"

Silas tosses a tater tot at my head and laughs. "You're an idiot."

I laugh. "What? I wanna know." Obviously, I'm joking, but I wanted to divert from anyone asking Chelsea more about her experience. "I never had a pet, so I have no idea."

They all stop eating and look at me.

"You've never had a pet? Of any kind? Not even a goldfish that died the next day?" Charlie asks, looking dumbfounded.

"Not even a goldfish. Although when I was little, I had a stuffed dog that I carried around with me everywhere, and I think one of my aunts bought a leash for it, so I would take it for walks." I smile and shrug. "I loved Spike."

Charlie brings her hands to her chest and pouts her lips. "Spike? Oh, bless your heart, Bo Callaway. You walked your stuffie. Didn't it get, like, really dirty?"

"Yep, but my mom washed it every day for me." I look at Chelsea and smile. "My dad is allergic to animals of all kinds, apparently, so we couldn't have them."

She leans her head on my shoulder. "My poor guy."

Casey holds out a hand. "Okay, but who else is picturing a little Bo dragging a stuffed animal behind him on the sidewalk?"

Everyone raises their hand and laughs.

"Ha-ha. Laugh it up. He was a good friend. A loyal friend." I try to stay serious, but I can't, and I bark out a laugh.

"You should definitely get a dog or something someday." Chelsea squeezes my arm.

"We should," I say and watch her eyes widen in surprise.

"Oh! I'd better go get us tickets for the mechanical bull so we don't have to wait forever." Noelle stands and swings her legs over the bench seat.

"I'll go with you," Brooke says, standing to follow her.

Charlie takes a bite of her pretzel. "I'll leave you girls to do that, but, hey," she calls out as they walk away, "I don't want a ticket! I just want to watch you guys fall off." She laughs and nearly chokes on her pretzel.

"Noelle won't fall." Casey defends her.

Charlie drops her head and looks down her nose at him. "Case, I love Noelle, but she doesn't have an athletic bone in her body. She won't last a minute on there."

He lifts his shoulder. "I think she will."

"I have faith too, Casey," Chelsea says.

Charlie has a piece of pretzel in her hand and uses it to point at Chelsea. "You're doing it, right?"

Chelsea nods. "Yeah. Why not? I'll probably make a fool of myself, but I don't really care."

"I mean, it's not like you're dragging it around by a leash or anything," Silas teases me.

"Fuck off." I chuckle.

A few minutes later, the girls come back with three tickets.

"You guys didn't want to try, right?" Noelle asks, looking at us guys.

"Pretty girl, Coach would be pissed if one of us got hurt by messing around on that thing. Even for fun." He holds her hand as she climbs back over the bench.

"That's what I thought, so I only got these three since Charlie's a party pooper." Noelle sticks her tongue out at Charlie.

My girl sets her turkey leg down on her plate and wipes off her hands. "I probably shouldn't eat any more of this if I'm going to be going up soon. What number are they on?" She looks over toward the mat where the bull is.

"I think there are, like, five people in front of us." Brooke glances over at Noelle. "Right?"

"Yeah, I think so. Are you guys done? We should probably go over there." Noelle stands again, holding on to Casey's hand.

I grab my plate and look at Chelsea. "Are you done with your leg, or do you think you'll want more?"

She giggles. "I'm done with my leg. I'm saving room for that funnel cake. And I might switch out the Twinkie for a fried Oreo instead." She drops her mouth open and wiggles her brows.

"Living dangerously. I like it. But please don't puke on the way home. I'm a sympathetic puker, and I really don't want to do that in front of you." I scrunch my face in disgust.

When I stand, I hold out my hand for her so she can climb over the bench. Once she's standing behind it, I pick up my plate and hers as the others walk ahead of us.

She looks up at me while we walk. "So, you really never had any pets growing up?"

I drop our plates in the trash, then take her hand in mine. "I really didn't. My mom's sisters and her parents had dogs, so when we visited, we'd get our puppy fix, I guess. Never really bothered me much as I got older because I was so busy playing sports."

"Did you play anything other than football?"

I nod. "Yeah, I played baseball and a little basketball. By the time I got to high school, I was only playing baseball and football."

Casey calls my name to tell me where they are, and I lift my chin to acknowledge him as we make our way over to the group.

"I actually almost went to school to play baseball instead. And they tried to get me to play here, too, but football is what I really love and part of my long-term plan."

"That's fun. I can see you as a baseball player. You have the perfect baseball butt." She smacks my ass.

My mouth lifts up on one side, and I wink at her. "Thanks, Lucky. I'm a big fan of your butt too." I release her hand, then run my hand over her ass in these skintight jeans that are driving me wild. "Have I told you yet that I can't wait to get these off of you tonight?"

We reach our friends and stand around the mat that the mechanical bull sits on. It has a rope around it, like you see in a boxing ring. There's a girl our age on it right now, and she looks like she knows what she's doing. Her arm is up in the air, and her other hand is holding on to a horn on top of the machine. She rocks with it as it slowly speeds up. When she flicks her wrist, the bull starts to get faster. There's a group of girls on the other side, watching her and cheering her on.

Chelsea leans toward me and tugs my shirt. "I'm not sure I can do this. She's really good, and I think I'll embarrass myself." She does look a little nervous.

"You don't have to do it if you're scared." I wrap my arms

around her and turn her to face me. "Give your ticket to someone else in line or something. And if you're looking for something to ride, I'll gladly give you plenty of time to do that at home." I kiss her.

She kisses me back but pushes me away. "That was cheesy, Bo." But she laughs. "No, I'm gonna do it. She's just really good. I'll let Brooke and Noelle go before me." She turns in my arms so her back is to my chest, leaning into me.

The girl on the bull finishes her ride, and they call the next number.

"Oh, that's me!" Noelle claps. She ducks under the rope and walks across the mat to the bull. She grabs it by the horn, slips her foot in the bootstrap, and pushes up and over the top of it.

"That's my girl!" Casey yells, then whistles loudly. Right next to my ear.

The girls cheer for her, too, and Noelle looks over at us, wide smile on her face. The guy running it walks over to her and seems to give her some instruction because she raises her arm in the air, just like the other girl did. Then he walks back over to the controls and looks at Noelle, who's watching him. He gives her a thumbs-up, and she nods.

The bull starts out slow, but gets faster, and she can't hold on and falls off within a few minutes. Casey whistles and cheers for her anyway and ducks under the rope as she gets closer and lifts her in his arms and kisses her.

Brooke's number is called next, and when she gets on the bull, she waves the guy off and gives him a nod. I look over at Charlie, who has her phone out, filming it with a shit-eating grin on her face. Then I look at Silas, and his mouth is open, but his hand is covering most of it, eyes wide.

"Let's go, Brooke!" Charlie holds her hands on either side of her mouth to yell.

Noelle and Chelsea cheer for her too.

I nudge Casey with my elbow and nod to Silas. "You see this?"

He turns his head and looks, then leans back into me. "Yeah, I'm not sure what Beck would think of it." He winces. "She's been coming around the house a lot. I don't think he's done anything about it though."

"Well, he might after tonight," I say quietly between the two of us.

Casey shakes his head. "Man, I don't even want to know. Brooke is like a little sister to me."

"Well, your little sister is rocking that bull right now," Chelsea says, looking over her shoulder at us.

The bull slows after a few minutes, Brooke completely killing it. As she dismounts and walks toward us, I hear Charlie tell Silas to wipe the drool off his face.

Chelsea's number is called, and I lean down to her ear. "You don't have to do this if you don't want to."

She nods. "No, I want to try it. I'm good." When she crouches down to get through the rope, she looks back at me and winks. "I got this."

"Yeah, you do, Lucky!" I clap for her, and the others join in too.

Chelsea is short, but she's strong. With little effort, she gets herself on top of the bull and wiggles in the seat to get comfortable. I can't lie and say it's not affecting me, seeing her up there, straddling that machine.

She looks fucking hot, sitting up there like she's done this a million times. Her cowboy hat sits low on her forehead, and when she lifts her arm, her shirt pulls tighter, outlining her breasts.

Goddamn, this girl is perfect.

She waves at the guy and nods, signaling that she's ready.

Like the others, it starts off slow, but I watch a little more closely this time. The way her hips roll with the movement of the machine. The way her tits strain against her shirt. The way she smiles like she's having the time of her life. The way she looks …

free. She finds the perfect rhythm, and I can see her start laughing. She's loving this.

She stays on the whole time, like Brooke did, but when she hops down, she tosses her hat in the air and laughs. Her hat lands close to our group, so she grabs it on her way toward us. I duck under the rope and open my arms to her, and she runs and jumps into me.

"Oh my God, Bo. That was so much fun!" She giggles and tucks her face into my neck and kisses me there.

"You looked like a natural up there, baby." I smack her ass. "Who knew I was dating a bona fide cowgirl?!"

She lifts her head and looks at me, laughing. "I'd hardly call myself a cowgirl, but that was super fun." She wiggles in my arms. "Not gonna lie though; my ass is a little sore."

"You're gonna have to stop wiggling. I'm already trying to keep my hard-on under wraps. That was so fucking hot." I pull her into me a little tighter, rubbing her against my dick. "Can we leave now?"

"Not before I get my funnel cake." She presses a kiss on my lips.

CHAPTER
FIFTEEN

BO

IT WAS NOT our night tonight. We lost our away game by two touchdowns. Sometimes, when we get a break in the schedule, like our bye week last weekend, I think it disrupts our chemistry on the field. It might sound weird, but I swear it's true.

To make things worse, our flight is delayed, getting back to Oklahoma, due to tornadoes there and heavy storms here in Tennessee. It fucking sucks. All I want to do is get home and crawl into my bed—or Chelsea's—and sleep for hours.

Coach stands and faces us, then pockets his phone. "Okay, boys. Looks like we're going to have to stay another night. They're shutting down the airport here for the night. We'll go back to the hotel we stayed in last night and hope to get out of here in the morning."

I look at Casey, who's sitting next to me. "Fuck. I hate traveling sometimes. I just want to go home."

"Same. I want to see my girl and climb into my own bed. I'm supposed to turn in a paper tomorrow, too, so don't let me forget to email my professor when we get to the hotel. I think I can send it to him that way." He pulls out his phone from his bag. "I'm gonna text Noelle and tell her we'll be here another night."

"Yeah, I'd better do the same." I grab my phone from my bag and see a text from my dad that I'll look at later and text Chelsea.

> Bo: Hey, we're staying here one more night because of the weather here and there.

Chelsea: I was wondering if they would change your flight. The weather is pretty bad here. It's been that crazy green hazy color that happens right before a tornado hits.

> Bo: Are you somewhere safe?

Chelsea: Yeah, I'm actually at your house for the night.

> Bo: In my bed?

Chelsea: Not yet, but I will be. Is that okay?

> Bo: Of course it is. I just wish I were there with you.

Chelsea: Me too. Are you doing okay after the game? That was a tough one.

> Bo: It fucking sucks, but we can't dwell on it. We need to fix our mistakes and keep moving forward.

Chelsea: That's some leadership right there.

> Bo: Does it turn you on?

Chelsea: I'll let you know when you call me when you get in your hotel room.

"Excuse me, Bo?" One of the producers of the docuseries comes over to me. "Would you mind if we interviewed you back at the hotel? We figured we could move your slot tomorrow to tonight since we'll be here anyway."

"Oh, yeah, that's fine. Can we make it short? I'm exhausted, and I need to make some calls before bed."

"Of course. We just want to do a recap of the week and the game. We already have our questions ready for you." She nods and points to her tablet in her hand.

My phone buzzes in my hand. "Okay, thanks. Sorry, I gotta take this."

"We'll call for you when we get the room set up. It's likely we'll do it in the conference room where we ate at the hotel." She turns and walks away before I can respond.

I look at my phone again.

> Chelsea: Call me later if you can. Or in the morning if that's easier.

> Bo: Sorry, I had to talk to the producer. They want to do my interview tonight instead of tomorrow. I'll call you when I'm done if it's not too late.

> Chelsea: Okay, talk to you soon. X

I close out our thread and pull up my dad's message. I'm not really in the mood to get his critiques tonight, but if I don't answer, he'll keep messaging me until I do.

> Dad: Tough loss, son. You held the ball too long in the pocket again. You've got to read the defense faster, son. When that safety drops, you should already be moving.

I exhale a heavy sigh. Not in the mood to do this with him at all.

> Bo: Yeah, I know. I saw it on film. I'll work on getting the ball out quicker next week.

Dad: Assume you're on the bus to the hotel?
Call when you're settled in for the night.

> Bo: Okay, but it will be late. I need to do some
> film for the show tonight.

Dad: I'll be up.

Great.

A few hours later, I make my way back up to my hotel room and decide I'd better call my dad before I get on the phone with Chelsea. He answers on the first ring, as if he was waiting for me.

"Hey, son. Are you finished with your filming?"

"Yeah, I'm on my way back to my room. What are you up to?"

"We've just been at home today. Watched the game. Then the girls had some friends over, so I escaped into my office." He laughs.

"Fun. Did everyone watch the game?"

"Yes, your mom and sisters watched with me. You looked good out there, but it seemed like the team was not communicating well today. Our defense wasn't reading Tennessee the way they should have and made mistakes, which cost us the game."

"It was a rough game. It's always hard coming back from a bye week. But to their credit, Tennessee is a great team."

I reach my room and tap my key card to open the door. Casey is sitting on his bed, and he's on the phone, no doubt with Noelle.

"They are good, and their coach is a fine man. You would have played well for him too." He says it like me going there was actually a possibility.

"Nah, you know Walker was always my endgame. I'm exactly where I should be." I clear my throat. "So, anything else you want to talk about? I'm pretty tired, and I need to make another call."

I haven't really said much to my parents, specifically my dad, about Chelsea since the last time we talked about me not having any distractions, but I'm itching to talk to her after this spectacularly shitty day. She just makes everything better.

"Just wanted to check in. It wasn't the best game, but you're playing well. See what happens when there's no distractions?"

Distractions. There's that concern again. I know where it comes from, but if anything, the girl who he thinks is a distraction has been the complete opposite. Knowing I get to see her at the end of the day has made me extra focused. I've kept my nose clean. Worked hard and kept my girl and football family tight.

"About that, Dad, I know you had concerns about me dating anyone, but I met a great girl. She's been good to me, and I'd really like you to meet her."

I let out a breath because it feels good to share this with my dad. He may come off as uptight at times, but we've always been really close, and telling him about a girl feels normal for us.

"A girl? A new girl?"

"Chelsea. She's the one you saw with me in the photo. I know you want me to be careful but ... Dad, she's amazing. When you meet her, you'll—"

"Hold on. You're seeing her against my wishes?"

I don't know why he's even asking. He knows the answers to

his questions ninety-nine percent of the time. I hated when he did this to me as a kid and like it even less now as an adult.

"Dad, can I ask why this bothers you so much? You have never had any concern, or interest frankly, about my girlfriends or girls I've spent time with. Not that there has been anyone serious since I've been here. Or ever really."

"Bo, I just don't want to see you … how do I say it?" I hear him tapping something. "Potentially ruin your future in the NFL by letting a new relationship interfere with that. I don't want to see her derail your plans."

My defenses are up now. Not only for Chelsea, but for myself. "You don't even know her, Dad. She could very well be the best thing that's ever happened to me. I honestly can't wait for you all to meet her. She's special, Dad."

I glance over at Casey, who's off his call now, trying not to look at me, but he hears everything I'm saying and can probably hear my dad's deep timbre through the phone too.

"Son, I'm sure she's lovely, but do you even know who she is? Anything about her past?" He lingers on that last word.

"What are you getting at, Dad?" I'm pacing back and forth, practically burning holes in the carpet.

"Look, my patience has run out about this. You *cannot* see her anymore for multiple reasons. One of which is, you two are just kids. You have a lot going for you—and it sounds like she does too. You're going into the NFL; she's going to law school. I suggest you leave your … connection or whatever it is as a friendship." He clears his throat. "I'm going to say it again, and I suggest you listen this time. I insist that you let her go."

"Dad, respectfully, I'm not a child anymore, and I don't need to do anything you tell me. You understand that, right? And I don't know where this is coming from, and I don't appreciate it after a really fucking shitty day. If there is something you know that you think I need to know, tell me, but just to be clear, whatever you have to say or whatever you think you know, you're wrong because you don't know her. So, Dad, I'm not going to talk to you about this anymore tonight. Tell Mom and the girls I said hello and I love them. I'll talk to you soon."

I pull the phone away from my ear, but I still hear him say, "Bo, please think about what I'm saying."

I end the call and throw my phone on my bed, tilt my head back, and blow out a breath. "Fuck."

"You okay, man?" I look over at Casey, and he moves from lying on his bed to sitting up, legs to the side of the bed, facing me.

I look over at him and shake my head. "I don't fucking know. My dad is being really weird about me being with Chelsea, and I can't figure out why. It's starting to piss me off actually."

"But why? It's not like she's a bad influence." He chuckles. "She's like the perfect girl. Other than my girl, of course." He places his hand on his chest.

"No, I know. She is perfect, but also perfect for me. I'm crazy about her, so it doesn't really matter what he says or thinks. Especially when he doesn't know her. It just bothers me that he won't leave it alone. I'm not sure what he's so worried about. She couldn't care less that I play football, and she has no intention of getting in the way of my goals. It's just pissing me off. I feel like … protective of her or something. I can't explain it." I sit on my bed and kick off my shoes, then flop back onto the mattress.

"Oh, I understand feeling protective. When I had to watch Noelle date her asshole ex, knowing he was a douchebag, it was brutal. Not that yours is the same issue, but I get it, man." He stands up and grabs his phone from his bed. "Why don't you call her? It'll make you feel better, I'm sure. I'll head over to Silas's room and give you some time to talk to her." He holds out his fist to me, and I bump it.

"Thanks, brother. I know you're tired, too, so I'll try to keep it short."

"Just text me when you're done. Call your girl." He opens the door and walks out.

I lie there for a minute, collecting myself before I call Chelsea. She's very intuitive, and I don't want her to hear the stress in my voice. I hate to even admit it to myself, but my curiosity is piqued. I can't figure out why my dad is so insistent on this. And more importantly, what does he think he knows about my girl that I don't?

After I pull in a few deep breaths, I lift my phone and press Call on her name. She answers after a few rings.

"Hey," she answers.

Instantly, when I hear her voice, I feel myself relax.

"Hi," I say, smiling. "Can I just say something before we start talking about other stuff?"

"Yeah, of course. Are you okay?" she asks, sounding concerned.

"I'm fine. I just wanted to tell you I miss you. I hope that doesn't freak you out or anything. I know we haven't been dating all that long, but I really fucking miss you right now." I let out a hoarse chuckle. "You just make everything … better."

I hear her take a deep breath in, and she pauses for a minute.

"I miss you too. Especially since I'm lying here in your bed and I can smell you on your pillow, and I'm surrounded by all your things, but you aren't here. I gotta say, it's a bummer. But I know it was a rough day, and I'm sure it sucks ass, being stranded there. Hopefully, you'll be able to get home early tomorrow though."

"You're in my bed?" I can't help the stupid smile on my face.

"Well … yeah. I *really* miss you."

It's one thing to be with her and be able to see how she responds to me, but to hear her say it? Makes me feel like I just won the Heisman. I mean, I feel like she likes being around me the same way I do with her, but honestly, I'm still letting her work up to letting me in more, and I think we're getting closer. She's definitely more open with me than she was when we first got together.

"I'm not sure if you're making it better or worse. Is it weird that I'm jealous of my pillow right now?" I sigh.

She lets out a soft giggle, and I can hear her shifting around. Getting under the sheets maybe.

"Weird? Nah. I mean, I guess some people might think it was weird, but I don't."

"If we don't think it's weird, that's all that matters." I sit up and swing my legs to the side of the bed. "So, what's your schedule tomorrow? You have class most of the day, right?"

"Yeah, I'll be in class all day, and then I need to go to the library to study. I feel like I'm a little behind with my law school applications, so I need to try to get in some hours at the library over the next few months."

"I'm not distracting you from that, am I? You just say the word, and I'll give you the time you need. This is important to you." I run my hand through my hair in worry, but also a little frustration. Frustration because my dad's words are running through my head.

"Bo, I'm a big girl who can make my own decisions, but I appreciate you acknowledging that it's important to me. And I think you know me well enough by now to know that this is a priority to me and I won't let anything get in the way of it. But I'm also starting to feel like you're"—she pauses, as if she's trying to think of the right words—"important to me too."

These confessions feel significant to me and really just solidify my growing feelings for her because the truth is ... she's *more* than important to me.

"You know how I feel about you, Chelsea. I'm all in."

The silence lingers between us for a minute, but it's not awkward. It's a comfortable silence.

"I'd better let you go. As much as I don't want to, I'm sure Casey wants to get to bed soon. It's been a long day, and I know he's feeling a little battered after today."

"I bet. He took a few hits that made Noelle throw popcorn at the TV. I'm not sure I've ever seen her so mad. She was ready to hop into that TV and defend her man." She laughs, but it's cut off by a yawn.

I nod even though she can't see me. "Yeah, I can see that."

"Okay, well, I guess I'll see you tomorrow at some point? And if not, will you just let me know you got home safely?"

"Yeah, for sure. I'll text you when I know what the plans are since you'll be in class. Then we can meet up after you're done studying." I stand and move to my duffel bag. I unzip it and pull out my toothbrush and face wash. "I'm gonna go get ready for bed before he comes back in."

"You mean wash your face and moisturize?" She tries to hold in a giggle, but she can't and ends up snort-laughing.

"Skin care is important to men too. I can't be letting all this sun exposure age me prematurely." I mean, that is part of it, but also I just like to feel clean before I go to bed at night.

"Hey, I totally get it. It's cute, really, that you have a routine with it. You won't have as many wrinkles as you get older. So, you go take care of that. I'm going to bed myself since I have a busy day tomorrow." I hear her moving around, and it sounds like she just plugged something in.

"All right. Sleep well. I'll talk to you tomorrow." I walk in to the bathroom and set my things on the counter.

"You too. Bye," she says softly and disconnects.

I set my phone down, brace myself on my hands, and look in the mirror. I have a few little scrapes from the game, and I definitely look tired. With a huff, I pick my phone back up and shoot off a text to Casey, letting him know I'm off my call, then look at the Weather app to track the storms. As much as I wish there were better news, it looks like we might be waiting here a while tomorrow. Fuck.

CHAPTER
SIXTEEN

CHELSEA

SCHOOL HAS ALWAYS BEEN easy for me. Even with all the chaos of my home life, or maybe because I craved some kind of structure, I've always excelled in my education. I was tested in elementary school and was considered to be gifted—whatever that means—and took all honors classes throughout the rest of my middle school and high school years. I'm in the honors program here as well. But for some reason, I've been struggling a little with studying lately. It's not that I don't know the material; it's more the focusing part of it that's starting to stress me out.

I know I've been a bit preoccupied with a certain quarterback. But Aunt Laura has brought up this letter almost every time we've spoken lately. I just don't want to read it. I haven't read a single letter from my father since he's been in prison, so I don't understand what the urgency is now.

For me, there are more important things to be focused on, like law school applications, what my next steps are, and now ... Bo. I never expected to fall for a guy like Bo, and—let's be honest—the timing couldn't be worse. Where do we go from here? With him going to the NFL and me not knowing where I'm going to law school yet, it kinda feels like we have a timer set for when our relationship will end. And I really don't like this feeling.

I haven't seen him since Friday, before he left for his away game, and I … miss him. And not just in a casual *oh, I miss you so much* kind of way that you tell your friends or family in conversation. Like I miss him in a *I breathe easier when he's around* kind of way. It's foreign to me, this feeling. Bo isn't the type of guy who will be easy to walk away from—ever. And I don't want to. Usually, by this point in a relationship, I'm ready to move on, but with Bo, what I feel is the complete opposite. But for the first time in my life, the idea of being in a committed relationship doesn't make me feel anxious. Although I'm anxious to see him now.

He hasn't texted since this morning, which I'm hoping means he's on his way back since the weather has cleared here. I know he wasn't happy about being stuck in Tennessee, especially after a loss.

Trying to study in the library and not look at my phone every few minutes isn't very productive, but I blocked out this time for the library, so I need to get my shit together instead of staring blankly at my laptop.

Maybe if I just start typing, I can get refocused.

Although I do need a book for my research before I get too deep into it. So, I stand and unzip my hoodie and hang it over my chair, then slip my phone, just in case Bo calls or texts, and my wallet in my back pocket and make my way to the row where the book I need should be.

The Law section is in the back, where I can find a book on torts and US private law. I find my book, which is on the right side, but not the right spot, and reach up to grab it, but it's a little too high for me.

"Fuck."

"Do you need some help with that?" a low and very sexy voice asks in my ear.

It's a smooth baritone I know well and have been having

eargasms to the last few nights while he was away. Strong hands run up my sides and to the front, up to my breasts, making me freeze.

A shiver rushes through me, and I feel it all the way down to my toes. If it were anyone else, I'd freak. But I know this man. This man is mine.

I turn to face Bo, and we have matching smiles. I reach up to wrap my arms around him, and he lifts me in his arms.

"Hi," he says, then kisses my neck.

"Hi." With my head tucked into his neck, I breathe him in. He smells like citrus, a little sweaty, but not in a stinky way, and a hint of something sweet.

"Do you need help getting that book, or can I give you a kiss first?" He pulls his head back to look at me.

Instead of answering him, I grab the back of his head and seal my mouth to his. I trace the seam of his lips with my tongue, and he opens for me. I twirl my tongue around his, savoring the taste of him, and I feel like I can't kiss him hard enough or deep enough.

He sets my feet on the floor, but only so he can grab the back of my thighs and lift me up. My back hits the book stacks, and I use the shelf to brace my weight, not that Bo can't hold me with his strength. The wall of books makes it easier for me to wrap my legs around him, bunching the skirt I'm wearing practically to my waist, but I don't care. He rocks me against his hard-on that I can feel straining against the zipper.

When he breaks the kiss, we're both breathing hard. His lips are wet from our kiss.

"I fucking missed you so much. This weekend was brutal in every way." He sets his forehead against mine.

"I missed you too. I don't care much for you being away for long." I kiss his lips again.

He chuckles deep in his chest. "Same, baby. I couldn't wait to see you. I practically ran here from the stadium." His hands inch up higher on my thighs. "You're wearing a skirt?"

I nod, biting my lip. I didn't think much about it when I got dressed earlier today, but now, I'm pretty happy with my choice. Especially seeing the heat in Bo's eyes, which only turns me on more than I already was from that kiss.

"Goddamn, Lucky. I'm not sure I can wait till we get home to fuck you." He looks to the left, then to the right.

"So, don't." I roll my hips against him, making him groan.

Honestly, this isn't a risk I would normally take since I work here and I've never been one for public displays. But I can't lie and say the thought of someone catching us doesn't turn me on a little. Or maybe it's the rush of needing to have him fuck me fast and hard that makes me lose all common sense.

He captures my mouth again, and this kiss is just as frantic. We're devouring each other, almost desperate. His hold on me shifts, and he wraps an arm under my butt to hold me. He unbuttons his jeans and pushes them down far enough to free his hard, thick cock. Then he runs his hand under my thigh, reaching my center, pulling my panties to the side.

"Fuck, you're wet." His fingers run from my opening to my clit, then back, and he thrusts one finger inside me. Then another.

"Bo, I need you." My voice is a hurried whisper.

I pull his head toward me and take his lips again, licking, biting, sucking. Rolling my hips against his hand, seeking the friction I need.

His mouth is on my ear, so his spoken words are hushed, deep, and intense. "I got you, baby." He pulls his fingers out of me and takes hold of his cock, then runs the head through my slit. "This might hurt a little," he says, pushing into me in short thrusts.

"I'm good, I promise." I tilt my hips down to push him into me more.

He pushes in deeper, and, yeah, it stings a little, but I'm so wet at this point that it won't last long. His hand moves up to my tank top, and he pushes it up, exposing my bra. He pulls one of the cups down and covers my breast completely with his hand, squeezing. "You're so fucking perfect."

"Bo, I love that you think so, but we need to hurry. Fuck me."

I'm low-key getting a little nervous about someone walking by and seeing us now. My boob is completely out, and his pants are down far enough to look suspicious. There's literally no hiding what we're doing.

He starts to pump faster and faster, his fingers digging into the backs of my thighs. "I'm not gonna last, so I hope you're close. I missed this pussy too much. You're so tight. Fuck."

"Kiss me," I say, panting.

I move my hands to the sides of his face, and I can feel sweat beading at his temples.

He tilts his head and seals his mouth over mine in a searing kiss.

Being in this position, my clit hits his pubic bone in just the right spot to drive me wild and closer to coming. I moan into his mouth as the first pulse of my orgasm starts.

His hips are moving so fast now; he's almost out of control as I start to come. We're both panting with our mouths hovering over each other, and within seconds, we both fall.

I kiss him, tongue moving slowly around his as my orgasm rolls through me. It feels even better because I can feel him pulsing inside me too. He pushes up once more and stills as he comes.

We take a minute to catch our breath. Then he pulls out of me and sets me on my feet. I feel slightly wobbly while I adjust my panties and pull my shirt back down. His dick is still slightly hard when I look over to see him pulling up his boxers and jeans.

Once he's tucked in, he grabs my waist in his hands and tugs me closer, placing a soft kiss on my lips. "Well, that was a first for me."

I let out a loud laugh, then cover my mouth with my hand. "Yeah, me too. We're lucky it's so quiet in here right now." I wrap my arms around his neck again and tip my chin to kiss him.

"Are you almost done, or do you still have a lot to do? I was hungry before, but now I'm really hungry." He pats his stomach.

I turn and look at the book I need on the shelf, then back to Bo. "I mean, technically, I have a paper to write, but it's not due until Friday. I could wrap up." I take his hand and lead him back to the table.

"Let's grab some food and go to your place. Noelle is on her way to our place, according to Casey, so we'll have your apartment to ourselves, and I'm not done with you yet." He smacks my butt playfully.

I gather my laptop and notebook and slide them both into my backpack. Then I put my hoodie back on and zip it halfway up. "Sounds good to me. And I might not be done with you yet either."

I point a finger into his chest, and he takes it in his hand, pulls it up to his mouth, and kisses the tip.

"Let me have your bag." He holds out his hand, and I give him my bag. Then he slings it over his shoulder. "Ready?"

"Yep, let's go."

We walk out of the library together, and no one gives us funny looks or anything—thank God. That would have been bad for me if we had gotten caught, but probably worse for him. I can't deny it was hotter than hell though, and I don't regret taking the risk. Not one bit.

We picked up our order of food from The Font on our way back to my place, and we're finishing up our meals now. Bo has been kind of quiet or maybe contemplative since we left the library. I don't know if he's just tired or he has something on his mind.

He's told me about the game from his perspective, and something that I admire about Bo is that he is a true team leader in every sense, but he's also humble. He talks about the mistakes he made in the game and how he could have played better. And I don't have much to offer in terms of advice or feedback so I just listen.

"So, what should we do tonight?" He gathers his trash and puts it in the empty container, then reaches for mine. "You done?"

"Yeah, I'm done. Thank you." I wipe my mouth one more time and put the napkin in the container in his hands. "And I don't care. I'm sure you're tired, so why don't we just chill and watch a movie or something?"

He throws away our containers, then washes his hands. "That sounds good. I could also use a shower."

"Okay, that's fine. You know where the towels are." I point toward the hallway where the closet is that holds our towels and other miscellaneous items for the apartment.

Bo walks back over to me and holds out his hands to grab

mine. So, I put my hands in his, and he pulls me up from my chair.

"I think you should join me." He walks backward toward the bathroom.

"You do, huh?" I smirk. "I could do that."

We haven't showered together yet. We've had sex on almost every surface of this apartment and most of his, but never showered together.

"I do." He releases one of my hands and keeps the other in his as he enters the bathroom, which he looks huge in because it's not that big of a room.

I drop his hand and slide the shower door open to turn the water on. We have a bathtub-shower combo, which should give us both room to fit. When I turn around to face him, he's pulling his shirt off, and I take a minute to admire him. He's got muscles for days and a trimmed trail of hair below his belly button, going down into his jeans. Seriously, just looking at him turns me on. My eyes drop to his groin, and I see an outline of his dick already hardening in his pants. Which gives me another idea. I haven't given him a blow job yet, and I suddenly have a craving to taste him.

He smirks at me, like he can read my mind, and slowly unbuttons his pants while I take my tank top and bra off. He pushes down his jeans and boxers at the same time, and his cock springs free, erect against his stomach. It's very possible that I'm drooling.

We've gotten naked with each other before, but somehow, this seems more sensual than ever. In a move that makes me feel more confident than I am, I lightly run my fingers over my skin, from my breasts to the waistband of my short, ruffled skirt. I tuck my fingers inside and slide my skirt and my panties down my legs, watching Bo's face as I do it.

His blue eyes roam over my body in appreciation, and he walks toward me. Framing my face in his hands, he leans in and kisses me slowly, deeply.

I brush my fingers from his chest down to his cock, making goose bumps appear on his skin. When I wrap my hand around him, he breaks the kiss and sucks in a breath.

"Let's get in the shower." I release him and take his hand, and we step into the shower together.

I stand under the water first, letting it rain down my body, and he trails the water with his fingers, tracing every curve. With my hair completely wet now, I twist it and tuck it into a bun at the top of my head. Then I reach over to the body wash and squirt some in my hand.

Opening his palm, I wipe the body wash into his hand. "Wash me."

"Yes, ma'am." He rubs his hands together to spread it evenly, and then he starts at my shoulders and moves down to my breasts. He takes both breasts in his hands and squeezes. "Perfect handful."

His gaze meets mine, and he has a devilish grin. He massages my breasts, paying special attention to my pebbled nipples, pinching and tugging on them, which only turns me on even more.

My breathing is getting faster with every pull. I slide my hands up his sides, then down to his waist and around to his butt, bringing him in closer to me. "Do you like washing me?"

Who is this breathy siren?

He nods, smile widening on his face. "It might just be my new favorite thing. Everything about you turns me on, but touching you like this makes me feel like I'm gonna lose control."

"You're doing so good, making me clean and turning me on. Getting me ready for your thick cock." I move one of my hands around to take hold of his erection at the base and start to slide my hand up and down.

"Fuck, baby. You can't say things like that and expect me to make it to the main event." His hand moves from my breast to my center, cupping me and sliding his middle finger through my folds. Then he pushes his finger inside of me as he bends down to kiss me.

Our tongues tangle, and then I suck on his tongue, making him groan. I turn us in the water, still moving my hand up and down his shaft, making it so he's standing under the spray. I break the kiss to let the water run over him, and with his hand that's not pumping into my pussy, he wipes the water from his face and brushes back his hair. Why that's so sexy, I don't know, but it fucking is.

I look down at his cock, and for a second, I worry I won't be able to fit my mouth over him. But I'm going to try anyway because I absolutely need to taste him. And I'm kind of mad at myself for not doing this sooner. So, I drop to my knees and look up at him.

"Oh shit. Baby, you don't need to do that." He cups my chin and tilts it up so I'm looking at him. "I mean, I'm not gonna stop you." He laughs. "But you don't have to."

"I know I don't have to. I want to. Desperately." I slide my hand down to his base and tilt his cock toward my mouth and run my tongue over the tip, then circle his thick crown.

He groans and thrusts into my mouth, like he can't control it. "Fuck me, that feels so good."

Bo is long and thick, and I'm not sure how deep I'll be able to take him. But I wrap my lips around the head and stretch my mouth as wide as I can to get around him, then work my way down as far as I can, which isn't very far. Then he thrusts into my mouth, hitting the back of my throat, making me choke and my eyes water.

He hears me choke and starts to pull out of my mouth, but I stop him with my other hand on his ass, holding him in place. I look up at him through my lashes and shake my head as much as I can, letting him know I don't plan to stop.

So, he grabs hold of the twisted knot on the top of my head and pulls my hair just enough to make me moan around his dick. The sting of the pull surprisingly goes straight to my pussy.

I drop my hand from his ass and bring my fingers to my center, rubbing my clit in the same tempo that I'm pumping his cock. I'm soaked—and not just from the water of the shower. My mouth barely goes past his crown, so I take short, shallow pulls on his head, and I can feel him as he twitches in my hand.

He continues to fuck my mouth as I suck, both hands on top of my head, holding me in place. My eyes are watering, and I can feel the saliva dripping out of my mouth, but I don't stop. His hips start to piston a little faster, and then he abruptly pulls his dick out of my mouth.

"I need to finish inside you." He bends slightly and pulls me up from under my arms. He kisses me quickly, then turns me around to face the wall. "Get ready, baby, I'm going hard."

I put my hands on the tiles and look over my shoulder at him and smile. He has a feral look on his face as his eyes roam over my body. I spread my legs as his hands run down my back to my butt. He squeezes, then spreads my cheeks apart. One of his thumbs presses on my tight hole. I've never been taken there, and I don't think that's the plan right now because I think I'd need a whole lotta prep work to go there with his size. But I can't deny that the pressure of it feels kinda … good.

With his other hand, he takes his cock and runs the head through my center to my opening. Without hesitation, he pushes in, all the way to the hilt, making me gasp. "You ready, baby?"

I nod and push my hips into him. "Fuck me, Bo."

He pulls out slowly, his hand holding his erection as he withdraws, then slams back into me, hard. When he pulls back again, he comes out completely, then puts his thumb that was pressing on my other hole inside my pussy, pumping, soaking it with my arousal. He replaces his thumb with his dick, and the pressure on my ass is there again. This time, his thumb breaks through the barrier of the opening.

It's sort of an odd feeling, but also really fucking hot. It's almost a sensation overload actually. His dick is sliding in and out, and his thumb is pumping in and out of my ass. I feel full in the very best way. I push against his dick and thumb, forcing them both deeper, and moan.

He grabs my hair again and pulls my head back and thrusts faster. The need to touch him overwhelms me, so I move one hand to his thigh, feeling the muscles in his leg flex as we fuck. My grip tightens on him as my orgasm hits me in a rush.

Bo lets go of my hair and removes his thumb, then grabs my waist, squeezing as he pumps faster into me, chasing his orgasm. He yells out as he comes, "You feel so good, baby. Holy fuck!"

With one last thrust, he releases inside of me. He pulls me up so my back is against his chest, and he wraps his arms around my waist. His lips find my neck, and he kisses me reverently, his breathing evening out.

I turn my head to find his lips, and we kiss softly, slowly. My hands rest on his arms, and I'm not sure I've ever felt so close to him. We didn't just fuck; we made love.

As we stand there, kissing, he pulls out of my body. The water starts to run colder, and he leans back and breaks the kiss. "We'd better finish up before we turn to ice cubes."

I step under the spray and make quick work of washing my body—again—rinsing off his cum that's dripping down my legs while he washes his hair. When I'm done, I move so he can finish, and then I step out of the shower, grabbing my towel off the bar. He comes out while I'm wrapping my towel around me, and I knot it on top of my head.

I bend down to grab my clothes, and he reaches for me.

"Let's leave the clothes. We can clean up later."

"Okay, but let me get you a towel. We forgot to grab one for you before we came in here." I stand and go out of the bathroom and grab him a towel from the hall closet.

He's standing in front of the mirror when I return, running his hands through his hair. If I had washed my hair, it would have been a whole process, but for him, a simple finger-combing works just fine. And literally everything he does looks sexy, including this.

I hand him the towel, and he wraps it around his waist and doesn't bother drying his body. Then he takes my hand in his and we walk to my bedroom. It's not too late yet, but I get the feeling he's just ready to be in bed.

We separate, and he walks to the other side of the bed. Together, we pull the sheet and comforter back. I untie my towel and climb in at the same time he does. I lie on my side, facing him. Once I get comfortable, he faces me, too, one of his arms tucked under the pillow.

His hand touches my face as we look into each other's eyes. "Chelsea, I ..." He pauses and sucks in a deep breath. "I just need you to know that I'm really invested in this. Us." He exhales.

I'm not sure that's what I expected him to say, but I'm glad he did. We haven't really defined our relationship; we have just been living in the moment—or at least I thought so. But I think this weekend apart had us both thinking about more than what might happen tomorrow.

"I feel the same." I'm not really sure how to articulate it without getting into my past—that I might not be the best at knowing what to do about all these feelings or what we should do from here.

"Good. I'm relieved." He chuckles as his hand moves down my arm, and he takes my hand in his. "I just feel like it's really important for me to lay it out there because I don't ever want you to doubt that you're a priority for me. I know I have a lot going on this year with the draft, and you have to figure out where you're going to law school, but I want us to be there for each other. I guess I just wanted you to know that, and I want to see where your head is."

I'm starting to wonder if this is why he was quiet on our way home.

"Yes, we both have a lot going on, and I do feel invested in us. It's definitely not something I expected, but I'm happy I have you in my life. I don't know that I can even imagine life without you now, honestly."

"Really?" he asks, eyebrows raised, looking hopeful.

I'm not sure Bo Callaway has ever had to feel like the world wasn't his, so I'm sure this is a foreign feeling to him, just like it is for me to open up to someone. Yet I still don't think I'm ready to tell him all of it.

"Really." I let go of his hand and trace his face with my finger.

He really is the most beautiful man I've ever seen, and I can't believe he's mine.

He sits up and rests his weight on his elbow and forearm. "Can I tell you something else without you getting freaked out?"

Oh shit.

"Yeah, of course." I swallow.

He tucks a loose piece of hair behind my ear. "I'm in love with you, Chelsea. Like, crazy in love with you. I don't expect you to say anything back. I just need you to know that's where I am."

I'm not sure if I feel elated or terrified. Maybe a little of both. But I know I don't want to lose this man because I love him too. So, despite my fears about losing myself to someone else, I let go.

"I love you too."

CHAPTER
SEVENTEEN

CHELSEA

IT'S Bo's birthday this weekend, and since he has a game, we're celebrating early. I have a little get-together planned with our friends later, but I wanted to do something for him alone first. And today is their only day off practice this week, so I took the opportunity to do something special with him off campus.

"You're really not telling me where we're going?" Bo looks over at me, smirking.

I tap the address into the GPS screen in his car. We had to take his SUV since he wouldn't fit comfortably in my Honda Civic.

"Nope. I want you to be surprised when we pull up." I giggle.

"But it's not a surprise party, right? I hate those."

"No, it's just us. Well, and some other people that we don't know, but the day is just for us." I finish putting the address in and sit back in my seat. "Okay, let's roll, Callaway." I clap my hands.

He pulls out of the parking space in front of his house, and we head to our destination. We make small talk on the way. He tells me about his past birthdays and about his circus-themed party for his tenth birthday, which was his favorite even though he doesn't like circuses. There were live animals, trapeze artists, clowns, and other circus performers, and I'm sure the food served was incredible. His cake alone, he said, was the size of a small, round kitchen table.

Let's just say, my tenth birthday looked a whole lot different from his. My sister and I celebrated my birthday that year with social services. It was super fun. My parents had gotten into a fight, and it turned physical, which was normal for us. But one of our old neighbors heard it and called the cops. My parents were arrested because they both assaulted the officers. So, social services was called, and we were picked up from the police station and taken to a shelter for the night. I didn't have a cake or presents at all. Not that I would have had we been at home anyway because my parents forgot that it was my birthday.

Twenty minutes later, we arrive at the farm where I'm taking Bo to play with golden retrievers. Hearing about him dragging that stuffed animal around when he was little made me sad that he never had a pet.

"What is this? A dog farm?"

We pass through the gates of Golden Prairie Farm, where we see puppies and dogs running through the fields.

"Yes!" I turn in my seat, and I can hardly contain my excitement. I mean, this is like giving myself a present too. I love dogs, and I'm dying to cuddle with some puppies.

He laughs. "Okay, so what are we doing here? You're not buying a dog, are you?"

"No, silly. So, you know how you told us about your stuffie, Spike?" I lean over the console.

He pulls into a parking spot and puts the car in park, then faces me, smiling. "Yeah, I remember."

"Okay, well, I got to thinking about what I could get you for your birthday, and then I remembered you telling us that story. So, I looked online to see what puppy farms were in the area that we could just, like, hang out at. Then this place came up, and it was like I won the doggy lottery!" I'm practically bouncing in my seat.

"But what do we do, just play with them or what?"

"I'm glad you asked, Bo." I pull out my phone from my crossbody. "Our golden experience includes play time with the dogs, a prairie picnic—I'm not sure what that involves other than food—and a tour of the little store they have here. I guess it is a working farm and not just the puppy part." I set my phone on my lap.

"Come here." He wiggles his finger toward himself.

I bend further over the console until my face is in front of his.

Bo cups my face and leans into me. "This is possibly the best birthday I've ever had." Then he kisses me softly, tenderly.

When I pull back, I take his face in my hands. "I doubt that, but I felt so bad that you never had a pet, and since neither of us can actually get a dog right now, I thought this could be a temporary fix." I kiss him again.

"Lucky, this seriously is the best birthday because I get to be with you, but also, I'm not sure anyone has ever done anything so thoughtful for me. Thank you, baby." He unbuckles his seat belt. "Let's go see some puppies." He opens his door.

"You're welcome! I'm so excited." I unbuckle my seat belt, tuck my phone back in my bag, get out of the car, and meet him in the back of the car.

He takes my hand in his, and we walk to the entrance.

"Hi. We have a reservation for today," I tell the girl at the counter.

"Welcome to Golden Prairie Farms. What is the reservation under?" She looks at me with her tablet in hand.

"Callaway," I tell her.

"Perfect. I have you checked in. You can go outside this door here, and the trail will lead you down to the play area with the dogs. Here's your bag of treats and a map of the property, so you know where to go for the picnic and where the store is located. Have fun!" She hands everything over to me.

"Great. Thank you so much."

"Here, I'll take it." Bo takes the treats and the map from me.

"Okay, thanks." I grab his free hand. "Come on. Puppies are waiting!"

He lets out a deep chuckle. "Let's go see the puppies."

An hour later, we make our way to the store to pick up our picnic basket and stroll around to see what they have. The building is an old wood building that has a rich, earthy smell to it. There are rows of baskets, filled with different nuts and dried fruits. They grow pecans, apricots, figs, and apples here. We're out of picking season, but they have all the fruit available to buy in various dried mixes. It smells amazing in here, honestly.

They also have T-shirts, sweatshirts, and hats available, so I pick us out matching shirts. Bo wants to buy them, but I insist on paying for them.

We go to the counter to check out and get our basket for the picnic.

"Is this all for you today?" the cashier asks.

"No, we also have the sampler basket under Callaway." I pull out my phone and show her the receipt in case she needs to see that it's already paid.

"Okay, I see it here, honey. You're all good." She hands me the bag with the shirts, then turns and tells the teenage-looking kid to go in the back and get our basket, but he's staring at Bo, not responding.

"Are you Bo Callaway?" the teen asks him.

"I am. You a Stallions fan?" Bo smiles what I call his TV smile at the boy.

"Hell yeah, I am."

"Peter David, language," the lady at the counter scolds.

"Sorry, Mama." He laughs. "You're killing it this season, man. You think you guys will make the playoffs?"

Bo nods. "I do. We have a really great team this year. We have to take it one game at a time, but I think we'll take the championship this year."

"Peter, you leave them alone and go get their basket," his mom tells him.

"Oh yeah, sorry. Be right back, but, hey, can I get your autograph?" he asks Bo as he walks away.

"Yeah, of course. I just need a paper and pen." Bo leans in toward the counter.

The woman rips off a paper from under the counter and hands it to Bo, along with a pen. "Here you go. Thanks for doing this."

Bo writes a little note to Peter and then signs his name. "It's no problem. Love meeting fans."

"Well, good luck with the rest of the season. We'll be cheering for y'all for sure!"

"Thank you so much. We appreciate the support. And we're having a great time here today. I assume this is your farm?" Bo asks.

"Oh good. That's what we like to hear. Yes, this is our family farm. It's been in my husband's family for over one hundred years. Started out as a pecan farm, but over time, it expanded. Then, in our early years of marriage, we decided to turn it into what it is now with the pups and other activities," she tells us.

"It's amazing. And everything looks so good. I wanted to grab everything to take home with us," I tell her. "It smells so good in here too."

"Thank you. That's the pies. We make everything in the baskets, but the pecan pie is our specialty, secret family recipe and all." She giggles, then turns when she sees her son walk back in with the basket in his hand.

"Here you go." He hands the basket to Bo.

"Thanks, man." He nods to the counter. "There's the signature for you."

"Awesome. Thank you." The teen reaches out his hand to shake Bo's.

"Of course. Have a good one." Bo takes my hand, and we start to walk out of the store.

Once we're out and walking toward the picnic area, I turn to him and really look at him. Sometimes, I forget that people around the country know who he is. It's kind of wild to think about. "You're really good with people. Like, you're a good man, Bo Callaway."

He smiles down at me. "Thanks, baby. I try to be."

"No, you are. And you're genuine, which I think is one of the best things about you." I pull his hand up and kiss the back of his.

"Where's this coming from? Don't get me wrong; I love it."

We reach the tables, and he sets the basket down on one.

"I don't know. I just like watching you and see how you interact with people. You're a special guy, and I feel really lucky to be in your orbit." I pull in a deep breath, suddenly feeling emotional.

He sits down on the bench, legs on either side. "Come here," he says, and he holds my hand as I climb over and straddle the bench too. He takes the bag from my other hand and places it next to the basket, then takes both my hands in his. "Chelsea, if anyone is lucky, it's me."

Instead of replying, I just kiss him. Even though I started this open conversation, we're getting into a territory that I don't know that I'm ready for. "Let's eat. I'm sure you're hungry, and I'm dying to try the pie."

I pull out a bottle of local organic red wine. Neither of us really drinks though, so we'll probably take it home for the girls. There's a packet of crackers, some cheese, some of the dried fruits, along with some slices of summer sausage. Small square sandwiches are neatly wrapped, and they have what looks like cream cheese, fig jam, and a slice of ham. As I take everything out, Bo sets it up on the table.

"Okay, now, this all looks really good. Probably won't keep you satisfied for long though, but we have dinner and cake tonight with our friends." I look at him, and he has a smile on his face and nods.

"This all looks great. Thank you for bringing me here. This is the best date and birthday I've ever had." He leans over and kisses my cheek.

"I'm glad. I wanted to do something special and different." I pull out the slices of pie and set them on the table, and then I clear my throat, deciding to give him more of my story. "So, after my mom died, we went to live with my aunt." I look over at him, and he nods. "My sister and I had to go into counseling, and I was struggling to connect with anyone, so they suggested animal therapy. My aunt found a farm near where we lived that worked with kids who'd had traumatic events in their lives. I started going when I was thirteen, and when my program was completed, I decided to stay on and work with kids who came in like I had."

I turn my head and look out over the beautiful landscape. The sun is starting to set, and there is a pink glow in the sky.

"Working there is how I decided I wanted to be a lawyer. Some of those kids who came in had no one to speak for them, and I guess I just want to feel like I can make a difference and be that voice for them when they can't. Does that make sense?" I look back at him.

"It does make sense." He nods. "Can I ask about your mom?"

My first instinct is to say no, but I brought it up, so I should tell him something. "You can."

"How did she die?" he asks cautiously.

I take a deep breath, my fingers tightening around his, almost without me noticing. My gaze drops to our joined hands because it's easier than looking at his eyes. The words feel heavy in my mouth. I can't bring myself to tell him the whole story right now, especially on his birthday.

"She was shot."

When I look up, he's watching me—not staring, but *waiting*. His brows knit together just a little, and the silence between us feels like it's stretching.

"I'm really sorry. Were you close with her?"

I shake my head. "Not in the way you should be close to your mother. My sister and I didn't have a great life before living with my aunt."

"You know you can tell me anything, right?" he prods.

A lump rises in my throat. Part of me wants to run, and part of me wants to collapse into his chest and spill everything. "I do know that. It's just … not always easy for me to talk about."

He nods. "I get that. But I just want you to know that you can. I want to know you in every way."

I nod and bite down on my lip to try not to cry. I don't want his birthday to become something sad.

"I love you, Bo. I hope you feel that."

I know I need to give him more of myself. He's always so open and honest with me. And while I've been authentically myself with him, there's a lot he doesn't know about me. But I don't ever want him to doubt how I feel because it isn't easy for me to let someone in like this.

"I do. And I love you too," he says, then leans in to kiss me.

He pulls back and watches me for a minute, and I think he can sense that's all he's getting from me today.

When we pull apart, I turn on the bench and reach for the pie and clear my throat. "I think because it's your birthday, we should eat dessert first. What do you think?" I look over at him and smile, opening the container.

He smiles at me knowingly and nods. "I think we should eat the pie."

CHAPTER
EIGHTEEN

BO

MY PARENTS DECIDED to surprise me and come for a visit the week of Thanksgiving. I couldn't go home because we have a game the day after. Chelsea stayed here, too, instead of going home to Florida so that we could be together; plus, she didn't want to miss my game since it's the last regular season home game. She's gotten really into coming to the games, and I love seeing her in my jersey that I gave her.

We already have plans with our friends for dinner, but I told my parents we could have an early lunch with them. So, they made a reservation at the hotel where they're staying, and we're on our way there now. They haven't gotten to meet Chelsea yet because she's been busy with school and she took on another student to tutor. This one is a basketball player, and I know him. Nice guy, but I don't love that he's hanging out with my girl twice a week.

Chelsea wiggles in her seat and pulls the visor down to look in the mirror for the third time.

"Babe, it's gonna be fine. Are you worried?"

"Bo, meeting the parents … and sisters is kind of a big deal, no?" She looks at me, wide-eyed and with her mouth open.

And I don't want to minimize it because it is kind of a big deal, but I also know they're gonna love her. Or at least my mom and sisters will.

"You're right; it is a big deal, but you're amazing, and they'll love you." I reach over and take her hand. "And I'll be there with you, so you have nothing to worry about."

"I'm not scared; I just have never met the parents before. I've never dated anyone long enough or cared enough to get that invested. This feels big, Bo."

"If it makes you feel any better, I guarantee that my sisters will do most of the talking. They're talkers." I squeeze her hand.

"It's fine. I'll be fine." She takes a deep breath and exhales.

I've never seen her like this. She's usually so confident and not so … anxious.

"Just be yourself. Try to have fun." I pull into the parking lot of the hotel and find a spot. "Okay, let's get this done, so we can go back to the house and watch football with everyone. Archie plays tonight."

She nods and unbuckles her seat belt.

"Wait here." I get out of the car and round it so I can open her door.

Chelsea always looks beautiful, but today, she's wearing a tight, long-sleeved black bodysuit—I think that's what it's called —and a tan-colored skirt that has a little belt and hits mid-thigh, which is driving me crazy. Her knee-high black boots have a little heel to them.

I take her hand as she gets out of the car.

We walk into the hotel and toward the restaurant where we're meeting my family.

Before we walk in, I stop her. "Hey, I love you. It'll be okay." I frame her face in my hands and kiss her.

She nods as she takes my hand again, and we walk to the table.

"Hey, everyone."

My mom, sisters, and dad all stand and give a collective hello.

My mom rounds the table. "Hey, sugar." She pulls me in for a hug, then turns to Chelsea and takes her hands. "You must be Chelsea. We've heard so much about you. I was just dyin' to meet you." My mom still has a pretty heavy Southern accent.

Chelsea smiles and seems to relax a little. "I am. It's so nice to meet you, Mrs. Callaway."

"Oh, honey, you can call me Lola." My mom waves her off, then goes back to her seat.

My sisters come over next and hug her, which seems to take her by surprise, and then they hug me.

Caroline whispers in my ear, "She's too pretty for you. You struck gold, brother."

I laugh and nod. "Don't I know it?"

My dad walks over to us, and he seems a little tenser than usual, but I'm not going to let it get to me.

"Chelsea, Jon Callaway," he says formally, holding his hand out to her.

"It's a pleasure to meet you, Your Honor."

"Oh, no, no. Call me Jon. No formalities, please." He chuckles as he walks back to his seat.

I pull out a seat for Chelsea, and she sits down. Then I pull my chair out next to her and take her hand in mine under the table.

"So, Chelsea, Bo tells us you're from Florida?" my mom asks.

"Yes, I'm from the Naples area." Chelsea picks up her water from the table and takes a drink.

"Oh, Naples is lovely. So, you're a Southern girl like me then." She winks at Chelsea.

"I am, born and raised." Chelsea smiles and nods.

"And you have a sister?" Mom asks.

"Yes, I have a younger sister. She just turned eighteen."

"I did too!" Savannah says. "So, is she graduating this year too then?"

"She is."

"Does she know where she wants to go to school yet?" Caroline asks.

Chelsea shakes her head. "I'm not sure she's decided, but she wants to stay in Florida. I know Miami is on the table and University of Florida."

"I'll probably stay in state too. University of Southern California is my first choice, but we'll see." Savannah shrugs.

"That's a great school. I applied there for law school," Chelsea adds.

I look over at my dad and see him watching her with a look I can't read. Like he's trying to figure something out.

"What other schools have you applied to?" he asks her.

She clears her throat. "Um, well, USC, Penn, NYU, and Walker, just in case I want to stay here." She lifts a shoulder.

"All great schools. What were your LSAT scores?" he asks her.

"Dad," I interrupt.

She laughs. "It's okay; he can ask. I got a one seventy-one, so I'm hoping it should get me into any of my choices."

My dad nods. "Strong score. Well done."

"Thank you," Chelsea says.

"I bet your parents are proud," my dad says.

I lean back in my chair. "Dad."

Chelsea touches my arm. "It's okay." She looks at my dad. "My aunt raised us. My mother died when I was young."

"Oh, I'm so sorry, Chelsea. Is your dad still living?" Mom asks her.

Chelsea shakes her head. "My dad isn't in the picture."

"Why not?" My dad asks.

"Dad!" I look over at him again, and he looks back at me like I'm the one being rude.

My mom clears her throat, reading the room pretty fast. "So, what does your aunt do?" she asks, trying to redirect the conversation.

Chelsea looks down at her lap for a minute, then back up at my mom. "She's a pediatrician. One of the best in the state actually."

"That's amazin'. Good for her!" Mom claps her hands together.

The rest of the meal goes smoothly, but I catch my dad and Chelsea looking at each other more than once. Almost like they're in a staredown. I'm not sure if I should be proud of my girl for not being intimidated by him or be angry with my dad for making things awkward for her.

After we eat, we go into a cocktail area with smaller tables. The girls sit down first, and my dad grabs my arm and leans into me.

"I need to speak with you upstairs for a moment."

"Now?" I look down at his hand on my arm. Then I look up and see the look in his eye that tells me this isn't up for debate.

I lean down and give Chelsea a kiss on the cheek. "I'll be right back. You'll be okay?"

She nods and smiles tightly. "Yeah, I'm fine."

"This won't take long." I kiss her again.

My dad and I make it to the elevator before either of us speaks.

"Dad, what is going on? You're acting strange and honestly rude, and I don't appreciate it. Is this because you told me not to date her?"

He laughs, but it's not because it's funny. "Oh, son, you directly disobeyed me. And in a way, if the circumstances were different, I'd be proud of you for it. But the fact of the matter is, they're not."

"What does that mean?"

The elevator doors open to the penthouse, and I follow him in.

"Bo, we don't want to keep the girls waiting, so I'm just

going to get to it. I'm officially being nominated for the United States Supreme Court. I got the call from the president yesterday. We knew this was a possibility, of course, but the time has come since Justice Blackburn passed away last month."

"Oh my God ... okay ... congratulations! This is amazing news, Dad." I throw my arms around him, expecting him to give the kind of hug you give when you've just achieved your life's dream.

But his arms barely come up. He pats me on the back—brief, mechanical.

I pull back, brows furrowing. "What's going on, Dad?" I take a small step back, hands open in front of me. "I still don't understand what the problem is here."

"Son, you know what the process is. They will dig into every part of my life, my career. All of it."

"And there's nothing to be worried about, so again, what's the problem?"

"Chelsea. She's the problem."

"What?" I shake my head. "How is Chelsea the problem?"

"Bo, have you ever asked her about her parents?"

"Yes, her mom was killed, and then she and her sister went to live with her aunt."

"You're not answering my question. Have you ever asked her about her dad? Like, why didn't they go live with him?"

"No, I've been letting her tell me things about her family at her own pace because I could sense there was more to the story and I didn't want to push her."

"Well, let me give you the full picture. And, Bo, let me just say again that if the circumstances were different, I would give you my full blessing, but they are what they are, and we have to deal with this the best way we can. She really is a lovely girl, and I really am sorry."

"Dad, I'm losing my patience here. What do you think I don't know?"

"You might not remember, but when you were about eleven,

there was a national manhunt. A man had brutally shot and killed his wife, then fled the scene. This man, who was a career criminal, as well as an addict, an alcoholic, and the list goes on—anyway, he was a bad man, and he managed to evade authorities for weeks. They would get leads, then he would be gone. Well, they finally caught him in Arizona. He was on *America's Most Wanted*, and it was all over the news. As the FBI was getting closer to catching him, they thought he might be heading to California. I don't know why, but for some reason, I had a fascination with this guy, so I watched and read every alert that came through to California authorities. As I was researching him, I found out that he and the wife had two young daughters." He pauses and looks at me.

I do remember that happening, but vaguely because I was so young. I know where he's going with this, and the pieces of the Chelsea puzzle fall into place. I wave him on to continue.

"Bo, those little girls were in the house when it happened. Do you know what kind of psychological damage that can do to anyone, but specifically a child? And don't get me wrong; my heart breaks for her and her sister, but, Bo, that was a national manhunt. This will be brought up in the hearings."

He walks over to me and puts a hand on my shoulder. I pick it up and remove it immediately.

"Respectfully, Dad, I don't give a fuck about any of that. That's your life, not mine. You want me to be involved in your life? Then you have to accept that Chelsea is part of my life. Because I don't give a flying fuck about any of this. And, yes, it is absolutely important in her story, but it doesn't define who she is. You don't even know her. You don't know how strong she is, and you telling me all of this makes me admire her even more for everything she's accomplished. So, no, Dad, I'm not letting her go now or ever."

I start to walk away, but he stops me with his next words.

"Bo, you have to think about this. Please. If you don't care about the family, that's fine. I get it; you love her. But don't for a second think this won't affect you too." He huffs. "You're on national television every weekend and for the foreseeable future as well. Do you think people won't find out who she is? Her past? No, she's not on any of the public records for the case, but, Bo, her father is on her birth certificate, and that is public record. If anyone wants to find out who she is, they can get that information. Do you really think she wants all that aired out on TV? Because my guess is, she doesn't, and that's why she hasn't even told you about it. If you really want to be with her, she needs to tell you the truth about everything, and then *you* need to lay out a very realistic picture for her of what your life will be like. Because you won't just be a famous quarterback. You'll always be my son, and like it or not, you have familial responsibilities. Let her make that choice before you drag her into the spotlight."

We stand there, staring at each other. My heart pounding in my chest. And I'm angry because he's not completely wrong. I need to know why she hasn't told me any of this. Why she's fed me pieces of information instead of everything. Why she can say she loves me, but doesn't trust me completely to share this with me. And, maybe worst of all, I need to know if her being with me is going to break the beautiful, carefully guarded heart of the woman I can't stop falling for.

"I have to go." I turn and press the button to the elevator, and my dad doesn't say another word.

CHAPTER
NINETEEN

CHELSEA

I KNEW something was wrong before Bo even went upstairs with his dad. The way his dad had looked at me during the meal, I just knew. He knows who I am. And he's probably upstairs, telling Bo everything right now.

His mom and sisters are talking, mostly to each other, and I'm smiling and nodding like I should, but dread is brewing in my belly the longer I sit here, waiting for Bo to come back. Honestly, I'm half tempted to just walk out and get an Uber back to my apartment.

I keep glancing over toward the elevators, trying not to be obvious about my growing discomfort. And when his mom asks me a question, I'm so lost in thought that I miss hearing it.

"I'm sorry. I didn't hear you. The music seems to be getting louder in here."

"Right? I thought so too. I can barely hear myself." Caroline giggles.

"I just asked if you were going back to Florida for Christmas." His mom lays her hand on top of mine. She's very touchy.

"Oh, I'm not really sure yet. Maybe." I try to smile, but it probably looks more like a grimace.

I look back at the elevators just as the doors to one slide open and Bo steps out. His jaw is tight, eyes stormy, and the first thing he does is drag a hand through his hair.

He strides toward me, his shoulders rigid, his steps quick and deliberate. I push up from my seat, heart kicking hard against my ribs because I'm not sure if I should stay put … or start running.

"Mom, Sav, Caroline, we have to go. Mom, thank you for lunch. I'm sure I'll talk to you soon." He takes my hand and starts to pull me away.

I look over my shoulder at them and wave. "Thank you so much. It was nice to meet y'all."

They wave back, and I can see their mouths moving, but I can't hear what they're saying because we walk right by the loud piano playing. I try to pull my hand from his, but he holds tighter.

When we get outside the hotel, I stop walking and yank my hand out of his hold. "Bo, stop." My heart is racing. "What is going on?"

I just want him to tell me something. I want to know if I'm right.

He paces for a minute, then turns to look at me, hands on his hips. "I'm sorry. Let's just go. I'll tell you about it in the car."

He holds out his hand to me again, but I walk by and head toward the car.

I can hear him following me, but he doesn't try to reach for my hand again. I stand outside my door, and he comes up behind me to open it. When I climb into the car, I buckle my seat belt and look up at Bo when he gets into the driver's side.

He doesn't look at me. He just buckles in and starts the car.

Neither of us speaks until we pull up to his house.

"I'm sorry about that. I just … my dad has been nominated

for the US Supreme Court, and he needed to discuss some things with me."

I swallow the lump in my throat. "Wow, Bo. That's huge. Like, really huge."

"Yeah, I know. It, uh, comes with a lot of pressure for the family too." He looks out the window. "Please don't say anything to anyone in the house yet. I really don't want to talk about it anymore today."

I nod, but I have a feeling there's more to it. "Yeah, of course."

I don't wait for him to say anything else. I unbuckle and get out of the car and go into the house.

Noelle and Brooke are in the kitchen when I walk in, laughing and making a mess that Casey will no doubt clean up. They both turn when they hear the door open, and I see Casey and Silas look over from the couch.

"Hey, Chels! How was meet the family?" Noelle smiles at me like she's actually excited to hear about it.

"It was fine. I'm gonna go change out of these clothes though."

I hook a thumb over my shoulder and walk to Bo's room. I keep a few things over here for when I stay the night, so I grab a pair of lounge pants from the dresser and a T-shirt. I toss my crossbody on the bed and quickly undress. Just as I pull the shirt over my head, Bo walks in and shuts the door behind him.

"Chelsea ..." He stands, leaning against the door. "We need to talk."

Nope. No, I don't want to do this right now.

"Bo, I don't feel like this is a good time to talk about anything important. Our friends are right outside the door. Maybe I should just go back to my place tonight. I'm not really hungry anymore anyway."

"Why would you go home? I just want to talk to you about a few things." He sounds tired more than upset.

"Bo …" I sit down on the bed and let out a heavy sigh. "What? What do you want to talk about that can't wait?"

"Why didn't your dad take care of you and your sister after your mom died?" He pushes off the door and walks toward me slowly.

"I think you already know the answer to your question." I look down and start to bite on the inside of my lip.

"But I want to hear your story from you." He shakes his head and runs his hand through his hair. "I don't understand why you won't tell me. You know I love you. Nothing you tell me could change that."

I bark out a laugh. "Okay, if that's true, why does it really matter why my dad didn't take care of us? Is this what you were talking to your dad about upstairs, or was he really nominated for the Supreme Court?" I gasp. "Oh my God. I get it. He doesn't want you to be with me."

"Chelsea, baby, I want you to trust me enough to tell me everything. And the problem is, I don't think you do, and I'm trying to figure out why you haven't told me. I suspected there was more than what you were sharing. Sure, you've given me pieces, but not the whole story. And I've been patient, and I haven't pushed. I wanted you to talk to me and tell me more when you felt ready. But things are changing, and I think the time to lay it all out has come."

He kneels down in front of me and tries to take my hands, but I pull them away.

"You want to know why? Okay, I'll tell you what you clearly already know. Paint you a pretty picture so you can see just how fucked up my life was." I look him in the eye. "My father and my mother were not good people, Bo. They were addicts, alcoholics, and abusive to each other mostly, but also to me and my sister. We didn't have birthday parties and vacations and private schools like you did. We didn't have parents who loved us and wanted to make sure we were fed and tucked in safely at night. I had to grow up a lot faster than you did because I didn't have a choice. I needed to survive, and I needed to keep my sister alive. And unfortunately, we have a very failed legal system, and no one ever saved us."

I cross my arms over my chest. If I could protect my heart, my past, and all my secrets with that one simple motion, I would. But this is my truth, and he wants it. He's been asking for months to really know me, to see every part of me I keep hidden. And now he's getting it. I just hope it's not too much ... that the weight of who I am doesn't scare him away.

"The night my father killed my mother started out the same as all the others. They were drunk or high or a combination of both. They fought, I took my sister to our room, and then he left. I'm not sure how long he was gone because my sister and I fell asleep. But when they started fighting, I knew something was really wrong. On bad nights like that, I would take my sister into our closet, and we would hide there until our parents stopped fighting or passed out. Except it didn't stop. We heard a bang, then yelling, then another set of banging. My sister and I sat in that closet and listened to our father kill our mother, and we couldn't do anything about it."

I stand and start pacing the room, the memories rushing back so vividly that they almost knock me off-balance. I can smell the mildewed carpet and the walls, thick with the permanent residue of nicotine and anger.

"My sister peed in her pants while I was holding her in my arms. I know now that we were both in shock, but we stayed in that closet until the police came. I couldn't move, and I was terrified of walking out of our room and seeing what had happened, even though I knew it in my gut." I stop and look at him. "Even after the police got there, they had to physically remove us from the closet and practically pry my sister from my arms. I didn't trust anyone because ... no one ever saved us."

Bo stands and tries to reach for me. "Chelsea, I'm so sorry that happened to you. Truly. I can't imagine."

"No, Bo, you can't. And I wouldn't want to wish what we

went through on anyone." I walk over to his dresser and lift up the picture of his family. "See this? You had a perfect life. And believe me, I'm glad you did. But most people, Bo, aren't as fortunate as you are. Most families have deep, dark, dirty, and very ugly secrets. Unfortunately for me, mine was all over the news for a long time. Thankfully, my and my sister's identities were concealed since we were minors. But people knew anyway and always looked at us just a little different. With judgment and pity."

"I would never judge you by your past, and I think you know that. And I hate that you went through all of that. I wish I could erase it all."

"But you can't, Bo. It's part of my story, and it has shaped who I am as a person. In some twisted way, I'm almost glad that it all happened because my aunt got us. We were saved by her because of a terrible act of violence between two people who'd had no business having children at all. They were consumed by each other, by their addictions. And that, Bo, is terrifying to me. That you can lose yourself so much in someone else."

"Chelsea, love isn't like that though, and what you and I are building isn't like that. I'm giving you everything that I have. You have my heart completely, and I want to build a life with you. I just need to know you're in this in the same way that I am because, baby, it's not always going to be easy. There are people that will find out about your past, and you will be in the public eye by being with me. Can you do this with me?"

I love him. I really, truly do, but even that scares me. The thought of opening up to him is one thing; the thought of everyone else knowing—my past, my sister's life, my aunt's secrets—is almost too much to bear. My chest feels tight, my stomach twists, and I can't stop imagining the world prying into parts of my life I've worked so hard to protect. I want him to see me, to love me, but the weight of it all feels crushing. I'm not sure I can handle letting him in … or letting anyone else see what's been hidden for so long.

"Bo, what is it you want from me?" I take in a shuddering breath because this beautiful man in front of me deserves everything that he is asking of me. And it should be an easy answer, but I just … can't.

"I want everything you have to give. Because I will give you every part of me. I need you to trust me and trust us."

"Bo, I want you to tell me the truth. Did your dad ask you to stop seeing me?"

He drops his head back and closes his eyes. "It doesn't matter. This is about us."

"Tell me."

Bo looks up at me with sadness in his eyes, like it hurts him to tell me. "Yes, but I told him it wasn't gonna happen."

I believe what he's saying—I really do. But I also can't be the cause for creating problems for him and his family. So, this is just another reason why I need to go. If I stay in this, it will hurt us eventually. I can't stop the tears that start to run down my face.

He rushes to me and wipes the wetness from my cheeks. "Baby, don't cry. It will be okay. As long as we're together and give each other everything we have, it will always be okay."

I turn my face and kiss his wet palm. "But I can't give *you* everything. I'm sorry."

I pull away from him, grab my bag from the bed, and rush out the door. Noelle sees me and drops the potato in her hand and tries to follow me, but I stop her.

As I close the door behind me, I hear her yell, "What the fuck did you do, Bo Callaway?"

But I keep walking, get into my car, and cry all the way to my apartment.

CHAPTER
TWENTY

CHELSEA

THE LAST FEW weeks have been pretty fucking terrible. Bo texts me every day, but I don't respond. He's come by the apartment and waited for me, but when I see his car, I keep driving. If I'm home, I don't answer the door.

Noelle has been staying at the apartment with me more than usual because I think she's worried about me. Casey stays here a lot, too, but he never says anything to me about Bo.

I gave Noelle a watered-down version of what had happened and shared some more about my past that she hadn't known. She's been really great, and Charlie has come over a few times to hang out with us too.

I called my aunt last week and told her I wouldn't be coming home for Christmas. She and my sister were disappointed and tried convincing me to change my mind. They've been sending me texts of various vacation spots to try to get me to spend Christmas with them anywhere. I just ... have no interest in doing anything.

I've gotten emails from two of the law schools I applied to, but I don't even care about opening those. I'm sad, and I can't figure a way out of it.

Noelle thinks I should just talk to Bo, but I don't know what I would even say.

The Stallions have made it to the playoffs, so I've been torturing myself by watching every interview and highlight that has Bo in it, which is a lot. He's always professional and courteous, but I can tell he's not completely himself. And I feel like I'm responsible for it.

I'm watching an interview right now, and he's talking about the upcoming game, and just hearing his voice makes me want to cry. And I'm not a crier. I literally hate everything about life right now. I'm so focused on what he's saying that I don't even hear the knock on my door at first.

"Chelsea! Stop flicking your bean and open up!" a female voice says, giggling.

"Jesus, Torie. Do you have to be so crass? I swear, you and your sister are too much for me," another voice says.

What the hell? Is that my sister? And my aunt?

I jump up from the couch and look through the peephole in the door. I can hear them now on the other side of the door, but I can't see them because someone is covering the hole with their finger.

"I don't open the door to strangers," I tease.

The finger moves, and I see my sister's smiling face. "Open the door! It's cold out here!"

I unlock the door, and we all squeal and hug. "Oh my God! What are you guys doing here?"

My sister is in shorts, flip-flops, and a sweatshirt. Completely inappropriate attire for the cold here in Oklahoma.

"What on earth are you wearing, Tor? It's freezing here."

"What am I wearing? What are you wearing? You look like a grandma. And your hair. Is there a bird living in it? I can loan you my brush." She walks past me and into my apartment.

"Don't hold back, Torie." My aunt shakes her head. "It's not that bad, sweetie. But have you showered today?" She kisses the side of my head.

I'm so happy they're here. I didn't realize how much I needed to see them until, well, I saw them. "Yes, I did. But I didn't dry my hair, which is why it looks like"—I pat my head—"this."

"I'll brush it out for you. But first, I need some pants and some fuzzy socks. I'm frozen." She walks back toward my room.

I look at my aunt, and we both laugh at my sister.

"I told her it would be cold, but she didn't believe me."

"I believed you, but, like, I didn't fully understand the level of cold," she says from my room.

"What are you guys doing here? Not that I'm not so excited that you're here, but why didn't you tell me you were coming?" I walk into the kitchen and open the fridge. "Do you want anything to drink?"

"Yeah, I'll take a water," my aunt says. "Well, we were really bummed that you weren't coming home for Christmas, and I could just tell that something was wrong and you weren't going to tell me about it, so I thought we should come and see what was going on."

I hand her a water and grab one for me and my sister. "I'm fine. Really. Just stressed about the last few weeks of school and finishing finals and stuff."

Torie comes back into the room wearing a pair of my pants and socks, with my brush in her hand. "I call bullshit. Something is going on, and you're gonna tell us what it is." She takes the water from me and moves over to the couch. "Come sit. Let me help you with this hair."

I follow her and push the coffee table out so I can sit between her legs. My aunt joins us and sits in the chair so I can look at her while Torie brushes my hair.

"I'm so happy to see you guys." My eyes start to water.

"Okay, see this?" My aunt points at me. "You don't do this. This crying thing. Being overly emotional. That's not our girl."

She gasps. "Chelsea Sullivan. Are you pregnant?" Her hands cover her mouth, eyes wide.

"What? No!" I shake my head and laugh.

"OMG, can you imagine?!" Torie cackles.

I turn my head. "I'm not, but why would that be so funny?" I have no idea why I'm getting defensive.

She stops laughing when she sees my face. "It's not, Chels. Talk to us." She puts her hand on my cheek.

I take a deep breath and sigh.

For the last decade, it's been the three of us, and I've never known my aunt or sister to hop on a plane on a whim. In fact, Aunt Laura keeps pretty strict office hours and hardly ever takes vacations. They're here. They came for me. It's like when I was the little girl locked in a closet, waiting in silence for someone to come along and find me, and Aunt Laura is here … again. I don't want to hide my feelings from her. Not this time.

"It's over between me and Bo."

Torie points at my aunt and says, "I told you that was it."

"That my relationship was totally screwed?" I ask her.

"Well, not necessarily that, but I bet it had to do with him. You usually drop about five *Bo does this, and Bo said that* in every conversation we have, and you haven't done that in a few weeks, so I figured it out." Torie puts her hand on the top of my head and turns it forward.

"How do you think you messed it up?" my aunt asks.

So, I tell them everything—from meeting his family to the conversation after. All of it.

"Oh, Chels. I'm sorry, sweetie. But if I may, I'd like to say a few things." My aunt sits up in the chair and leans forward, her elbows on her knees. "I think you're making a mistake."

"Yeah, I mean, I kinda already feel bad about it, but thanks."

"No, I mean, I think you're making a mistake about not letting him in, Chelsea." She picks up her water and takes a sip, then sets it back down.

"You know, your dad and I didn't have the best childhood.

Now, he was a lot older than me, so I don't really remember what it was like for him, and honestly, I think I got the better end of the stick because my parents weren't in good health by the time I was old enough to understand that they were alcoholics.

"Now, your dad, he chose a path similar to our parents. Became victimized by it actually. Probably because that's what was familiar to him, but also, some people are just predisposed to being addicts, whether it's alcohol or another substance.

"And then when our mom died when I was fourteen, your dad stopped coming around completely because he and your grandpa didn't get along at all." She drops her head and shakes it.

"My dad, like yours, wasn't a nice man. So, I was quiet, did what I was supposed to, and stayed away from home as much as possible. And then my junior year of high school, my math teacher told me I was smart." She looks at us and smiles. "No one had ever said anything like that to me before."

"No one? Not even other teachers?" Torie asks her.

"Nope. I was quiet and kept to myself. I did my assignments on time and did well in school, but no one ever noticed me, I guess. Either way, that's not the point of my story. My point is, I didn't let my circumstances define me, and I don't want you to let yours or your past determine yours. By watching my friends' families and—it sounds silly—TV shows, I recognized that I wanted more out of my life than what I was living. And all I needed was that one little nudge from a teacher to give me the confidence to do it. Now, I hope in the time you girls have been with me, I have shown you that, but maybe I haven't done a good job of it." Her voice cracks.

We both move over to her and hug her.

"No, you've been our biggest cheerleader, and I know how lucky we are that the social worker found you. And that you gave us and do give us so much love and support." I tell her.

"I hope so." She wipes her eyes, smiling faintly. "I just don't ever want to see either of you to see yourself as victim. You're fighters."

I gnaw on my lip and look to the side. *Fighter. Drama.* Doesn't she see it's all so connected? There's a name for it in psychology —the way we become our parents without even realizing it. They call it intergenerational transmission or sometimes intergenerational trauma when what gets passed down is the pain.

It's not just the drinking or the tempers; it's the craving for chaos. The kind of love that burns instead of warms. Addictive personalities feed on passion and fear and the high of being wanted one minute and worthless the next. It's in our blood.

And based on how hard and fast I fell for Bo, I have no doubt I could end up just like them.

I glance back at her. "In your medical training, did you ever learn about intergenerational trauma? How we repeat our parents' patterns over and over—what's it called, repetition compulsion?"

Her brow furrows as she studies me. "Is that what all that adoption talk was about a few weeks ago? You think your dad's behavior is something that's been passed down to you?"

I let out a shaky breath. "You said your childhood was fucked too. It's clearly generational."

She reaches out, resting a hand over mine. "Generational trauma stops with us." Her voice softens, steady but sure.

Tears start to fall down my cheeks. "You sound so positive. And, well, fine … we aren't our pasts, but the past is still ours, and there's no hiding it once people know. I don't trust anyone not to exploit our secrets."

"Oh, kiddo, that is my one regret. I think I should have given you girls an example of what a healthy relationship looks like. I was so focused on you both that I never took the time for myself to find love, which, in turn, you also missed out on. I mean, I'm not an expert on relationships, especially since I haven't had more than hookups in the last twelve years, but"—she pauses—

"you both need love. Healthy love. But you have to be willing to give in return too."

"I know that, and it's not that I don't want to give everything to Bo because I do. I think I'm just scared. I know we're not my parents, but I also feel like I could get completely lost in him." I shrug.

"Let me ask you something though. Why would that be so bad? He sounds like a good guy, he's definitely handsome, he comes from a good family—oh, and he's going to be a professional football player. I don't see what the problem is." She puts her hand on my shoulder.

"I mean, when you put it like that, I'll step in and take over from here, Chelsea," my sister teases.

"Not a chance, little sister." I playfully push her. "Aren't you worried about any of this stuff, Torie? Do you ever worry about someone finding out what Dad did or where he is or how Mom died?"

She shakes her head. "No, I really don't. It's probably because I don't remember as much as you do. And my memories of that night are fuzzy. I'm sorry that you do remember more and that you lived it. I hate to say it, but like Aunt Laura, I got the better end of the stick because most of my memories are us with her and not Mom and Dad. But, Chels, if he knows all of that and still wants to be with you, support you, I think you should let him. I think he would protect you too."

"I agree with Torie. I think you need to trust him and let him love you and take care of you. But you also need to be able to do the same for him." Aunt Laura sucks in a deep breath. "You're going to hate that I'm saying this, but I really think you need to read that letter from your dad. I think it might help you in this situation with Bo."

"Torie, did you get a letter too?" I turn and look at her.

"No, I never got letters like you did, thankfully." She shrugs.

"You girls know I would write to him once a year, right?" My aunt takes our hands in hers. "I would tell him about your accomplishments and how beautiful you both were, how happy you were. At first, I felt like I needed to do it because I thought he would care and want to know all of those things were true. But then, one time, he asked me for money for a new lawyer to try to get his sentence reduced, and I wouldn't give it to him because I honestly believe he's where he should be." She looks at us both. "He stopped writing me back after that, but I kept writing and giving him yearly updates. Because you girls haven't let what he did define you. You're out there, making your dreams come true, Chelsea. Wouldn't it be great to have someone by your side, cheering you on? Don't give him or the memory of your parents any power over your future. Not giving Bo everything in return is them winning in a way. Do you know what I mean?"

"Aunt Laura, you're like a love doctor too. You should have a podcast," Torie chimes in.

"Torie, we're trying to be serious here. Although I don't hate the idea of a podcast. We'll put a cap on that for later." She reaches for my hand. "Read the letter. And then think about what I'm saying."

"Okay, I'll think about it." I hug her, and then Torie wraps her arms around us both.

The door opens, and Noelle walks in with a bag in her hand. "Oh my God! Laura! Torie! What are you guys doing here?" She drops the bag and comes over to us to join in on the hug.

"We came to get our girl out of this funk." Torie tells her.

"Oh good. She wasn't listening to me, so I'm glad you came to talk some sense into her." Noelle pulls out of the hug, but reaches for my hand. "You know I love you."

"I do know, and I love you back." I squeeze her hand and let it go. "What's in the bag?" I tip my head toward the bag on the floor.

"That would be for you." She walks over to it and picks it up, then hands it to me. "Open it."

I set the bag on my lap and pull out the tissue paper first.

There's a note inside, so I take that out and set it to the side. A black shirt and a pair of red-and-black checkered pants are inside the bag.

"What is this?" After pulling out the pants, I lay them next to me.

"Oh, it's for the Christmas PJ party!" Noelle claps her hands. "My birthday is coming up, and we're doing a Christmas slash B-day party for me."

"But who—" My words stop when I pull out the shirt. There's a Christmas tree on the front of it, and sitting under the tree is the word *everything* in a fancy script. "Bo." I lift up the card and open it.

Chelsea,
I'm not giving up on us.
Please come back to me.
I love you.
Bo

"What does it say?" Torie looks over my shoulder. "Oh, Chels, you have to go. When is the party?"

"In two days," Noelle says.

"Perfect. We leave that morning, so you can go! Although if we were going to be here, I would have crashed your party, Noelle." Torie wraps an arm around her.

"I wish you could stay and come! It'll be fun. I'm so excited." Noelle claps her hands.

Aunt Laura stands up from the chair. "We'd better get going and get checked in to our hotel."

"You guys can stay here if you want. I can sleep on the couch," I offer.

"Oh, no. We got a room, but we'll pick you up tomorrow. Get you out of the apartment for a while. Maybe we'll do a little

Christmas shopping." She pulls me up and gives me a hug. "I love you, sweet girl. After you read the letter, you can call me. But, Chels, get it done."

"Okay, I will. Love you guys. I'm so happy you're here." I hug my sister next.

"Me too, but I'm keeping these pants until we leave."

I walk them to the door. "Call me in the morning when you're ready to get me or I can meet you at your hotel."

"Okay, talk to you tomorrow!" my aunt says.

I shut the door and go sit down on the couch.

Noelle comes over and sits next to me and wraps an arm around me. "You good?" she asks.

I nod. "Yeah, I'm good. Surprised to see them for sure. But also surprised by these." I hold up the shirt.

"I'm not at all surprised by the PJs. He really misses you." She scrunches her nose.

"I really miss him too. It's scary though. You're with your forever person, and you already knew him, so there wasn't all the unknown, like there is with us. And your past isn't like mine."

"Well, no, but it was still scary. You were there, ma'am. You know I was scared about ruining our friendship, but then it got to a point that I knew I had to take the chance anyway. And it wasn't easy or without our share of issues. Trey was a lot of baggage—different from yours, yes, but still a lot." She shakes her head. "You just need to give him the chance to show you he's the man he says he is, and honestly, I think he has the whole time. Bo's not the kind of guy to play games. Trust him. Believe him."

"I'm working through it." I nod.

"Okay, good. Are you okay if I go to Casey's tonight? I can stay here if you need me to." She takes my hand in hers.

"No, I'm good, I promise. Go be with your man. I'm probably just gonna go to bed anyway. It sounds like I have a busy day tomorrow." I stand and let go of her hand.

She starts to walk toward her room. "You'll have fun tomorrow."

I put the PJs back in the bag and walk toward my room and meet her in the hall. "I'll see you tomorrow maybe, and if not, I'll see you at your party."

"You're coming?" She bounces on her feet.

"Well, yeah. I always planned to come."

"I wasn't totally sure, but I'm really glad you're coming. It wouldn't be the same without you." She hugs me. "I'll come over and get you. My PJs haven't arrived yet, so if they don't show up, I'll have to wear my backup pair."

"You have a backup pair of Christmas PJs?"

"Uh, yeah. My name is Noelle, and my birthday is right before Christmas. Of course I have backups. Multiple." She laughs. "But I really want to wear these new ones."

"Right, yeah. That makes sense. I guess I never paid attention to your Christmas PJ collection." I push her toward the door. "Go see your man."

"Love you, Chels." She blows me a kiss.

"Love you back." I pretend to catch her kiss.

I watch her leave and when I hear her lock the door, I go into my room. My phone is on the charger on the nightstand next to my bed and I pick it up to see if Bo has texted me tonight. And he has.

Bo: Good night, Lucky.

I hesitate for a minute, but type out a reply.

Chelsea: Thanks for the PJs. Night.

He replies instantly.

Bo: You're welcome. And just so you know, I
have the matching set, and I really want to see
you wearing them for the party.

Matching? So, they both say everything?

I don't reply because if I do, we'll just end up going back and forth, and then we'll get on the phone, and I just need to think a little more. And I need to read this letter from my dad, as much as I don't want to.

I set the bag on my bed, and then I go to my closet and pull the shoebox off the shelf that has the letter from my dad in it.

My fingers are shaking as I open the envelope. I can see his handwriting through the paper, and I recognize it immediately. It's been years since I've seen it though. I sit down on my bed and then pull it out and unfold the white paper. I suck in a deep breath and start to read.

Chelsea,

I know you probably won't read this, since Laura says you haven't read any of my other letters. Can't say I blame you. But I wanted you to know I'm dying. Got stage four lung cancer. They say I don't have much time left, so I better get my affairs in order. Not that I got many affairs to take care of, but I did want to make sure I said goodbye to you.

Torie probably don't remember much about me, which is for the best. But I hope you'll tell her what I'm saying here.

I don't know if you know this, but your aunt's been writing me over the years. She's told me about the things you've done, and I just want you to know I'm proud of both of you. I know that might not mean much coming from me, but it's the truth.

I've been busy these last fifteen years. Got my high school diploma and even took some college classes, mostly just to pass the time. Had a few jobs here and there and even started up a little gardening club. Keeps me busy. Most of my days are spent in Bible study now.

I know it seems too late to be finding guidance, but a man like me needs something to hold on to. What I've learned over the years is that I wasn't a good man. Wasn't raised by a good man, who wasn't raised by one either. Guess it just kept going down the line.

The best thing that ever happened to you and your sister was being put with my sister.

I'm glad Laura gave you the kind of life your mom and I never could. She's done right by you, like I always figured she would. She was always the smart one and from what I hear you take after her more than you ever did your old man.

I ain't gonna waste your time with some long apology. Don't think that'd fix anything anyway. But I am sorry —for what you and your sister went through because of me and your mom. You didn't deserve that.

I've been trying to make peace with the Lord before I go, and I hope maybe one day you can find it in your heart to forgive me, even just a little.

Goodbye, Chelsea. You and your sister take care of each other, and always follow the light.
Robert Sullivan

Not Dad. Robert Sullivan. He has never been a father to me or my sister though, and I guess he knows that and has at least an ounce of respect for us not to insult us by calling himself Dad.

I fold up the paper and put it back inside the envelope. My hands are no longer shaking, and I'm not really sure what I should feel right now. I thought maybe I would be a little more … upset, but all I feel is detached.

I set the letter next to me on the bed and walk around to the other side of my bed and get my phone off the charger.

> Chelsea: I read it.

Aunt Laura: And?

> Chelsea: He's dying.

Aunt Laura: I know, he told me in his letter to me. What else did he say?

> Chelsea: Hang on.

I pick up the letter, take a picture of it, and send it to her.

Aunt Laura: How do you feel?

> Chelsea: I feel…nothing. Nothing may be a good thing. I honestly thought I'd feel distraught after reading.

Aunt Laura: Okay, that's fair. Do you want me to come back over?

> Chelsea: No, I'm fine. Honestly.

> Aunt Laura: If you change your mind and need me, I'll be there.

> Chelsea: I know, and I love you for it.

> Aunt Laura: I love you. So much.

> Chelsea: I'll see you tomorrow.

> Aunt Laura: Night.

The letter is still in my hand from taking the picture of it, but I have the overwhelming urge to burn it. I don't want any part of this man to touch the life I'm creating for myself. And just having this here feels like poison.

I take the letter and envelope in my hand and walk into the kitchen and grab the lighter we use for candles. I definitely can't set off the smoke alarms, so I go to the sliding doors leading out to the tiny porch we have and open it. The burst of cold hits me, nearly taking my breath away.

Flicking the lighter, I watch the flame glow. Then I place the letter under it and watch it catch fire. I set the paper on the ground, then toss the envelope on top of it. I stand there, watching it burn until the fire goes out. The ashes scatter as a gust of icy air blows through.

I look up into the sky and see a million stars shining and smile. For the first time in my life, I finally feel free.

I walk back into the apartment, lock the door, and walk back into my room and pick up my phone off the bed.

> Chelsea: I burned it.

> Aunt Laura: Well done.

CHAPTER
TWENTY-ONE

BO

I KNOW she's coming tonight, and the anticipation is making me crazy. I'm wearing a hole in the carpet, and I'm probably driving Charlie nuts. But I think something else is going on because Casey is acting a little squirrelly too. He and Charlie have been doing a lot of whispering today.

Silas has noticed it, too, but he just shrugs and shakes his head.

"Dude, settle down. She's coming. Come watch TV with us." Silas waves me over to the couch, but I sit in the chair I've basically claimed as mine.

Aston and Ace Griffith are on the other side of the couch anyway.

"Yeah, what's your deal, Callaway?" Ace asks me.

I ignore him.

"I know she's coming, but I want her to be wearing the PJs I bought for us. But what if she doesn't?" I sit up in the chair and rest my elbows on my knees and lean toward Silas.

"Then she doesn't, and you keep trying." He looks at me pointedly. "Right?"

"Okay." I nod. "Yeah, you're totally right. But what do I do if she doesn't?"

"Callaway, you're killing me. I've never seen you this nervous, even in a playoff game when the championship is on the line."

"Well, that's because I have some control over the outcome. This? It's all up to her. She's it for me, you know?" I flop back in my chair.

"I get it. I mean, I haven't experienced that yet, but I get it." He nods, smirking at me.

But he looks over his shoulder toward Brooke, who's in the kitchen with Charlie, Arbor and Lily, wearing pajameralls, like he is.

"Oh yeah?" I tip my head toward the kitchen.

He holds his hands out. "What?"

The front door opens, and Noelle comes into the house first, and then … she's here.

"Hey, y'all!" Noelle says, holding some packages.

"Happy birthday, Noelle!" everyone shouts, except me.

My eyes are locked on Chelsea. Who's wearing my PJs.

Thank fuck.

"Aww, thanks!" she says, handing Casey the packages to put under the tree.

"Charlie, it smells so good in here," Chelsea says, walking into the kitchen.

"Hey, girl. Thank you so much, and I agree! The food will be ready in just a few minutes. We have snacks that Silas helped with, and Bo made some apps if you want to eat something before dinner." Charlie turns to look from the oven and looks at Chelsea. "Love your PJs, Chels. Looks like you have a match in the house, huh?" Charlie glances over at me and gives me a wink.

I can't hear what she says because something is happening with Noelle and Casey, and then Charlie is yelling at Casey about not ruining her plans, and it's all too much for me to follow because all I want to see is her.

"Holy shit, is he proposing?" Ace whispers loudly and pulls out his phone.

"Shut up, dumbass." Aston elbows him.

"Ow, asshole. I'm telling Mom." Ace shoves back.

"Would you both shut the fuck up?" Silas glares at them.

Brooke looks over at Silas and smiles.

I look back toward the kitchen to look for Chelsea and see she's standing near Casey and Noelle, her hands covering her mouth, and it looks like her eyes are a little glassy. She looks over at me, and I can see her smile behind her hands.

If I didn't want to ruin Casey's moment, I would run over and grab my girl, but I'm polite. I'll wait another few seconds for them to wrap this up.

Between the chatter from the twins and Charlie's friends, I can barely hear what Casey is saying, but then they're both kneeling, then kissing, so I'm gonna go with my gut and say we have a newly engaged couple in the house.

Everyone stands and cheers, running over to congratulate the couple.

Charlie is going on about Casey ruining her plans, but then they all start laughing, and Charlie announces that we're having birthday cake before dinner.

Chelsea is still looking at me, and when I stand and she sees my PJs, she smiles softly at me.

I walk toward her and stop close enough that she can hear me over everyone singing happy birthday to Noelle.

"Hi." I reach out and loop her pinkie with mine.

"Hi." She tugs my hand toward her body. "I like your PJs." She nods toward my shirt.

"Thanks. I like yours." I tilt my head toward the direction of my room. "Can we talk?"

She nods and lets me lead her down the hall. I release her

hand just so I can close the door. When I turn back to her, she's sitting on my bed.

"When you said we had matching PJs, I was picturing yours also saying *everything*, but this is much better." She tugs at the hem of my shirt. "*I Have Everything I Need.*"

"It's true." I kneel down in front of her, and she opens her legs so I can fit between them. "You're everything to me."

She puts her hands on my face, then pushes them through my hair. "I've missed you."

"I've been here, waiting. You didn't have to miss me." I take hold of her wrists. "But I missed you too."

"I know." Her thumbs brush over my cheeks. "I'm sorry, Bo. There were a lot of feelings rolling around, and it was … uncomfortable to me because it scared me. And I know we have a lot to talk about, but I'm here. And I'm ready to give you everything."

I drop my head and let out a rush of air. "Thank fuck."

"Can you kiss me now?" She cups my face and traces my bottom lip with her thumb. "I really missed these lips."

"They're yours."

We lean in at the same time, and our mouths crash together. I slide my hands under her shirt just so I can feel her skin.

We break apart, panting.

"Tell me you're staying tonight?" I rest my forehead against hers.

"Yes. Besides, I imagine Casey and Noelle will want some privacy tonight, right?" She laughs.

"Yeah, I'm sure they do. He's probably ready to throw her over his shoulder by now." I stand and hold my hand out for her to take.

"Oh, for sure."

We walk out of my room, hand in hand.

Brooke looks over at us as we come into the room. "Nice of you guys to join us. Now, can we open presents?" she asks Charlie.

"Y'all have ruined all my plans for tonight, so do whatever

you want to do. But I want it on the record that I had an amazing night planned for us. And I'm not cleaning the kitchen, so, Griffith boys, you're both on dish duty after presents." She points at them.

"Wait, why do we have to do it?" Ace asks.

Aston rolls his eyes. "No problem, Charlie. We got it."

Silas raises his hand. "Even though I helped with food prep, I'll help too."

The guys look at me, and I look at Charlie. "I made the appetizers."

"Bo, you get a pass tonight so you and your girl can make up." She winks at me.

Silas stands up and walks over to the tree. "Who wants to go first?"

All the girls, except mine, yell, "Me!"

After presents, we ate and watched *Elf*. Casey and Noelle ducked out before the movie started though. And Arbor, Lily, and the twins just left. Then Charlie went into her room. But Brooke is asleep on the couch, next to Silas, who is also asleep.

"Do you think we should wake them?" Chelsea asks, tilting her head to see me.

"Nah, I'm sure he'll wake up soon and go to his room. And Brooke won't leave this late. She'll probably just go into Charlie's room. You ready for bed?" I kiss the tip of her nose.

"Yeah, I'm ready." She wraps her arms around my neck as I start to stand.

I carry her bridal-style down the hallway toward my room. "You need to go to the bathroom or anything?"

"Actually, yeah. You didn't throw away my toothbrush, did you?" She winces. "I probably should have brought a little bag with me, I guess."

I bark out a laugh. "No, I didn't throw away your toothbrush." I set her down in the bathroom. "I had to believe I would get you to come back to me." I give her a peck on the lips.

She grabs my shirt and pulls me down to her face again. "Thank you for not giving up on me."

"Chelsea, I will never give up on you. I will always stand by you; you just have to let me." I cup her face and kiss her again, deeper this time.

She pulls away first. "Let me brush my teeth, and then we can talk?"

"Can I brush mine too, or do you want privacy?" I smirk at her.

She nods. "I think we can brush our teeth together."

We both prepare our brushes with toothpaste.

I watch her in the mirror and smile. "I know you're gonna tell me I'm cheesy, but I love doing life things with you. Brushing our teeth together is a little thing and probably weird, but it's also pretty personal, and I like doing it with you."

She smiles around her toothbrush. "That is cheesy, but I love it."

When we finish, I leave the bathroom so she can finish doing what she needs to do in private. Chelsea said we're not quite at the stage where we can pee in front of each other. She said we need to have a little mystery, and we both laughed.

I take off my shirt as I walk into my room, then pull the covers back on the bed. I sit on the edge of the bed and take my socks off, then climb in, leaving the covers off for now. I'll get too hot in these pants. But also, I'm dying to get my hands on her, but I'll let her set the pace. We do need to talk. I want to understand where her head is, but I also want to know that she's not going to change her mind about us.

She walks in a few minutes later and closes the door behind her. Chelsea never gets nervous, but she seems a bit timid or something about getting into bed with me, so I pat the spot next to me and smile at her.

"I won't bite. Well, unless you tell me to." I wink at her to try to make her laugh and ease her nerves, and it works.

She sits on the bed and faces me, sitting crisscross. Her elbows rest on her knees, and she nervously picks at her fingernails. So, I sit up and face her, mimicking her position, even though it's not really comfortable for me with my long legs. I reach over and take her hands in mine.

"Talk to me." I bring one of her hands to my mouth and kiss her fingers.

"Bo, I'm really sorry I hurt you. Not that it's an excuse, but I think the whole day was a little overwhelming for me, and then when I felt like I was being backed into a corner, my guard went up." She sucks in a deep breath, then exhales. "And to be clear, it had nothing at all to do with you or me wanting to be with you. It's childhood trauma stuff that, honestly, I'll probably always have to deal with in some way or another. But this"—she waves her hand between us—"was new territory because I'd never allowed myself to love someone the way I love you. And honestly, it scared me. Still does a little, but not enough that I don't want to push through that fear."

I sit and listen patiently because I want to hear everything she has to say before I respond.

"I told you about my parents, and logically, I know that not all relationships are toxic like theirs was, but that's the only example that I lived with. Even during the rare times they tried to get sober, they were still chaotic. They would fight, then make up. And they were completely in their own little world. It was like nothing else existed for them except each other and their addiction." She shakes her head. "That's scary when you see that as a kid, and you don't really understand any of it. As I got older and started to realize that this wasn't a normal family dynamic, I decided that I never wanted to lose myself like that to anyone. Does that make sense?"

I nod. "It does, and I can't say that I understand because I didn't have that experience, but I can say that I promise you that we will never be like that. I mean, I am obsessed with you." I smile at her softly. "But I think instead of getting lost in each other, we'll grow together. And I know we'll face a lot of challenges, but I want to face them together. Because I think you and I will be stronger together. And when you can't be, I'll hold you up."

"Yeah, I can see that now, but it's just hard to believe that it can be real sometimes. You know?"

"Chelsea, I want you to trust me, trust in us, and know I'll always have your back. And I know you'll have mine too. Because that's just who you are, but I also know you love me for me and not because of my last name or because I'm on TV every weekend. And that's how I know in my gut that this is where I want to be."

"I do love you, and I will always have your back, too, but, Bo, you also need to take into consideration that there is a chance people will find out about my past. A past that I've worked hard to run away from. I came here to escape the memories, to be a normal girl going to college. And not the girl who was found in a closet while her mom lay dead in the next room." She swallows. "The girl whose dad was on national television, running from the law, with his picture all over the news."

"None of that matters to *me* though. Do you understand that? I don't give a fuck what anyone says or thinks about us because what we have is ours only. But don't think for a second that I won't protect you. Because I will destroy anyone who hurts you in any way."

"You really mean that, don't you?" She tilts her head to the side, eyes roaming over my face like she's trying, hoping, to see the truth there.

"I absolutely mean it to my bones. Trust me, baby. Believe in us. Let go of your fears, and if you can't, give them to me to shoulder."

She smiles and squeezes my hands. "I do trust you. And I want to be all of these things for you too. I want to be your protector, but also your partner. I want ..." She swallows. "I want to do this life with you."

I pull her by her hands into my lap because I can't wait another second to have her in my arms. "That's good because you're mine, and I had no intention of letting you go."

"You were pretty confident that I would come over tonight in these PJs, weren't you?" She pulls her head back to look at me.

I tilt my head from side to side. "I mean, I might have been pacing the house a little. I knew you wouldn't miss Noelle's birthday, and I was hopeful after you texted me the other night, thanking me for the PJs, but until I saw you walk in the door, I was holding my breath. And if that hadn't worked, I would have tried something else."

"Oh, yeah? Like what?" She lays her head on my shoulder.

"I didn't get that far, but I would have done something." I brush my hand through her hair.

"Well, lucky for us both, you don't have to try to figure out the next thing." She laughs. "I am kind of bummed that you didn't get to meet my aunt and my sister. They surprised me this week for a quick visit."

"Really? That sucks that I missed them, but I'm glad you got to see them."

"Me too. I didn't realize how much I'd needed it until I was hugging them. My aunt gave me a lot to think about. And she told me I should trust you."

"Smart lady. Remind me to thank her for being on my side when I meet her." I kiss her forehead.

"I also read a letter from my dad that I'd been avoiding. He's dying."

That's heavy. My dad and I might not always agree, but I love him, and losing him would be really hard.

"How do you feel about that?"

"It was weird, Bo. I read the letter and felt nothing. But what I realized was that even having that letter in my apartment was like a noose or poisonous. So, I burned it, and when I was standing outside, watching the ashes blow away, I felt an overwhelming sense of peace. Like I could finally move on."

"That's a lot. But I'm really glad you felt that weight lifted off of you."

"Me too. And I think between my aunt and sister coming, then burning that letter, it made me realize how much I didn't want to let you go."

I tip her face up. "I love you. Completely. Every piece of you is mine."

I slant my mouth over hers and trace the seam of her lips, seeking entrance. She opens for me, and our tongues move slowly against each other, savoring. I deepen the kiss, and she moans into my mouth.

She turns her body so she's straddling me, and I take hold of her ass and lift her so I can turn on the bed and lay us down. She breaks the kiss and sits up, running her hands over my chest and down my stomach, making me suck in a breath.

"God, Bo, I missed you so much. I don't ever want to be apart like that again. I just can't."

I grip the hem of her shirt and pull it over her head. Then trace the curve of her breasts with my hands and pull down the cups of her bra. "I missed you too, baby. Never again."

She reaches behind her and unclasps her bra, then tosses it to the floor. Her hand moves her hair to the side, and she bends to kiss me again, and my hands roam up and down her back, feeling her soft skin.

Her hips start to rock against my hard-on, but then she stops abruptly and lifts off of me onto her knees.

"I need to get these off of you."

She grips the waistband of my pants and scoots down the bed to pull them off of me, and then she steps off the bed and takes her pants off. It's possible that I'm drooling. Her perfect breasts, her smooth and bare pussy, her long black hair hanging over her shoulder … she looks like a goddess.

My dick twitches as she climbs back up my legs and straddles my waist. When she drops her hips, her wet pussy cradles my dick, and she shivers. I grab on to her hips and rock her against me, and we both moan.

She bends to kiss me again, deep, wet, hot, as her pussy slides against me. My crown hits her clit with every stroke. I can feel her getting more aroused, making her slide up and down my shaft easily.

She pulls up again, her hands resting on my chest. "You feel so good like this, Bo. Does it feel good for you?"

"Baby, everything feels good with you. Take what you need. Stroke that pussy with my dick."

"Fuck," she says as she tosses her head back as she grinds against me.

Her hips move faster, and I can't deny that my balls are starting to tighten. When she leans back and puts her hands behind her on my thighs, I nearly lose it. I can see everything like this. Her pretty pink clit sliding over my crown …

Fuck.

"Are you gonna come like this?" I'm not opposed to it at all; it's fucking hotter than hell, watching her grind on me.

"I'm close, but I want you inside me when I come."

She pushes off her hands and puts them back on my chest, but then she lifts her hips off my cock and grabs me by the base, lining me up with her opening. And I watch the whole thing. Every fucking move. And as she sinks down on me, I nearly lose my breath from how tight she feels.

"I don't think I'll ever get over how big you are. You have the most perfect cock. And it's all mine."

She starts to bounce up and down on me, and I slide my hands from her hips to her taut stomach before cupping her breasts.

"All yours, baby." I can't help but piston into her as she comes down, hitting her deep.

"I'm gonna come. Don't stop." She leans over me, and her hips start rocking, almost out of control.

I reach between us and circle her clit with my thumb. "Come for me, baby."

She tucks her head into my neck and moans. "Bo. Oh God. Bo!"

I thrust into her as her orgasm pulses around me. "That's it. Come all over my cock."

I pump once, twice, and then I can't hold back any longer. I take her hips in my hands and hold her in place while I fill her.

Chelsea looks up and drops a soft kiss on my lips. "I love you, Bo."

I'm still breathing heavy. "I love you too, Chelsea. Always."

She moves off of me, and I see my cum drip out of her and down her leg. I hold my arm out across the pillow so she can lie on my chest.

"As much as I'm happy about where we are right now, I think we still have a lot to talk about, no? I mean, I guess a lot will be determined by where you get drafted to, but I might need to change my plans for law school based on where you go."

My hand runs up and down her arm while I listen and think about what she's saying. "Chelsea, I don't want you to put your dreams on hold for mine. I don't know yet where I'm going, but wherever I land, we'll make it work. Charlie and Beck are working it out until she finishes this year."

"Yeah, but I don't think I want to do that. Do you have any idea on when you might know where you might go?"

I shake my head. "Not exactly. I mean, I've had meetings

with my agent, but right now, I'm focused on the championship game. Once I get through that, I'll have more meetings and prep for the combine. By then, I should have a pretty good idea. But when I get back from the combine, I'll come back here so I can be with you until the draft. And then you and I can decide if we want to go to the live draft or be home."

"It's a lot to think about. But I guess it's not something we can figure out today." She props her head on my chest and looks at me.

"Nope, not a today problem." I roll my body so I'm aligned with hers. "But you know what we can do?"

She smirks. "What can we do?"

"We can make up for the last few weeks apart."

"And how are we gonna do that?" She smiles at me and brushes her hand up my arm to my shoulder and into my hair.

"For starters, I think you should sit on my face. I need to taste you. It's been too long."

"But you just came inside me. I should probably go clean up first."

"Why?" I put my hand between her thighs, and she opens for me. I run my finger through her and push my cum back inside of her. I pump my finger a few times, then pull it out of her and bring it to her lips. "Nothing wrong with it. It's us. Open," I say as I slip my finger inside her mouth. She wraps her lips around it and sucks. "Fuck."

She pulls my finger out slowly. "Us."

I nod, too turned on to speak.

She sits up and turns her body and straddles my head. "Well, I certainly don't want to deny you, but I can't let you have all the fun either." She takes my cock in her hand and swirls her tongue over my crown.

I don't waste another second; I pull her hips down on my face and devour her.

EPILOGUE

BO

THIS GAME SHOULDN'T BE AS tight as it is. Our defense made a lot of mistakes in the first half, and we've been trying to fight back, but it seems like with every touchdown we make, they come back in and score too. It's really fucking pissing me off.

I'm tired, my foot hurts from getting stepped on, and my nose is sore from getting smashed in the third quarter. It was nasty. Blood literally burst from my nose, and I had to keep playing through it because it happened right after the ball was snapped. And I have no doubt I'll have some pretty nice bruises on my chest, even through my pads. They're gunning for me tonight, and I've taken more hits than I should be taking.

It's third down and one, with two minutes left on the clock, at their forty-yard line. We don't have any time-outs left, and we're down by a touchdown. If I can get down the field and also slow the clock down, we can win.

"Come on, guys! Wake up! I need every single one of you to lock in and get this done. Do you want this trophy?" I walk around the huddle, getting in their faces.

"Yeah!"

"Then prove it! Slant route on three. Break."

We all clap, then go to the line of scrimmage. I look across and see where the defense is moving to determine which receiver I'll throw to. They're heavy on the left, which is where Casey is positioned. They expect me to throw it to him, so he's getting guarded heavily today. He's hurting just as much as I am, if not more.

I check my line and start the call. "Red thirty-three." I look to my left first to let Casey know he's not getting the ball. "Red thirty-three." I look to my right and make eye contact with my other receiver, Isaac Johnson. He makes no move to indicate that the ball is coming to him. "Set. Hut!"

The center fires the ball to me, and I move to my right, outside the pocket, and look for Johnson.

He breaks through the defense and makes a sharp angle across one of the linemen toward the middle of the field. I bounce on my feet and spin to avoid a tackle. When I see Johnson is where I need him, I throw him a diagonal pass, and he takes off running and gets us the first down before he's taken down with a tackle.

The clock is down to a minute thirty-five, and now's our chance to get into the end zone and win this.

"Huddle, huddle, huddle," I call out and wave my guys over. The noise of the crowd is almost deafening, and I can't hear the calls coming through my headset. "Let's shut this down." I look at Casey, and he nods. "Trips Left Nine-Eighty-Seven Fade Susie. Break."

We all clap.

This play should put Casey far enough down the field to get into the end zone, and Susie is our code for a silent count, which means my right guard, Davis Taylor, will watch for my signal and then tap the center to snap the ball. Once the center gets the tap, he'll count silently to three before he snaps the ball to me.

At the line of scrimmage, my receivers position themselves

on the left, with Casey as my intended target. The defense sees the formation and adjusts to bring more coverage to the left. And I look to my right to make sure we're all ready to go. I lift my leg to signal to Taylor.

I watch the defense shift again as I silently count, *One. Two. Three.*

Then the ball snaps to me. I move out of the pocket to my left and watch as Casey breaks left and starts to run near the sideline. I launch a rocket to him; his arms reach above his head, and he has to jump to grab it. When he lands on his feet, he takes off and runs right into the end zone.

We all rush down the field.

"Fuck yeah, King!" I slap his helmet. "That's my guy!"

"Let's fucking go!" he yells, then flexes into the camera in the end zone and tosses the ball to the ref.

We opt for the two-point conversion and line up again without the huddle. We practice this pattern so many times; everyone knows where they need to be and when. And we almost always use a silent count on two-point conversions, and this play is no different. I lift my leg again, and Taylor taps my center.

I count to three in my head. *One. Two. Three.*

I catch the ball from my center, then turn to my right as my running back runs behind me. I send a toss pass to him, and he runs to the right, diving over the defense to make it into the end zone.

"Hell yeah!" I pump my fist into the air.

The game is all but over now, and our teammates start to run out onto the field to celebrate. It quickly becomes out of control as our fans also start to rush the field. State troopers start to create a circle around us, so we can move to the safe zone.

Red and white confetti starts to fall from the domed ceiling all around us. I try to make my way through my teammates so I can go shake the other quarterback's hand and also their coach's.

It's almost impossible to make it through, and then I'm swept away by our media specialist to be interviewed.

I give a quick interview, recalling the game, and then it's time for us to make our way to the stage they've set up out of nowhere. Someone hands me a T-shirt and a hat that reads *National Champions Walker University* and has the Stallions logo in the center, but I don't put it on just yet. I notice some family members and girlfriends making their way into the group and start looking for Chelsea and my parents—who made the trip after a very long conversation about where Chelsea and I stood —over the crowd.

I spot her walking toward the stage, in her number six jersey, with Noelle and Charlie. They're all excited, looking around at everything and trying to find me and Casey. I spot him over on the other side of the stage. And when I turn back to look at the girls, Chelsea sees me, and I point to Casey. She tells Noelle and Charlie, and they split off to go see him, and she makes her way to me. I still don't see my parents though.

When she reaches me, I lift her into my arms.

"Congratulations!" she yells over the crowd noise.

I lean in and kiss her, not caring who might be watching. And keep kissing her until I feel a tap on the shoulder.

"Bo, excuse me. Can we get a few questions in real quick?" our media manager asks me, then winks at me, letting me know it's time.

Chelsea and I pull apart.

"Yeah, that's fine."

I lower Chelsea to the ground and take her hand in mine. She tries to pull away, but I don't want her to get lost in the crowd so I bring her with me.

"Bo, I can wait for you here so you can do what you need to do, or I can go find the girls."

"Not a chance. You're staying with me." I tug on her hand, pulling her along with me.

When we reach the reporter near the sideline, I lean into her.

"If you don't want to be on camera, you can stand to my left, out of the frame." I know she's been a little nervous about all the media exposure, so I don't want her to feel pressured to stand next to me while I'm on camera.

"I'm good, I promise." She leans up and kisses my cheek. "I'm so proud of you and proud to stand by your side."

"Okay, if you're sure." I lift my eyebrows in question. "You know I've got you."

"I'm sure!" She laughs and wraps her arm around mine.

I look at the interviewer, who I know from other games over the years; she's also a well-known broadcaster. "Hey, Holly. How're you doing?"

"Awesome game, Bo! Really incredible." She shakes my hand.

"Thank you. It was memorable for sure." I laugh.

"I bet." She looks at the cameraman, then at me and nods. "Bo, congratulations on your second national championship! How does this one feel compared to the first one?"

I lean down to hear her over the noise and nod as she speaks. "Thanks, Holly. Yeah, I mean, it was a great game today." I look up at her.

"Your defense missed some crucial errors in the first half. What did you have to do to compensate for those?" She tilts her microphone to me.

"We all made some mistakes out there, but we just had to keep getting out there, executing play after play, and it paid off in the end."

She holds the microphone toward her mouth. "Is this your girlfriend, Bo?" Then she moves it to me.

I look at Chelsea, but I'm not sure if she heard Holly because she smiling like she's fascinated by it all. "This is my fiancée, Chelsea."

Chelsea's mouth drops open, and she whips her head up, looking at me. And I just smile down at her.

"Well, I mean, she will be here in a second." I look over

Holly's shoulder and see one of our trainers, Sarah, standing behind her. "Thanks, Holly."

"Congrats on the win and the engagement, Bo!" She backs away.

I tip my chin, and Sarah rushes over to me. "You got it?"

"Yep, I got it." She pulls out a ring box from her fanny pack, and then she looks at Chelsea, whose mouth is still hanging open, and smiles as she hands it to me.

"Thanks, Sar. You're the best." I give her a nod and take the ring out of the box, then set the box on the ground next to me.

"I know," she says as she backs away, still watching.

When I turn back to Chelsea, her hands are covering her mouth, but I pull them away and take one of her hands in mine.

"Lucky," I say as I get down on one knee, "you are the love of my life, my partner in all things, and my best friend. And I'm so excited to walk through this life with you. Will you marry me?"

She starts to cry and nods. "Yes!"

"Thank fuck." I bark out a laugh. Then I slide the engagement ring onto her finger. When I stand, I lift her in my arms and kiss her. "I love you."

"Holy shit, Bo! I love you too! I was not expecting this at all. There are cameras everywhere aimed at us."

I look around and notice that she's right. "Oops." I shrug, smiling, not sorry.

My teammates, who are nearby, all rush us, while cameramen fight to get a shot of Chelsea and me.

Then my parents come into the circle, and they hug me first.

"Congratulations, sugar!" my mom says, then hugs Chelsea. "And congratulations to you too! Welcome to the family!"

"Thank you," Chelsea says, a smile breaking across her face.

"Bo," my dad says, grabbing my hand, then pulling me in to hug me. "You were amazing out there today. We're so proud of you." He turns to Chelsea. "Welcome to the family, Chelsea," he says, then leans in to hug her.

"Thank you, sir," she says politely.

It's been hard for her to know that my dad wasn't on board with us at first, but we're all in a good place now, so I know it will work out.

"Bo!" Coach yells. "Callaway! Get your ass over here so we can get this trophy!"

"Go." Chelsea tries to push me away, but I don't let her.

"Uh-uh. I want my fiancée where I can see her."

I kiss her finger with the ring and pull her along with me toward the stage, cameras following us as we go.

I lean down to her ear. "You doing okay with all of this?"

"Which part? The ring or the cameras?" She giggles.

"Baby, I know you wouldn't have said yes if you didn't mean it, so I know you're okay with the ring. I mean the cameras."

"Bo, this is all part of being with you, and I don't want to miss a thing, so, yeah, I'm okay with all of it." As we reach the stairs, she stops. "Now go get that trophy!" She kisses me, then pushes me to climb the stairs.

After Coach gives his speech, he moves and waves me toward the mic. Chelsea is right where I left her, and Casey's family and Noelle are with her. My parents aren't far, but closer to the side, some state troopers standing near them.

I adjust the mic and bend down to speak into it. "Let's go, Stallions!"

Coach hands me the trophy, and I lift it up, and the crowd cheers again.

"First, I would like to thank God. I wouldn't be here without my faith. And I want to give a quick shout-out to my teammates, who killed it out there today and fought hard to bring this win home. Coach Pettys, you brought me to Walker three years ago, and we had a conversation about winning a national championship. But now ... we have TWO!"

My teammates cheer and jump around Coach.

"And I'd like to thank my family for always supporting me. And to my fiancée, you are my reason for everything. I love you,

Chelsea." I blow her a kiss, then lift up the trophy and kiss it. "Let's GO!"

The crowd roars again, and I pass off the trophy to someone else, then make my way off the stage to my girl.

"You ready to celebrate tonight?" I ask her as I lift her in my arms and kiss her.

She wraps her arms around my shoulders. "Hell yeah, I am." She kisses me fiercely. "Fiancé." She smirks.

I spin her around, and we laugh.

The first time I saw Chelsea Sullivan, she took my breath away. I thank God every day that I failed that quiz, because it led me to her.

She used to think love was supposed to be loud—fast, dramatic, full of highs and lows. And I guess that's what happens when you grow up around people who mistake chaos for care. But I'm trying to show her something different. I want to give her peace. The kind of silence where you don't have to fill the space—you just belong in it, together.

Chelsea was meant to be mine, and I was meant to be hers. And this love we have for each other, it's the kind of love that lasts.

Want to see what Bo and Chelsea are up to now? Read their bonus chapter here.
https://BookHip.com/SLSBWZA

Up next is Silas in **Lockdown Corner**!

Read on for a holiday SURPRISE!

SURPRISE!!! So many of you have asked for a book for Liam, and I listened! He was only supposed to be a side character, but alas…we all fell for him.

This is a sneak peek inside a holiday novella that will be a LIVE release at the beginning of December. It will lead into a new spinoff series with Liam's being the first book (date TBD). I hope you're as excited as I am!

SNOW BLITZ

Liam

Why am I standing on a rooftop in the middle of Winter, freezing my balls off? I did not sign up for this. I thought coming to some posh wedding meant we would at least be, you know, comfortable.

I take a hefty gulp of my Macallan Eighteen to try to warm myself up. Sure, there are heating lamps placed strategically around the rooftop and a glass wraparound to cut the wind, but it's still fucking cold. It's only supposed to be a short cocktail hour up here, then we'll go to the main dining room for dinner, but I've been standing in this same spot for close to an hour under one of the heaters. If I had been better prepared and maybe worn a thicker coat, I wouldn't be acting like a pussy about the whole thing.

Glancing around, I take in the all-white wedding theme. Even we, the guests, were asked to wear white. It almost feels like we're in a white-out blizzard —inside a snow globe that you can't get out of— because it also started snowing about ten minutes ago. *Fuck, I'm trapped in this snow globe world and starting to feel claustrophobic now.*

A few of my old teammates are hanging around, but almost everyone brought a date, except me. They've tried to include me, and I can carry on a conversation with the best of them, but

I'm just not feeling it tonight. I'll probably duck out after we eat.

My teammates from Michigan are all great guys, but I miss my guys from Walker. We're all on our own paths now, too, but we try to see each other now and then. Especially Archie Griffith. He's my best friend and the one I talk to the most.

I pull out my phone to text the big guy, because I'm getting bored, when I see a woman with long brown hair standing next to the bundled-up bride in a long, bright red coat. I'm guessing she didn't get the memo. Then I see my buddy, Aaron Muldoon, walk up to her. He places a hand on the small of her back, and when she turns her head to look up at him, I almost drop my whisky glass.

I've seen some beautiful women in my life, but she is unbelievably stunning, and I can't even see her whole face yet. But then they turn and walk away from the bride, and I get to see her head on. She's got long shiny brown hair that looks like silk, with piercing blue eyes, a perfectly symmetrical nose, and her lips...*fuck me*. They're full and painted in bright red lipstick that matches her coat.

They're walking toward me now, and he leans down to say something to her that makes her laugh, and I'm done for. By the time they reach me, I've managed to pick my jaw up off the floor and compose myself enough that I don't look like an idiot.

"Sup, man. How's it going? Good to see you." Aaron reaches his hand out and pulls me in for a bro-hug.

"Muldoon, good to see you. How's New York treating you?" I ask him, but glance her way.

"Good, good. The season's been—" Aaron stops talking when he looks behind me. "Oh, shit, I gotta go say hi to someone, I'll be right back." Aaron looks at the woman as he walks away.

"Okay then. No problem. I'll just stand here by myself freezing, but cool, cool." She tucks a piece of her hair behind her ear.

"Right?" I chuckle. "Whose idea was this? I mean, it does

look incredible, but these heating lamps aren't doing a whole lot to cut the chill."

She straightens her arms and holds her hands out. "Picture this...New York City, it's snowing, love and Christmas magic are in the air, but I feel like I'm standing in a cryo chamber."

"Ha! Pretty close to the truth there. You ever been in one?" I tilt my head toward her.

She nods, smirking. "Oh yeah. I'm a fan, but this is like really kinda crazy."

"Indeed, it is. I was just thinking about leaving after dinner. My hotel room is calling my name. I'll need a good thaw out after this." I lift my glass to my lips and take another pull of my whisky.

"Whatever you have in that, I might need some to warm up." She tips her head toward my glass.

"Do you want some of this while I go get you a drink?" I hand it out to her.

"Hmm...risky taking a drink from a stranger. But you like a trustworthy guy, and Aaron seems to know you, so why not?" She takes my offered glass and takes a sip. "Nice. Macallan. Eighteen?"

My mouth drops open, then I shut it so I can form words. "You know your whisky?"

"Mmm. I do. My father is a big fan. I also love a good whisky." She hands it back to me.

I'm just about to say something when a woman wearing a headset starts to speak. "Excuse me, everyone, can I have your attention please? Thank you so much for your patience tonight. There was a minor water issue that we're working to resolve. We should be able to go in shortly. In the meantime, we'll be bringing more appetizers out for you to enjoy. And don't forget to grab a drink at the bar." She waves her hand, then spins around and walks over to the bride and groom.

I glance over at this angel in red, and she meets my gaze.

"I have an idea," she says, grinning.

"Oh yeah, what's your idea?" I move in a little closer to her.

"How invested are you in staying here?"

I mean, is this a trick question? "Uhh, not very."

"Have you ever been to New York City at Christmas?" She rubs her gloved hands together.

I shake my head. "I have not. I'm from Kansas, and I don't live here."

"I..." She starts to say something, then stops.

"I..." I prompt her.

She laughs. "I was going to say, do you want to get out of here? Let me show you what a Manhattan Christmas is like."

Fuck. Yes. "Absolutely. But I don't even know your name."

She tilts her head to the side. "Let's go with...Vixen. And you can be...Blitzen."

"What? Why?" I chuckle.

"Because it's fun and Christmas is magical." She holds out her hand to me. "What do ya say, Blitzen? You wanna go make some Christmas magic with me?"

I place my hand in her small one. "Lead the way, Vixen."

www.avasuttonbooks.com

ACKNOWLEDGMENTS

To my family, thank you for your patience and encouragement. You're my reason for everything. I love you all, eternally.

Compass Press, thank you for walking me through the author journey. I can't wait to work on our next secret project!

Jovanna Shirley, once again, thank you for your patience and expertise. I promise one day I'll make a deadline.

Jeannine Colette, you are amazing and bring beauty to everything you touch. Thank you endlessly for working with me on this book. And thank you for giving me the motivation to keep going and get it done!

Sarah Sentz, you are a rock for Team Ava Sutton. You make our lives so much easier. And your feedback and love for these characters go beyond what is expected or asked. Thank you for literally...everything.

Sam R —Thank you for loving this book and your incredible feedback! I can't wait to send you the next surprise!

Rickie —Thank you for jumping in quickly to read Bo and Chelsea's story. Your love for this series is incredible and I can't thank you enough.

To all the readers, thank you for giving me a chance and reading more of my words! Your reviews, edits, and just knowing you're reading, still blows my mind. Thank you, thank you!

Wordsmith Publicity, Autumn and Roxie, thank you for helping me reach readers and your guidance and support!

ABOUT THE AUTHOR

Ava Sutton is a sports enthusiast and author of spicy college and professional sports romance.

When she's not writing, you can find her nose in a book, scrolling social media or planning dream vacations she someday hopes to take. She lives in Dallas, Texas with her two dogs. Connect with her on Facebook, Instagram, and TikTok. @avasuttonbooks

www.avasuttonbooks.com